Archangel: Raven's Card

Ed Adams

a firstelement production

First published in Great Britain in 2020 by firstelement
Copyright © 2020 Ed Adams
Directed by thesixtwenty

10 9 8 7 6 5 4 3 2 1

A CIP catalogue record for this book is available from the British Library.

ISBN 13 : 978-1-913818-00-5
eBook ISBN : 978-1-913818-01-2

Printed and bound in Great Britain by Ingram Spark

rashbre
an imprint of firstelement.co.uk
rashbre@mac.com

Mailing list: https://mailchi.mp/9f0b30712620/ed_adams

To John and Georgina

who provide socially distant advice

Thanks

A big thank you for the tolerance and bemused support from all of those around me. To those who know when it is time to say, " step away from the keyboard!" and to those who don't.

To Julie for that kind of understanding that only comes with really knowing me.

To thesixtwenty.co.uk for direction.

To the NaNoWriMo gang for the continued inspiration and encouragement.

To John, for many hours of intense scrutiny, whilst I was delicately scoffing asparagus. To Georgina for cover ideas. To MJ Cullinane for the Crow Tarot. To Alexej Ravski for inspirational cover art.

And, of course, thanks to the extensive support via the random scribbles of rashbre via http://rashbre2.blogspot.com and its cast of amazing and varied readers whether human, twittery, smoky, cool kats, photographic, dramatic, musical, anagrammed, globalized or simply maxed-out.

Not forgetting the cast of characters involved in producing this; they all have virtual lives of their own.

And of course, to you, dear reader, for at least 'giving it a go'.

Books by Ed Adams include:

Triangle Trilogy		About
1	The Triangle	Dirty money? Here's how to clean it
2	The Square	Weapons of Mass Destruction – don't let them get on your nerves
3	The Circle	The desert is no place to get lost
	The Ox Stunner	The Triangle Trilogy – thick enough to stun an ox
		(all feature Jake, Bigsy, Clare, Chuck Manners)
Archangel Trilogy		
1	Archangel	Sometimes I am necessary
2	Raven	An eye that sees all between darkness and light
3	Card Game	Throwing oil on a troubled market
	Magazine Clip	the above three in one heavy book.
		(all feature Jake, Bigsy, Clare, Chuck Manners)
Stand-Alone Novels		
1	Coin	Get rich quick with Cybercash – just don't tell GCHQ
2	Pulse	Want more? Just stay away from the edge
3	Edge	Power can't be left to trust
	Now the Science	the above three in one heavy book.

About Ed Adams Novels:

Triangle Trilogy		About
	Triangle	Money laundering within an international setting.
	Square	A viral nerve agent being shipped by terrorists and WMDs
	Circle	In the Arizona deserts, with the Navajo; about missiles stolen from storage.
	Ox Stunner	the above three in one heavy book.
		(all feature Jake, Bigsy, Clare, Chuck Manners)
Archangel Trilogy		
	Archangel	Biographical adventures of Russian trained Archangel, who, as Christina Nott, threads her way through other Triangle novels.
	Raven	Big business gone bad and being a freemason won't absolve you
	Card Game	Raven Pt 2 – Russian oligarchs attempt to take control
	Magazine Clip	the above three in one heavy book.
		(all feature Jake, Bigsy, Clare, Chuck Manners)
Stand-Alone Novels		
	Coin	cyber cash manipulation by the Russian state.
	Pulse	Sci-Fi dystopian blood management with nano-bots
	Edge	World end climate collapse and sham discovered during magnetite mining from Jupiter's moon Ganymede
	Now the Science	the above three in one heavy book.

TABLE OF CONTENTS

PART TWO – TOURNAMENT OF LIES 202

Secret Keeper

ἢ τὰν ἢ ἐπὶ τᾶς

Ḕ tãn ḕ ep" tâs

'Either with your shield, or on it'

annað hvort með skjöldnum þínum eða á honum

- *Plutarch*

Roberta

Christina was in the dark, underground vaults at Waterloo station waiting to see Roberta, the fortune teller.

Christina had originally visited Roberta in the Boxpark, where Roberta had a small gallery, and Roberta had given Christina some spirited advice, which had been useful when trying to understand the Raven situation.

Now Christina was standing in a crowded, bohemian bar, lit by fairy lights and waiting for Roberta's show to begin. They were all called through to a small black room, with rows of chairs arranged along the back wall. A black curtain marked the edges of a stage area.

With a flash of smoke, Roberta appeared as a pirate queen. Long, flowing brunette hair, a white bodice pulled tight with a leather corset and thigh-length leather boots. She carried a dangerous-looking sword which glinted in the spotlights.

"Of course you would," thought Christina.

Roberta winked when she spotted Christina in the

audience of about forty people. She flashed the sword through the air and a pirate flag appeared. She held the sword aloft, and the flag rose above the point of the sword, then fluttering down where it cut into halves. Then, suddenly, the two halves became bats fluttering upward.

A woman behind Christina screamed.

"The next one to scream will see me use my pistol," she cried and as suddenly as the bats appeared, a flintlock pistol was now in Roberta's hand.

She holstered the weapon and slapped her thigh, in good pantomime style.

"Imagine two ships, she said, A tall galleon and a smaller frigate. The smaller frigate holds the pirates. The tall galleon has a larger crew but is slow.

At that moment a back projection appeared. On the left was a galleon and on the right was a frigate.

"What type of audience do we have tonight? Are they King's supporters or Pirates? Think hard about this. Which ship do you want to win?"

... The story telling continued, of pirates, wreckers all along the coasts of Cornwall and Devon and then some stories from the Spanish Main.

"... Who is for this King's ship? Point to the ship. And who is for the Pirates? Now you point. And you that have not pointed, you will feel the anger of the sea."

There were several shouts from around the audience, some of whom were being soaked with jets of water.

"Come here," said Roberta to one of the people who had screamed, "For you must face my pistol."

Roberta pulled the female audience member still wearing her raincoat forward.

"Stand still," she said, and pointed the flintlock pistol.

There was a loud crack and glitter fell from the ceiling. A gasp from the audience as her victim's coat swept away, revealing a pirate costume.

"Now sit yourself down and behave," said Roberta, "But look at the ships. The King's ship survives. The pirate ship is burning. We cannot spare the souls of the pirates. It will become a ghost ship."

There was a scraping of chairs and three others of the audience stood. They each had bedraggled pirate costumes and grey skins.

"Look, for we have new ghosts tonight."

"And now, a song."

Roberta used a flourish to produce a black and silver ukulele. She played and sang Pirate Jenny - The Black Freighter.

…" And now, the chorus," she sang.

"And the ship, the black freighter
With the skull at the masthead
Sails into the bay"

And later "…another chorus…"

"And the ship, the black freighter
With fifty long cannons
Opens fire on the town"

She sang the verses of the song and then, "…this time the chorus…"

"And the ship, the black freighter
Runs a flag up her masthead
And cheer rings the air"

And, after a rousing ukelele solo, "… And we all go down together…" Roberta winked to Christina,

"And the ship, the black freighter
Sails away out to sea
And on it is me"

The pirates in the audience clapped and cheered and the rest of the audience followed.

"That's Kurt Weill and Bertolt Brecht for you," said Roberta.

"Tonight, I've been Pirate Jenny - the Pirate Queen - and thank you all!"

She carved her sword through the air. The pirate ships vanished, and a full stage-width pirate flag appeared and fell to the floor.

More applause. Christina clapped enthusiastically. Roberta knew how to work it.

The audience filed out. Christina realised that these were

short sets, in a 'Fringe-style' performance. A chance to get a taste of the artist rather than an extended show.

A tap on her shoulder. "You came along! - Christina? Isn't it? - I remember you - from the land of the ice and snow!"

Christina smiled, "Yes, a great show. How do you do those clever things with the sword?"

"I may have told you some trade secrets, but a magician never tells," answered Roberta, "Come on, a drink at the bar?"

"Sure," said Christina.

They found two seats at the bar and ordered two Sol beers, complete with lime.

"Did you find your ship of fools?" asked Roberta.

"Actually, I did," said Christina, "And I found out a lot of other things that I can link back to our conversation in the Boxpark."

"That's great," said Roberta, "I'm still there, you know, hanging on by good fortune!"

"Plus, this act, terrific," said Christina.

"Yes, and that's before you see our regular theatre show "Busy" or even see me serving in The Pure Ground - it's a coffee shop."

"Were those some of the actors?" asked Christina.

"Yes, and Celine from the coffee bar - they come along to

support me. I can't properly pay them, but we all help one another out with our solo projects."

"Look - after the last time we met, I wished I'd given you something," said Roberta.

"What's that?" asked Christina, intrigued.

"Well, you had natural abilities - we talked about it then - I think I have something in my bag. Wait, a moment."

"This isn't another magic trick where I get squirted with water? " asked Christina.

Roberta fiddled with the catch of a small bag. It was like a miniature-sized suitcase.

"Don't look inside," she said, "You'll spoil the magic."

Christina looked away.

Then, Roberta produced with a flourish, "Ta-da!" she said.

Christina looked puzzled. "What is it?"

Stacked on the bar was something small. It looked like playing cards.

"It's Rider Waite, " she said, "Tarot. These are the real deal. Look…draw two cards."

Christina fingered through the deck, looking at the backs of the cards and pulled two.

"Place one by you and one by me."

She did as she was asked and placed them on the bar.

"Now turn them over."

By Roberta was the Magician, by her The High Priestess.

"I knew it. You have the power. You pulled two of the most powerful cards from the Major Arcana - for me, the Magician, for you, The High Priestess, signifying Intuition and Wisdom. Together for you these two represent Willpower, Creation, Mastery, Adaptation, and Divine Truth. They are the powers of an Archangel."

Roberta smiled, "Take them. Take this deck of cards, This Tarot belongs to you. It is telling me to give them up. It has found its owner."

Christina smiled. She kissed Roberta on both cheeks.

"Robert/Roberta. Thank you."

The Tarot

Historie de la magie, du monde surnaturel et de la fatalité à travers les temps et le peuples (1870) - Jean-Baptiste Pitois

The tarot trumps can be considered as being the principle scenes of ancient Egyptian initiatory "tests".

At one stage in the initiation procedure, the postulant climbs down an iron ladder, with seventy-eight rungs, and enters a hall on either side of which are twelve statues, and, between each pair of statues, a painting.

These twenty-two paintings are Arcana or symbolic hieroglyphs. The Science of Will, the principle of all wisdom and source of all power, is in them.

Each corresponds to a "letter of the sacred language" and to a number, and each expresses a reality of the divine world, a reality of the intellectual world and a reality of the physical world.

Such claims, started by early freemasons, have today found their way into academic discourse.

Part 1 – Path of Mysteries

Cross Town Traffic

You jump in front of my car when you; you know all the time that
Ninety miles an hour, girl, is the speed I drive.
You tell me it's all right, you don't mind a little pain.
You say you just want me to take you for a ride.

You're just like crosstown traffic, so hard to get through to you.
Crosstown traffic, I don't need to runnin' over you.
Crosstown traffic, all you do is slow me down
And I'm trying to get on the other side of town.

Jimi Hendrix

Ten of Swords

Failure
Collapse
Defeat
Backstabbing

(Reversed)

The Worst
The Depths
Inevitable End

Unwrapping

"Look, " said Bigsy, reading from the newspaper, "Cabinet Minister in Fatal Car Crash"

The newspaper rustled as he held it up.

Bigsy continued, "Driscoll was on his way from his constituency to his family home, when his car suffered a puncture and crashed off the road, into a ditch, hitting an electricity sub-station. No seat belt and they found that his phone was on. They are calling it death by misadventure."

Christina looked up, "I wondered, you know, that we kept Marion Charlotte in for the entire dinner with Driscoll. She noticed a couple of things that I wouldn't expect. When I spoke Russian and when Amanda did, I could see her look of recognition.

"I think we were played."

"What? Do you think that Marion was working for Raven?" asked Bigsy.

Christina answered, " If so, then she would know that Driscoll was compromised. She could tell Raven. They could clean up after Driscoll's mistakes.

"They had got what they wanted from him. The company divestment and the ability to operate in Celarus. Removing him would mean they didn't have to pay him any longer. But now I'm concerned there seems to be a Russian angle on this."

Jake said, "We'd better call Amanda Miller at SI6 and warn her. She would also be compromised."

"If there is a Russian angle, then I think it is organised crime rather than pure state, " said Christina, "Russian organized crime or Russian mafia (российская мафия) otherwise known as Bratva (братва).

…

Sir Charles Frobisher sat in his ISMC office at Raven Corps with Michael Tovey, the MP.

"Interesting," said Sir Charles, "How useful to get a microphone into their temporary office."

"Just how did you manage that?" asked Michael Tovey.

"Well, it's all a matter of degree," answered, Frobisher, "I found a man who proved to be very helpful."

"Ah," answered Tovey, realising that Frobisher was alluding to his Masonic connections.

"Yes, and I've arranged with Brant Holdings that they

will run ongoing monitoring of the office from Minerva Station, out in east London."

"Is that the CIA station out by the Dome?" asked Tovey, "The one that seems to pay too much attention to the indiscretion of MPs."

"That's correct," answered Frobisher, "Although I have a sneaking suspicion that we have been compromised. And what's more, I think it is something to do with the same people."

"There are too many of them to meet the same fate as Driscoll," said Tovey.

"I agree, although I'm not sure if it involves the full office, the way they were talking it seems to point towards an American ex-marine, someone named 'Chuck'. We don't know who that is though, nor where he has gone. We are not even sure whether its an actual name or a codeword," answered Frobisher.

"I've asked the people at the listening station to monitor for longer to see if we can work out what is happening. However, I hear that one of them, Jake Lambers, is already looking for a new office space - we could lose our access if that were to happen."

"Not necessarily, " said Tovey, "Wouldn't one of the members have an attractive property somewhere in central London? - We could lure them to that location but also ensure that it is fully equipped. What do you think?"

"Well, if someone would like to assist us with a very special offer to the group of them, one they would be crazy to turn down?"

"I'd imagine we could assist the difference in the cost. We could add something from Brant into the deal as a sweetener?" added Tovey.

"So long as they didn't know or suspect anything?" answered Frobisher, "The sound quality from here is really rather exceptional!"

They listened, as Christina was speaking.

"… Yes, Bratva is a collective of various organised crime elements. Today, there are 6,000 distinct groups, with over 200 of them having a global reach. They are everywhere.

"They say that the United States is operated by Russian oligarchs. I believe this, both from my direct education but also after having lived in a range of other countries.

"Criminals of these groups are raw material to the Russian criminal operatives. They are often former prison members, corrupt officials and business leaders, people with ethnic ties, or people from the same region with shared criminal experiences and leaders. Some claim it is one of the best structured criminal organisations in Europe, with a quasi-military operation. Some say they are operating puppets in the White House. Back in Russia, those in charge of the schemes are quite amazed that they have not been found out.

"So, the Americans have got Raven installed in Celarus, under the name Brant. But you think there may be Russian influences there too?" said Bigsy, " That's one hell of a hot-spot".

Christina said, " Yes, I think we stumbled into something altogether more malevolent. I now have a feeling that Marion is about to disappear. If she was trained the way I've been trained, then she would know she was 'burned' and already be calling the FSB for a new identity."

Clare added, "We must take heed too and maybe lose our connections with this entire situation like Chuck has done."

Christina said, "Yes, at least you've been able to operate as unknown freelancers in all of this. It's people like Chuck, Amanda and me that get the scrutiny. We are the ones that people will watch."

"Or listen to," said Sir Charles, looking towards Michael Tovey.

Too good to be true?

Clare saw Jake staring intently into a computer screen.

"What's happened? Won't the inspiration come?" she asked.

"No, it's not that. I've been looking at so many offices I'm going slightly mad," answered Jake.

"Now that the insurance has come through and we have the option to sell the old plot for redevelopment, I'm keen to get us something even more central. Even with a lot of money we could end up stuck outside London if we are not careful. I asked Richard to give me a hand, and he's pulled in some favours from his agency, but most of them are further away from the centre. Look, Acton, Finsbury Park. We'd be further away than if we'd stayed in Triangle Works."

Clare looked at the properties on offer.

"I can see they are spacious, but not really what we are looking for. Ideally, we want central, good transport access, decent floor space, near to amenities, ideally some parking in case we need it."

"It is but a dream," answered Jake.

"Well, until this one came through… It looks a bit too good to be true."

He showed Clare the listing. She read out loud, "Well it has got security access, decent sized room; it is about 3 minute's walk from London Bridge train station! There's - wait a minute - riverside views towards St Pauls Cathedral. Amenities include - no way - two pubs downstairs, a restaurant, a pizza place, a wine cellar. This is bonkers, Jake,"

"I know, that's what I thought, I wondered if they had forgotten a digit in the pricing or something?"

"Yes, look at the neighbours. They are all rich financial services type organisations. Wait - Bigsy could commute to work by riverboat! This is amazing."

Just at that moment Bigsy walked into the office. "I could do what?" he asked.

"Look at this place - it's called Hay's Galleria - and has an office space."

"Hold on, I know Hays, it's just by London Bridge train station, " Quite an extensive complex of old tea warehouses that have been refitted as offices. They must go for an enormous sum?"

"I can get us a managed space in one of them here for a superb rate," said Jake, "Frankly it kicks everything else out of the way."

"Hays would be a top choice," said Bigsy. "London Bridge

is on the Jubilee, with fast links to the centre, west end and to docklands. The middle of the building complex is a huge atrium with restaurants and bars everywhere. You can walk along the river all the way to Westminster. Borough Market is only about 10 minutes away - on foot! Take it! - Wait, what about the office space - is there room for expansion?

"Well, we could get four adjoining air-conditioned individual offices, an open plan area, break-out areas, a crash bar with kitchen and access to managed meeting rooms, all for what we were paying at Triangle Works. It says it is all Category 6a wired and wi-fi ready. There's perimeter security, CCTV, washrooms with showers, a downstairs 24-hour security and concierge and access to onsite services such as a laundry and food delivery services."

"Can I live here too?" asked Bigsy, "It sounds too good to be true."

"What about gym membership?" asked Christina, who had just arrived.

"No there's no gym… but wait, there's access via an underground walkway to a nearby commercial gym, with preferential terms."

"It also says that parking is limited but can be pre-arranged on demand."

"No good for a daily commute then," said Bigsy.

"And when did any of us ever do a daily commute by car?" asked Clare, " Oh, I know, never."

"Visitors might need it and we'd need to make an occasional van run, I suppose," said Bigsy, "but we'd be better with the transport parked away, like it is now."

"Okay, do I sense a consensus?" asked Jake, "If so, I'll make a call."

"Agreed!" said Clare. Bigsy nodded. "I'd say yes, if I had a vote," said Christina, "Although I was always taught to beware of deals that look too good to be true."

Jake picked up the phone.

Emily Karankawa

Pete Burr was sweeping through the recordings. He'd listened to Triangle Yard for the last couple of weeks and felt he was getting to know the people there. He could recognise their individual voices and the banter. Pete had decided that the banter for this group was altogether more respectful of one another than the banter he'd had on his last listening case, which was of the inside of a police station.

The police had been investigating some kind of politician sleaze and he was supposed to find pieces that referred to the charges against a certain MP. But oh, the language in that police station was over-ripe. He knew they were dealing with some shady situations, but there didn't seem to be an end to the depths that they would sink when calling one another names.

He was used to it now, and thankful that the name calling was only something distant. Pete had worked his way through a whole range of call-centre jobs, from the sleaziest low-end hustler roles- working from home and paid by results. Then he had joined a corporate financial services call centre - which was still a hustle. - He was fed automatically with numbers to call and offers to make, usually driven from scripts.

Oh - the names they had called him when he did that. He was pleased and relieved to be doing something now that seem to be in the national interest, although he couldn't work out why the bosses all seemed to work for the CIA, instead of GCHQ. Still, the pay was hugely better than in the previous roles and his French and Italian language skills had given him a further boost. He worked out he was already a ten-year veteran of call centres in one form or another.

He had been DBS'd - that was Disclosure and Barring Service checked when he joined and had to sign various papers of Non-Disclosure Agreement and Official Secrets Act, but he had decided it was easiest to say nothing about what he did at the listening station. If he was called upon to describe anything, he would fall back on his earlier time in a call centre.

When he'd talked to others that worked at Minerva, they had all said the same thing. Just describe the previous employment as if it was current. The pay was too good to accidentally crash and burn the opportunity.

The American bosses he worked with all seemed to be so young to be in charge of things. He wondered sometimes if there was another shadowy one behind the scenes running everything but had never asked.

If the Americans went out socially with the team, it was usually to one of the places around the Dome or across to Canary Wharf. It was just one stop on the tube and several of the Americans had said the living underground of the Isle of Dogs reminded them of where they lived in America.

He noticed that many of the Americans seem to have small apartments around Docklands, so he guessed they were all well-paid. He also thought they seemed to be as scared as the call centre operators about doing something wrong.

He had briefly dated one of the Americans, Emily Karankawa. He was surprised when he had discovered she was eight years younger than him, yet already a higher grade. He remembered being on a date and asking if her name was middle-European and registering her surprise as she said instead that her name was native American and that her people had lived in Texas for many centuries.

Her father had worked for a company called EDS which was big in Plano, Texas. Pete had to look up Plano on google and found it to the north of Dallas.

Emily had explained that her father was a big shot in EDS but then they had been taken over by Hewlett-Packard and then HP had sold them to another company. The company's name had then changed from a world-renowned company to a three-letter acronym and eventually to another name like Perspective or something.

Her father had seen his role slide down as each new company appeared and from once being at the epicentre of a company employing 300,000 people centred in Plano, he was now on the periphery of a company based in Virginia and close to Washington. The old, majestic waterside Plano Head Office had been closed.

He remembered Emily describing the situation,

"Yes, when Father's firm moved out to Virginia, it reminded them of what happened to the family name. We were descended from the Karankawa, " she explained.

"Yes, sorry I thought it sounded middle European," responded Pete.

Emily continued, "When a Spanish explorer Álvar Núñez Cabeza de Vaca washed up on a Galveston beach in 1528, he was met by the island's American Indian inhabitants— the Karankawa. "

"This encounter, which Cabeza de Vaca wrote about in his diary," she explained to Pete, "It was the first recorded meeting of Europeans and Texas American Indians."

She continued, "Then In 1685, French explorer René-Robert Cavelier, Sieur de La Salle, also met the Karankawa when he established Fort St. Louis near Matagorda Bay."

"These places have such exotic names, " answered Pete.

Emily continued, " Yes, Matagorda Bay is a large Gulf of Mexico bay on the Texas coast. It is a major estuary along the Gulf Coast of Texas and serves as the mouth of the Colorado River. There's even a ghost town of Indianola, which was a major port before it was destroyed by two hurricanes in the late 19th century.

" The bay is separated from the Gulf of Mexico by Matagorda Peninsula. Its shore, especially near the Colorado River delta, provides a habitat for a wide variety of wildlife. It can look beautiful there in the evenings, watching the sunset from Jensen Point. And all of this was Karankawa land.

"The Karankawa were historically one of the most powerful American Indian peoples in early Texas, but by the 1850s, their numbers had been so reduced that they were considered extinct."

He remembered she'd said something heartfelt to him, "I find it great, here in London, not be greeted with the kind of entitlement that permeates many American encounters. People in the US see my skin, my facial shape, my dark hair and even my name and sometimes a quiet racism emerges."

Pete had only dated Emily for a brief time. He found being with her was just too intense and intermingled work and socialising. They still got along, but he felt that Emily had found going out with him just as much of a challenge.

Knight of Wands

Action
Adventure
Fearlessness

Pete Burr

Pete Burr was concentrating now. He had been listening to the recordings from Triangle Works and a pattern was emerging.

Two names had emerged, Amanda and Chuck, both of which seemed to be linked to security services, but the name Chuck, or Chuck Manners seemed to appear the most frequently.

'Chuck' seems to be an American, and it sounded as if he was a one-time soldier, now working on black Ops. This would fit the bill exactly with what had been the discovery of the Minerva Station.

Pete had called his bosses and one of them had come along to listen to the discovery work. Her name was Olivia Lang and Pete knew she was another one of the young transferees from Washington.

"Hi Pete, " she said, "What have you got for me?"

"It's an American running Black Ops inside the UK. Counter to the intentions of Brant and Raven. I've some recordings here, which I've down selected into a single file."

"I think you know Emily, don't you?" asked Olivia, "We're quite good friends, actually. She says you are very reliable."

"That's right," said Pete, concerned about what else Emily and Olivia might discuss.

Pete played the recordings, and Olivia listened.

"Well, that's quite some work to piece everything together. It seems to indicate that 'Chuck' could be a player here, " said Olivia.

"Yes, or it could just be my editing, " said Pete, "But I like to think I've done a good interpretation."

"One approach we can take now is to run the name through CIA searches to see what we get," said Olivia, "We don't know yet whether it is an actual name or a codeword?"

"I think it is his name, unless we've started to give people two-part code names," answered Pete, "see he is often referred to as Chuck Manners. One time he was called Colonel Chuck Manners."

"That should make any search easier," said Olivia, "Look, can we keep this quiet now? I don't want half the station latching on to this or we'll have comms flying back and forth to Washington."

"That's smart, I agree," said Pete, "Let's see what we can turn up."

42

Mastermind

Pete had called Olivia Lang back for another meeting. He had been doing some routine intel gathering.

"It looks as if I have been able to track down Colonel Chuck Manners, mainly from routine HUMINT files," said Pete Burr. His boss, Olivia Lang, looked interested, "So spill,"

Pete continued, "He's a bit of a hero. He's been in many campaigns and a few clandestine ops. Here, take a look," They both leaned over Pete's computer. Pete noticed the pleasant fragrance that Olivia was wearing.

Pete began, "Manners has been in Afghanistan, shown as from 2001 and as part of the War on Terror and the War in Afghanistan. He was in the Resolute Support Mission. It shows that he was fighting against the Haqqani network and then later against al-Qaeda and the Islamic Jihad Union. It doesn't say what role he played, although it also lists opposition to the Talibani Army, the Salafist extremists and the 055 Brigade. Whichever way you cut it, that would be intense."

"It sounds like groundwork too, rather than in planes?" asked Olivia.

"I'd think so, there would be some mention of hardware otherwise. They have been clever with their redaction too, because they have deleted all the dates - I suppose that assists deniability, although I suppose we could reassemble the dates from other records."

"Why would they do that?" queried Olivia

Pete continued, "It's an obvious way to disguise someone's movements and allows for little extra missions to be slipped in the gaps but conveniently not recorded."

Pete scrolled through the text for a moment, "Next he is shown as involved with the destruction of al-Qaeda and Taliban militant training camps, involved in the Fall of the Taliban government and the establishment of the Islamic Republic of Afghanistan under the Karzai administration."

Olivia picked him up on this, "'Involved with' is a somewhat vague term?"

Pete continued, "Yes, but 'destruction' isn't and suggests he was a shadow there doing something quite robust. I'm used to reading between the lines of these reports - even the redacted ones. Then there is a gap before he is involved with drone strikes in Pakistan."

"It also shows him in the invasion of Iraq and as Part of the War on Terror. It includes the invasion and occupation of Iraq and the Overthrow of Ba'ath Party government as well as the tracking and capture of

Saddam Hussein."

"Capture?" asked Olivia.

"That's what it says, it doesn't mention anything subsequent," answered Pete, "Then the combating of insurgency during the rise of al-Qaeda in Iraq with its severe sectarian violence. It shows him assisting the reduction in violence and depletion of al-Qaeda in Iraq. And being an instrument in establishment of democratic elections and formation of new Shia-led government."

"So that could be the hunting down of some of the 'playing cards'?" asked Olivia, referring to the playing card decks of Iraqi suspects handed out to the US fighting forces.

Pete replied, "Yes, although in-between this he seems to have served on a missile testing range in Arizona and during this time he learned to fly several classes of aircraft and helicopters at Kirtland, Arizona."

Pete looked further down the screen. "Then he transferred to East Pakistan where he was involved with some of the insurgency in the Northern tribal regions of Pakistan and in Khyber Pakhtunkhwa. That included more drone attacks."

"Drones? Any particular types?" asked Olivia.

Pete repelled, "It doesn't say, although I think these would be the big ones, you know like Predators and Scan Eagles - and not just used for surveillance either. Used to hunt and kill. "

Pete was studying the file again, "Then he took off for

Somalia where there were yet more drone strikes. I would say that Colonel Manners was a highly technically accomplished operator with a broad knowledge of combat territories and of drones, missiles and asymmetric warfare. "

"So, has he collected any medals during this time?" asked Olivia.

"Mainly the US and NATO service medals for some of the theatres he operated within," replied Pete, "Nothing that leaves an obvious trace or connection. I'd guess there's probably an Intelligence Star somewhere in Langley with his name on it too. But then, there is just this one hard-core anomaly. He was awarded a KBE for gallantry by the Brits."

"KBE - that's a serious medal - isn't it?" asked Olivia.

"You bet, A Knight Commander of the British Empire - He's officially a 'Sir' with that medal. - And it has been awarded for gallantry rather than merit, so he must have done something spectacular to get it."

"But nothing shown in the records?"

"Nothing. Nada. Nichts." Replied Pete, "Whatever it was must have been very secretive."

"Then he moved into Libya, where he worked for the overthrow of the Gaddafi government and the subsequent interim control by National Transitional Council(NTC). Despite diplomatic recognition of NTC as sole governing authority for Libya by 105 countries there was a lot of post-civil war violence in Libya leading to the restart of the main war in 2014."

"Colonel Manners seems to have cut loose by then though and it looks as if he then pops up in redacted reports, from London, Saint-Petersburg, Nice, Washington, Cali-Columbia and Paris.

"It says he was suspected of having got inside the violent drug cartel Los Urabeños, also known as the Autodefensas Gaitanistas, where he was trying to pinpoint Dario Antonio Úsuga David, also known as "Mao", the Colombian drug lord. That section is also redacted, but I suppose it ties in with Cali-Columbia."

Pete continued, "Then there's some other stuff about human trafficking and the Libyan refugee crisis , where he is thought to have run missions."

"These later reports position him as disrupter, designed to create waves which could ultimately bring empires down."

"What about private life, is he married, does he have kids?" asked Olivia.

"Divorced. He married a British woman, Melissa Skipton-Buxley, a member of the landed gentry. They had a child, Charlotte, aka Charlie. There is no reason given for the divorce, but I guess it must have been a consequence of Chuck's times away. I guess that's how he came to have a British passport too."

"Do we know anything else about Melissa?" asked Olivia.

"Well, for her it was a second marriage. She had married into wealth. Her first husband Anthony was a landowner with inherited wealth and made more money by selling off part of his estate to a builder. They built homes, schools and community building on the land, which seemed to enhance his reputation."

"Anthony was an ardent skier and had represented Britain in the Olympics. His love of skiing was what killed him. He was off-piste around Les Daiblerets, in Vaud, Switzerland when he crashed out. He was in a coma for a couple of days, but sadly died. I can't see how long afterwards Chuck met Melissa, but they seem to have got married about three years later. I guess Melissa liked her action-men!"

"And when did Charlie appear on the scene?"

"About two years later, but then they seemed to break up within another couple of years. According to Wiki, which lists the Skipton-Buxleys, the 'divorced second husband of Melissa' is also shown as 'estranged'."

"Wow, there's a book in there somewhere," said Olivia.

"Yes and it is noticeable that Chuck Manners would not even show up on a google search to this family record," said Pete.

"I see," said Olivia, "But now we see this Colonel Chuck Manners showing an interest in Minerva? We should be worried. I will need to escalate this. Please package your findings into a report for me, with a summary cover sheet."

Pete nodded to his 23-year old CIA boss.

Olivia climbs the pole

Pete wrote his report and summary of Chuck Manners and forwarded it to Olivia. She thanked him but said she would be tidying the summary sheet to make it punchier.

Pete had seen this before. He was all-too-aware aware of the Chilcott Report. How the Iraq Weapons of Mass Destruction report had allegedly been adapted by 'communicators'. He was concerned that his report into Chuck might be going through a similar process.

It was as he feared. The brigade of new millennials had worked it up into something altogether more sensational.

He read the new summary:

"Chuck Manners is a US-spy on British soil. A disrupter using a British passport to operate among the privileged classes. His range of skills made him an expert in asymmetric offensive measures, and he should now be considered a threat to the UK, USA and NATO-States. An immediate alert for his apprehension would be issued."

"Well," he thought, "The golden thread of justice of the

Universal Declaration of Human Rights is not so obvious in this case. The presumption of innocence until proven guilty has gone missing."

Pete wondered if he had done the right thing, by telling Olivia as much as he had discovered. She was already spinning her way up the greasy pole by now. Still, there were still a few more things which he had later unearthed. He doubted whether any of the other CIA millennials would dig as deeply as he had done, preferring to review, extrapolate and surf from the existing report.

Pete was even beginning to wonder about the pages beyond the summary. Did anyone really read them?

A convenient truth

The repackaged report about Chuck Manners was soon in circulation at higher levels inside the CIA. Several CIA people in higher positions saw it for what it was. A piece of cobbled together spin. Some had worked with Chuck or knew of his prior exploits and were certain that he would not jeopardise his career in the ways suggested in the report.

A copy also found its way across to the Raven Offices. It was marked "For the eyes of Sir Charles Frobisher Only," It had already gained a mystic sheen by the time he opened it.

Sir Charles had called his Ruler, the Freemason and MP Michael Tovey. He knew that Tovey was not supposed to hold a Freemason degree or membership whilst in Parliament, yet the secrecy of the Masons would protect him.

"Hello Charles, so what have you got today?"

"Michael, Some interesting news from Minerva. We've a report on Chuck Manners."

"Yes Charles, I think I might have already seen it."

Charles was taken aback by this statement. If he had only just received it as an 'Eyes Only' report than how on earth could Tovey have already seen it?

"Yes, I received it yesterday, direct from Minerva. I think one of our Brothers works there and decided it was worth plucking from the routine delivery chain."

"We need to decide what to do," said Frobisher, " He sounds like a loose cannon."

"I think you know what to do," said Tovey, "And I'll expect to see another report when it is ready."

There was a soft click as Tovey hung up his phone. Sir Charles was left with a difficult problem to resolve. He called his fixer, Gerhardt Schmidt.

"Hallo, Schmidt hier,"

"Hello Gerhardt, we've a little problem to fix." He explained the situation with Colonel Manners and that he felt direct action would be required.

"I can find out what is happening," said Gerhardt, "It might take me a couple of days to gather the intelligence, but I've a wide range of options - especially as this is linked with Qube and Brant. Leave it with me."

Eight of Pentacles

Diligence
Passion
High Standards

Blackbird

Her phone woke Christina, trilling early in her apartment. She recognised the voice. It was Blackbird, her handler.

"Hello," she said, deliberately deciding to stick to English. She secretly wondered that now she had re-awoken the FSB beast, whether things would be as straightforward for her.

"Privet, Arkhangelsk, mogu skazat', chto ty predpochitayesh' govorit' po-angliyski. Ya prines vam interesnyye novosti."

"Yes, I would prefer to speak English, and what is the interesting news that you bring?" asked Christina.

"Well, you know I mentioned that I thought Chuck Manners was trying to track you? And that we had brought a couple of embedded agents in to look? Well, they have found out something," said Blackbird.

"Our agents - you remember the man and woman team

аук и тупик er that's Auk and Puffin?"

"How could I forget them?" laughed Christina, "Although they never made any contact with me."

"Well, they continued to trace Chuck Manners until they finally caught up with him."

"And where was that?" asked Christina, intrigued at the thought of a near miss.

Blackbird continued, "They found out where he was working, but not where he was staying in London. Manners seemed to have a range of contacts spread across London, but аук и тупик could not even find out what he was doing. Well, it turns out that they have now intercepted a report from the Americans about him."

"At a listening station on the Thames, there's been some surveillance of an office that was used by Chuck Manners and a small team of other freelance operatives. The same station sent them as a hit squad into that team's prior office as a warning when they thought the team might have been on to something. To throw people of the trail, they used an American incendiary grenade."

"So you are telling me that these two agents were deployed for a live mission as well as to act as a tail?" asked Christina.

"Yes, to be truthful, the number of Russian agents in central London has diminished since the oligarchs gained power. They've bought up parts of the system for their own enforcement uses. Putin has just watched it happen."

So that implies that there are private armies out there now?" asked Christina.

"Yes, many of them. You know how street enforcement is managed in Moscow?"

"Yes, with small *Chastnaya armiya* patrolling the areas." answered Christina.

"Well, it is getting to be the same in London, and even down to the increasing costs. They don't want to be paid in roubles either, its USD, GBP and Euro all the way."

"I've seen some security in use. It's the flabby end of the GRU mostly. It looks as if the Silovik have been holding a fire sale to lose a few less-effective agents, " said Christina.

"Don't underestimate the security services though," said Blackbird, "They have a pretty tight grasp on things. Some would say they even have a grip on Putin."

"Ah yes, the Putin as a spook fan-boy theory?" asked Christina,

"Yes but watch out if offshoots of Wagner or Kramer turn up on the London scene. They are extremely dangerous," answered Blackbird

"The real 'men of force?' " asked Christina.

"Yes, not to be messed with," said Blackbird.

"What does this Listening Station have to say?" asked Christina, not prepared to reveal that she had already visited it.

"Well, they are putting together a dossier on Colonel Chuck Manners. It is nearly as impressive as yours, although he did more of his work in combat zones and only a scattering around in civilian situations."

"They are saying he needs to be brought in. There's not a strong reason, but he's being positioned as someone who knows the secrets of the Listening Station."

"Is the station one of ours? Asked Christina.

"Only indirectly, it has been set up with CIA fronting it and then uses the private contractor Brant to run it." Answered Blackbird.

"I see, we are supplying the staff into Brant?"

"We have a wrap-around Russian management structure for the station. Oh, the station is called Minerva."

"Roman goddess of wisdom, arts, poetry and notably, war," said Christina.

"That's right, myth has it she sprang from Jupiter's head and was borne fully grown and carrying armour." said Blackbird.

"Yes, and like all good Icelanders, I remember the stories of the gods. Minerva was a member of the Capitoline triad, a group named by the sacred Capitoline Hill in Rome, where Minerva is placed in a position of power and importance. The three gods were Jupiter- her father, Juno and Minerva." Said Christina, "I suspect there's a couple of other listening stations named Juno and Jupiter, somewhere in the world."

"Correct, and we are looking for them right now," said Blackbird.

"So what we get from your two agents is that Chuck Manners is wanted by the CIA, and that the CIA station in London is partly being run by Russian subcontractors?" asked Christina.

"That's right," said Blackbird, "And we just want you to sit tight at the moment. Let's see how the next stage of this plays out before taking any action."

"Okay, although can I meet аук и тупик - Auk and Puffin?" asked Christina, "I'd have a few questions for them."

"No, we want to keep the air gaps between you at the moment," said Blackbird, "Silent running."

Gerhardt

Sir Charles Frobisher's phone rang.

"Hello, Sir Charles, It is Gerhardt - I think I have tracked down what is happening with Colonel Chuck Manners.

"Someone from Minerva has already put out a hunt order for him. They have also dispatched two Russian operatives to find him. The two Russians have been tracking him for several weeks already, but their orders have been changed to terminate him now."

"I think you can let the system run its course on this situation," said Gerhardt.

"Whose orders are the Russians operating under?" asked Frobisher. He was mystified that there was already an order out on Chuck Manners.

"I couldn't find that out. The most likely would be the FSB, but I'm told these particular agents were partial to freelance work as well. I think their time in the west has corrupted their ideology."

Sir Charles considered for a moment. Minerva Station was supposedly being run by the CIA; Brant were positioned inside it as outsourcers. Someone was pulling the strings, but it sure wasn't him.

"This also seems somewhat clumsy," said Sir Charles.

"Clumsy?" asked Gerhardt,

"Maladroit, ungeschickt" answered Sir Charles.

"Ach Ja," said Gerhardt,"Unpassend - Yes I don't know who is running these agents, nor how they have issued a kill order - and I can't imagine it would be the CIA either - Colonel Chuck Manners is held in the highest regard inside the CIA."

"So now we have two loose cannons chasing one loose cannon?" asked Sir Charles.

Polystyrene peanuts

Back at the Triangle's temporary offices, Jake and Bigsy were unpacking a few containers of electronics.

"Do we really need all of this stuff?" asked Jake, looking at a Rode shotgun microphone.

"Oh yes," answered Bigsy, "That microphone, for example, is very omnidirectional. Great for picking up conversations. And look, I have some anti-surveillance equipment too. To stop people doing to us what we might want to do to them."

"Where do you get this stuff?" asked Jake.

"Literally, from the Spy Shop," answered Bigsy, "It's a place in Tottenham Court Road."

"What? Do they still have all those gadget shops along there?" asked Jake, "I remember when it was the place to go for hi-fi and TV equipment, before computers took over music and television."

"Yes, the spy gadgets thing has always been there too,"

answered Bigsy.

"Look at this," he plucked a large carton from a flutter of polystyrene packing peanuts.

"What is it?" asked Jake.

"I thought I'd get one for the new office," answered Bigsy, "It is a WAM-108t Multiband Wireless Activity Monitor. It is a high specification portable handheld multi-band detector for the detection and logging of all types of radio frequency devices. It provides coverage and logging of all radio activity in the surrounding area"

So, then, switch it on, "show what it does," asked Jake.

Bigsy quietly assembled a row of small antennae along the top of the unit.

"Right, here we go, but it shouldn't detect anything here, except our normal wi-fi and phone signals."

Jake was intrigued as Bigsy suddenly made series of 'silence' hand gestures to Jake.
    "Is everything okay?" asked Jake. Bigsy was shaking his head.

"Yes, its fine. Just as I thought. Nothing to report. Do you know what, all this unpacking has made me thirsty. Shall we go downstairs to the cafe?"

Bigsy was gesturing to Jake to go downstairs.

"Oh, Sure, Let's grab a coffee."

Bugged

"What was all that about?" asked Jake, looking towards Bigsy.

"Here, two lattes," answered Bigsy, "I can't be sure, but I think we are bugged."

"How so?" asked Jake.

"Well, that last gadget I was testing. It showed a huge amount of activity from a couple of spots in the office. Like there's a microphone been placed there."

"But how could that be?" asked Jake. "Since we've been in there, we've only had 'known' visitors and there's not been any perimeter alarms?"

"Yes, but we are in a managed facility," said Bigsy, "That means at night we have cleaners come around and in the day we might get someone visiting from the service desk."

"Can we track down the microphones?" asked Jake.

"Em, with four-thousand pounds worth of kit I jolly well hope so," answered Bigsy.

"Really?" said Jake, "I'd no idea those little gadgets were so expensive."

"Think about it…They help stop company secrets from being sold, so the guys that make them value price them," said Bigsy, "And I'd rather know that it works than build something that would leave a nagging doubt."

"Fair point," said Jake, "so what are we going to do about it?"

"A couple of things. First, we should see whether we can work out who is listening, and second we should stage an accident which somehow zaps the microphones, or at least their transmitters."

"We'd better tell the others too," said Jake.

"Not in the office though!" said Bigsy.

Mop-up operation

They were sitting together in the coffee bar across the street. Bigsy had just told Christina and Clare about the bugging. Jake returned with the coffees.

"What are we going to do to remove them?" asked Clare.

"Well, now I've found their base station, I think we have a simple solution," said Bigsy, "Whoever planted the devices gave each of them a big fat battery, which I reckon would last about a year. The signal from the microphone goes to a special base station outside one of our cupboards. It looks like an old landline telephone connector, to throw us off the trail. From there, it just sends the signal along the old telephone lines back to whoever is on the other end."

"Do we think there will be an accident of some kind?" laughed Christina, "Maybe a two-part demolition of the device?"

"Good idea," said Bigsy, "I can be quite clumsy with a mop and bucket.

"Okay, so one of us spills something on the floor, another one comes along with a galvanised steel bucket which just accidentally knocks the cover off the device. And oh dear, we've also dislodged the wires. It will all make sense to them listening to the recording too. Cause and effect - all innocent," said Christina.

"You've done this kind of thing before?" queried Jake.

"Maybe, but only in training situations," answered Christina, "Let's see now, what kind of sandwich should I buy? - One that is especially messy."

She settled for a BLT - Bacon, lettuce and tomato, which she said to the others represented the best payload for the upcoming mayhem.

They trooped back across to the office and Christina started to noisily unwrap the sandwich by the side of the cabinet at the foot of which was the phone adapter box.

"Oh no! I've dropped my sandwich all over the floor. The package must have been loose!" she cried and then Bigsy called out, "Hold on a minute, I'll get the cleaning mop."

He wheeled in a galvanised cleaner's bucket filled with soapy water and a rugged looking mop. Christina noticed he was also wearing a tool belt.

"Here we are, " he said, "I'll soon have this mess cleared up." He banged and crashed the bucket around a couple of times. Christina noticed that the top had already come loose from the phone adapter. Then she saw Bigsy snip through some wires. He replaced his cutters in the leather tool belt and continued the mopping sounds for another couple of minutes.

Then, gesturing to everyone for silence, he tiptoed around the office with his bug-detector.

Then, a thumbs-up.

"Well, that sea bit of a mess, but we've cleaned it up really well. I'd say we've made the office squeaky clean now, but I think we maybe need to check for any other dirt maybe once a week." Said Bigsy.

"Cool tool belt," said Jake, to Bigsy.

"Yes, brand new and leather - first time I've ever needed one," said Bigsy in reply, "I feel like I'm in some wild west show, instead of pushing a mop bucket around!"

Christina looked around. Everyone was looking relieved that they had removed the source of the bug.

"You know, I found out something today," she began.

She told everyone what she had heard about Chuck. She explained that she thought Minerva station was setting him up for capture. She also described the two people that had been chasing him and that they had a part in the fire-bombing of the original Triangle Offices.

"Well, maybe they did us a favour?" said Clare, "I mean I liked the old place, but if we are moving to Hay's Galleria then that is still a real step up."

The Lovers

Choices
Union
Love
Relationship

Kramer

"Something I can't properly understand," said Christina, "Is how Minerva is being run?"

"How do you mean?" asked Jake.

"Well, think about it. We know it is fronted as if it belongs to the CIA. We also know they are bringing in people from Brant to run most of it. Yet we know that the Brant people are being sourced with at least some Russian Agents."

"My handler, Blackbird, said that the big oligarch operated private armies were not present in London. I can see that is the case by the lack-lustre performance of the agents that I've seen. Auk and Puffin were the two firebombers. Neat work, but they still took an age to trace Chuck Manners and didn't make any connections between Chuck and the Triangle offices. Multi-lingual low-end workers in the Minerva offices - and incidentally being run by CIA children. It's all a bit *poshchechina* - er slap-dash."

"What's this about oligarch armies?" asked Clare, intrigued.

"As well as the Russian Army and the various Russian secret services, there's been some attempts at privatisation. For example, there is the Russian firm Wagner Group, which is a shadowy mercenary outfit waging secret wars on the Kremlin's behalf from Ukraine to Syria to the Central African Republic. It seems like something from a Tom Clancy novel.

"I visited one of their training camps once, " said Christina, "It was in the back of beyond, in Russia, sandwiched between the Ukraine and Georgia. They had a facility there. They called it a children's school, but it was a boot camp. We flew there by Anatov AN-148 from Vasil Levski National Military University in Bulgaria. It was a kind of away-day. We were told we were getting there on a MIL-26 so there was much relief when we found we would be on a jet plane with windows and seats instead of a helicopter with stretcher mounts and no view. The flight time was about two hours instead of what we guessed would have been 8 or 9 hours in the chopper."

"I was a little bit shocked at how basic the facilities were at Wagner. It was far more primitive that the capabilities we had at Vasil Levski NMU. We had a much better supply of weapon types, trainers and even the accommodation. Wagner was for tough guys and was all about the shouting with a loud frog voice over 22mm autocannon fire."

"Come to think of it, I was at that camp with Antanov Chekeryn. We had to stay there overnight, and we both decided to sleep out under the stars. - Yeah Yeah - stop it!" as both Jake and Bigsy moved in with questions.

"I'm going to try to call up Antanov for this one. He will have some inside information about this. He was pilot trained and would have gained other insights into the way the camp ran. Hold on while I try to reach him in Brussels."

She reached for her phone and they all waited to see whether he would pick up.

"Antanov - it's Christina - Great and how are you. Look, you remember the folk from The Triangle? I'm sitting with them now - but we are in a different office after the first one got fire-bombed."

"Yes, I know - cross town traffic - ninety miles an hour, is the speed I drive. Well - you remember that Anatov flight we did to *Mol'kino, Krasnodar Krai*? You remember, the one where they let you co-pilot part of the way back? Well, I'd like to describe the Wagner facility to the guys here and thought you could help me remember? Can I put you on speakerphone?"

"Sure Christina, hey guys, it sounds like you have been having some fun! Who is there? Jake, Bigsy, Clare? Chuck?"

"Hey Antanov - all of us except Chuck. He's in some hot water now and left London."

"Huh? I guess it makes sense. What about that woman of his? Does she know where he'll be now?"

Clare looked up, "Antonov - you are a star! I'll bet Amanda Miller has a way to find Chuck, we'll be on to it after this call!"

Christina asked Antanov, "So what can you remember about Wagner and Kramer?"

Antanov started, "Well, I think they liked to use names that were not particularly Russian - which is why they chose Wagner and Kramer. - The wagon makers and shopkeepers of middle Europe!"

He continued, "Putin has let Wagner and Kramer set up their outfits and a few smaller ones. They are born out of a need for plausible deniability in Moscow's military operations abroad."

" 'Plausible deniability' sounds like something out of a CIA movie," said Jake.

Antanov continued, "Take Wagner - Their contractors were at the forefront of some of the heaviest fighting in eastern Ukraine and Syria in recent years before hitting the headlines with their brazen assault on a U.S. military position in northeast Syria in February 2018."

Christina added, "There's been setbacks too, although Wagner seemed to herald a new reality, one in which it would form the spearhead of aggressive new Russian policies abroad, but it may be less influential than it seems."

Antanov continued, "Yes, the past few months have been filled with revelations about the group's reversal of fortune. A Russian independent media outlet Novaya Gazeta revealed that three Russian military contractors killed in central Syria in mid-June were not Wagner employees but part of another similar firm, called Shield."

"Like the Russian dolls?" said Bigsy, "Contracts within Contracts?"

Antanov continued, "*Babushka* – Yes. The casualties were the first confirmed non-Wagner-linked Russian contractors killed in the country, a fact made more significant by their presence in the central Syrian desert, previously one of Wagner's primary operations zones in Syria.

Antonov's tone changed, "Remember that Wagner played a pivotal role in capturing Palmyra and Deir Ezzor in 2016 and 2017?"

"Yes, they were tough fights too," added Christina, "But what with another Russian private military contractor apparently muscling in on Wagner's turf there was then another report the following day which painted the group in an unflattering light. It's incredible to think the subcontracts of the Russian army would become as factional as they did."

Antanov continued, "Yes, that report was from Meduza, a Russian independent news portal who spoke with one of the Russian contractors deployed to Venezuela."

Antanov added, "When a group of contractors arrived in the country in January, it was widely reported that they were Wagner mercenaries, sent to the country to shore up President Nicolás Maduro's rule in the face of sustained mass protests. Russia could be looking away while this was happening."

Christina added, " Yes, but some Western analysts, not unreasonably, took the move to indicate Wagner's growing status as a Kremlin policy instrument to militarily bolster a key allied regime whose survival was in serious doubt, furthering Moscow's foreign interests while remaining at arm's length."

"Kremlin Policy instrument? Now things were getting serious, particularly as they had rumbled Wagner," said Clare.

Antanov said, "That's why the Meduza report suggested the opposite. Their source, a Wagner employee, revealed that he and his fellow contractors had served merely as security guards for Rosneft office buildings in Caracas during an unremarkable year-long posting."

"There's plenty of evidence of the same operations on the streets of Moscow, outside of the headquarters buildings of the big conglomerates. It would make perfect sense to an average Muscovite reading about it in the papers." Added Christina.

Antanov added, "But then, other interviewees, including a long-time Wagner employee, confirmed that Wagner itself has played no role in Venezuela, contrary to initial reports. The outfit has reportedly haemorrhaged experienced veterans to several other such groups, including the firms Shield, Patriot and Kramer in recent months, while it has lost its autonomy in decision-making and was downgraded to guard duty in Syria."

Christina added, "Wagner became a shell of its former self, having had its wings clipped by the Kremlin and its most valuable personnel stripped away by competitors.

Not quite what Putin had in mind when he first embarked upon the idea of deniable private armies."

Antanov continued, "Well, seeing Wagner being discussed publicly in the Russian press finally prompted some direct action by the USA. Wagner's confrontation with U.S. troops in Deir Ezzor marked the beginning of the end for the firm."

He continued, "When roughly 600 Wagner contractors, armed with tanks and artillery, launched an assault on a position of the Syrian Democratic Forces, a largely Kurdish militia force that had worked closely with the U.S.-led anti-Islamic State coalition, in northeast Syria.

Antanov added "What they may not have known is that U.S. advisors were embedded with the unit and promptly called for air support."

"Could those advisors have included Chuck?" asked Clare.

"Well, he did claim to be a disruptor," said Christina.

Antanov continued, "Wagner forces maintained the assault for a full four hours, during which U.S. artillery, airstrikes, helicopters, and even an AC-130 gunship hammered them. When the dust cleared, about 300 of the 600 Russians were dead or wounded, in the first direct battle between Washington's and Moscow's forces since the Vietnam War."

"Whew, so the US had launched a counterattack using aircraft and obliterated the quasi-Russian force. That would be some disruption," said Bigsy.

Christina added, "The most astonishing aspect of this incident was that it evidently occurred without being ordered by, or even fully known to, the Kremlin itself - an illustration of what happened when Putin allowed deniable autonomy to armed forces."

Jake added, "I can see that, not wanting to become implicated in the mess, but I bet Putin was furious that someone had acted with such stupidity as to fall into an American military trap."

Antanov continued, "Yes, but leaked telephone conversations revealed that Yevgeny Prigozhin, a man referred to as President Vladimir Putin's 'chef' who is believed to lead Wagner, ordered the assault after conversing with several Syrian business colleagues."

Antanov added, "And that this could all be self-interest. Prigozhin also controls a company with oil and gas stakes in the region."

"Ahah, so it was a greed-driven mission by Wagner!" said Bigsy.

Christina agreed, "Yes, Prigozhin himself was sanctioned by the U.S. Treasury Department for his role in Russia's 2016 U.S. election interference several times. I know from first-hand about the Russian click-farms. We even had one when I lived in Arkhangelsk."

Antanov added, "Yes, and this marks the time when Putin was looking towards soft influence rather than purely warfare to get what he wanted. The start of the cyber-warfare."

Christina added, "The disjointed response from official

Moscow also suggests they were uninformed: It took a week for Kremlin officials to say that there 'may be citizens of the Russian Federation' not linked to the Russian armed forces fighting in Syria, before later saying that five Russians may have been killed, a number that later grew to 'several dozen' - still a long way short of the real number."

Antanov continued, "Sources close to the Russian Ministry of Defense said they were "simply stunned" when they learned the attack had occurred and that a deeply embarrassed Prigozhin then had to grovel to Kremlin officials that such an error would not happen again."

"I'm amazed that Putin didn't get crazy with Prigozhin after him doing something so stupid and revealing his corrupt hand," added Jake.

"It was a sign of the times," said Christina, "Corruption and pocket lining by Russian state officials with access to state industries."

She added, "This is where it gets interesting, vis-a-vis Brant. Viewed in this light, the Prigozhin's moves in places such as South Sudan and Mozambique appear almost pathetic, casting about desperately in a mostly futile search for opportunities that could come close to matching those they found in Syria and Ukraine. They had great opportunities but blew them."

Antanov nodded, " Yes, and the Russian model was not as sophisticated as an American one. The Americans would blow up everything, install a peacekeeping force and then set up contracts to rebuild everything damaged. That is the model that Brant and Raven want to operate in Celarus, for example."

Antanov continued, "Training a handful of minor militias in Central Africa and bidding, seemingly unsuccessfully, against Erik Prince of Blackwater fame for security contracts is a far cry from leading assaults backed by the Russian air force in a major civil war in the strategically sensitive Middle East."

"It shows a lack of imagination too," said Christina, "to just run the warfare but not the civil reconstruction - let alone the infrastructure."

Antanov agreed, "With a wealth of new competitors springing up, such as Shield, Patriot (allegedly directly linked to the Russian defence ministry), Kramer and Vega, Wagner's days as the top dog of Russian defence contractors are likely done and the waning of Wagner will elicit few tears in and around the Kremlin."

Antanov continued, "Wagner gets downgraded without major scandal, its personnel dispersed among similar groups, and its operations curtailed. It's punishment for Prigozhin, who was never one for the spotlight and not attempted to complicate matters in any remotely public manner, likely aware that doing so would only further jeopardise his position."

"Not least with Putin!" added Clare.

Christina added, "Out of Wagner's fall there is the opportunity for a new company to rise - Kramer springs to mind as the most likely. Wagner's fall has had few consequences for the Kremlin, which has no pressing need for a professional yet expendable military force."

"I agree," said Antanov, "Although I can't imagine Putin without a few useful strings to pull spread around Europe."

Jake questions, "So, with the Babushka dolls, do we think there is another layer? I was just getting my head around the Raven divestment of Qube, the merger of Qube into Brant and the stealthy outsourcing of a spy operation by the CIA to Brant. Now I'm wondering if there isn't a further wraparound of Kramer, which pushes the overall game to the Russians?"

Antanov Analysis Redux

"Can we position this against what is happening in Celarus?" asked Jake, "We know that Raven was up to no good when they hived off Qube to make Brant."

"Yes, although we thought this was Raven or Freemason inspired, with no strong thoughts about it being state-run," said Christina, "We'd found the link to the CIA but Anne-Marie who we questioned confirmed Minerva was running as a boiler house to blackmail and squeeze some MP influencers."

"I agree, it doesn't seem to set up a major foreign army outpost in east London," said Bigsy.

Antanov added, "The Kremlin has long jealously guarded the approaches to the security field, placing strict regulations on private security firms to maintain its monopoly on armed force in Russia."

"Hmm, there's still an ability to build up a private army on Russian soil though," said Jake.

Christina added, "We were taught that legally, Russia's

various private military contractors do not officially exist: Their presence remains illegal under Russian law, with various false-start attempts to draft and pass new legislation on the matter to allow their registration."

Jake queried, "So how did Wagner develop in this legal vacuum, transforming from an ad-hoc project into a full-fledged private military, replete with Russian tanks, artillery, and as many as 5,000 service members?"

Bigsy added, " Yes, if Wagner is the beta test, then maybe Kramer or Brant will become the first full release?"

Christina agreed, " Yes. If Wagner became one of the most powerful force structures in terms of fighters and material in the Russian Federation, outside of the Kremlin's own security apparatus.

Antanov said, "So a new Kramer or Brant could start to challenge Moscow's central authority. These challenges are bound to grow as Russia lurches toward the uncertainty of life beyond Putin."

Clare said, "Instead of the image of an omnipotent autocrat brandishing all levers of power, Putin may be forced to lead Russia through a series of compromises and understandings among powerful elites, from businesspeople to bureaucrats, with the all-powerful security officials. He's built a system with powerful thugs running things but now they are building their armies, it could be the beginning of a power grab."

Christina said, "The struggles to carve out turf and eliminate rivals with five years to go until this watershed moment have already begun and are certain to continue to deepen as the next presidential election approaches.

Putin's system, while stable and presenting the image of a monolithic entity to outsiders, is highly personalised. Russia's various security services are riven with factionalism, with the one controlling variable being their agreement to bow to the current president.

Christina said, "It is important to remember that it was not always this way: Putin's predecessor Boris Yeltsin had a famously difficult time controlling Russia's various armed services, and it took Putin years to bring them to heel and eradicate the various fiefdoms corrupt generals had established in Chechnya in the early 2000s, where trafficking in illegal oil sales became a popular pastime for commanders looking to enrich themselves."

Antanov agreed, "Firms such as Vega, Shield, Kramer and Patriot are a pale echo of what Wagner was at the height of its power, but they have a shining example of what they could one day become."

Christina smiled, "What remains of Wagner's service members are now acting as glorified bodyguards and mall cops. But its successors like Kramer will set their sights much higher—and in a less stable post-Putin future, that could pose a threat to Russian, and global security."

"Yikes," said Bigsy, "So we are all doomed?"

"Not exactly," said Antanov, "But there's a lot to unpack here. I always say to Christina that she runs at ninety miles per hour. This has just been another example. Now, I will sign off and tuck my children into bed. Night-night everyone!"

There was a click.

"Only ninety miles per hour?" said Jake.

Finding Chuck

Jake made the call to Amanda Miller at SI6. He had several past dealings with her including that time she had locked him up for his own protection and knew she would take the call. He was just slightly cautious about broaching the subject of Chuck to her.

"Hi Amanda," he began, "It's Jake, Jake Lambers,"

"Hello Jake, and, how are you?" asked Amanda. Jake was pleased that she at once recognised him, in amongst the hundreds of contacts she met in her role.

"Look, I need to talk to you about someone," he said, being suitably covert on an SI6 line, "It's a somewhat military matter."

"Can I meet you somewhere?" asked Amanda.

"Certainly," said Jake, relieved that Amanda had picked up on the delicate nature of the call, "The weather is nice. How about Jubilee Gardens?"

"That's very walkable for me, shall we say an hour?"

"Perfect," Jake was secretly delighted that he had a head of SI6 coming out to meet him at an hours' notice. He walked outside. He'd take a cab the short distance and if he was early, he could enjoy the sunshine.

…

An hour later, Jake could see Amanda walking towards the gardens. They were a large expanse of grass by the side of the London Eye. Londoners would sit on the curved walls next to the paths that cut through the gardens.

Jake could see the busy tourists walking in large groups along the embankment of the River Thames.

"Hello Jake!" said Amanda, "I've thought about your team a few times over the last few weeks."

"Well, this is about our honorary guest member, Chuck," said Jake, "And funnily enough, we first met him close to here. Just along Belvedere Road in the Sushi place. We didn't have a clue who we were dealing with back then."

"No, he's never told me how you all got intertwined, but I suppose he is a man of mystery."

"Well, we think he might be in some more trouble," said Jake, "And Clare thinks you might know how to contact him."

"Okay, you've got me," said Amanda, "We discussed a way to contact one another, where I'm static most of the time but Chuck moves around a lot."

"I'll respect your privacy on this," said Jake, switching into journalist mode, "But we think Chuck is being sought by a couple of Russian tracers."

"Tracers?"

"Yes, low level agents who have been tasked to find him," Jake looked serious, "If you remember that east London listening post, the one called Minerva? Well, we think its them that have requested a trace on Chuck."

"I'm confused now. The listening station was being operated by the CIA, in collaboration with Brant. Why would they put two Russians onto it?"

"That's what we thought, but we think there is already a hole in the Listening Station's security and that the Russians have access to what is happening. The Russians have been tipped off that Minerva is looking for Chuck and now want to get to him first."

Amanda nodded, "Okay. I think I can contact Chuck, to let him know. I don't know what he will do though, whether he will come in or go deeper into hiding?"

"Well, if you make contact, please try to find out his plans," said Jake, "and let him know that we are all- including Christina- rooting for him."

Yegorin protection

Amanda made her way back to Vauxhall Cross. She was scheduled on a video conference call with Jim Cavendish from SI6 and Grace Fielding at GCHQ.

They were discussing the case of Khramov Gavril (Gavy) Yegorin.

Jim Cavendish began, "After a bomb scare, Yegorin requested the protection of SO15, the counter-terrorism squad. Yegorin had once enjoyed the life in Moscow – high powered deal making, behind-the-scenes agreements, 'understandings' between friends in the Kremlin corridors of power. It was all good."

Grace continued, "Yes, then it looks as if the tide has turned. Yegorin is being squeezed. He asked for protection from the UK counter-terrorism squad. Like every good TV show cliché, his bodyguards found suspicious-looking boxes taped underneath his Rolls-Royce, and magnetically attached to the car used to transport his children to school."

Jim asked, "Do we think these were real, or was he trying to get our sympathy?"

Grace answered, "We don't know. The devices were real enough. Smart magnetics on the kid's car and a phone operated explosive on the Roller. UK were obligated to give him protection."

Amanda asked, "Could this be linked with that Minerva listening station out in south-east London?"

"We don't know. The profile of that listening station is confusing - fronted by CIA, staffed by Qube/Brant and possibly under Russian influence."

Jim added, "Well, as far as Yegorin goes, SO15 counter-terrorism squad has installed Yegorin's home with an attack alarm and perimeter protection. Frankly, he has enough security of his own. I think the alarm was a way for him to signal to those attacking him that he was linked with the UK security forces."

Grace added, "Let's not forget. Ten years ago, Yegorin was a Kremlin insider who'd manoeuvred to help bring Vladimir Putin to power. He would most likely be on someone's list by now,"

She continued, "Known as one of the Kremlin's financial advisors, he has been a master of the deals and the conjuring tricks that governed the way Russia operated."

Amanda agreed, " Yes, I had him pegged as one of Putin's untouchables. A member of Putin's inner circle that made and bent the rules to suit themselves, with law enforcement, the courts, and even elections twisted for their needs."

Grace added, "But now the Kremlin machine he'd once been part of has turned against him. He had become the latest victim of Putin's relentlessly expanding reach.

"The Kremlin had moved in on his business empire, taking it for itself. Television sketch shows and popular magazines show how Putin manoeuvres to take control, with prior owners of businesses taking a fall or disappearing in the process. We've seen some examples here in Britain."

Jim said, "Yegorin was smart and well-informed. When things stacked against him, he left Russia. First to France and then England as the Kremlin launched its seizure of his assets. Putin's men took the prestigious hotel projects the president had granted him in St Petersburg and in Moscow. Then his shipyards, among the largest in Russia, valued at $4 billion, were acquired by one of Putin's closest allies for a fraction of that sum.

Jim referred to his notes, "Then Yegorin's coal project, a huge coking-coal deposit in the Siberian region of Tuva, valued at $3 billion, was taken by a close associate of the Chechen president, for $150 million."

Amanda added, "Let's not forget, the manner that Yegorin acquired these projects in the first place is also a matter for question."

Grace added, "Yes, and so to put the boot in, Putin's men blamed Yegorin for the collapse of *Mezhdunarodnyy kommercheskiy* bank, that's *Mezhkommbank,* the international commercial bank Yegorin co-founded through his 'relationships' and that had once been the key to his power."

Amanda asked, "So were his relationships to the siloviks, or the blatnoy, or whom?"

Grace said, "We think, by definition, that Yegorin is a blatnoy - gangster - and his relations are to the silovik clans, but he has worked his relationships through the use of Freemasonry. It's not helping him much now, though."

Grace continued, "The Kremlin authorities were ruthless and opened a criminal case claiming Yegorin had caused the Mezhkommbank's bankruptcy by transferring $800 million from it to a Swiss bank account at the height of the 2008 financial crisis."

Jim said, "Yes, that's where it becomes very murky. The Kremlin paid no regard to Yegorin's claims that the money was his own. Nor that the takeover of the hotels and shipyards at a fraction of their value was the biggest reason for the shortfall in the bank's funds to creditors."

Grace said, "Honestly, it is hard to have any sympathy for Yegorin, it seems more like a case of rough justice."

Amanda said, "Yes, the state manipulated the rules against him to bring the bank down, unsurprisingly benefiting themselves. It is a typical story for a Kremlin machine that had become relentless in its reach. First, it had gone after political enemies. But now it is turning on Putin's one-time allies. Yegorin was just one of the inner circle to fall."

Amanda added, "But now the Kremlin is leveraging its campaign against him using the veneer of respectability of London's High Court. They know certain London lawyers can be coin-operated and so the Kremlin obtained a freezing order against Yegorin's assets, tying the tycoon up in knots in the courtroom along the way. Ever since Yegorin left Russia, the Kremlin has pursued him."

Grace said, "Yes, and we've been following the trail of breadcrumbs outside of Russia. Yegorin has links to Raven, via Brant in Celarus."

New Office

Jake decided to walk from his meeting with Amanda along the bank of the Thames towards the new offices in Hay's Galleria. He could do an early scout around to see whether there was anything they had missed. His general impression was that it was getting better and better.

Outside the building was a bustling glass atrium area. It had a range of small shops and cafes along it. It was all high-end and there was a discreet wine bar underground just along one side. At the end was the River Thames, with a tourist ship - The HMS Belfast - moored alongside and in the other direction there was a small dock where the Thames Clippers - high-speed glass-domed passenger boats came into dock. It was possible to go all the way to Chelsea or to Canary Wharf on the river, including passing right underneath the nearby Tower Bridge.

On the other side of Tooley Street was the huge conurbation of London Bridge complete with its myriad shops and hidden arches. There was also the tube line to the West End and across the bridge along the Thames was the start of the City of London.

Jake was surprised at the cost of the offices, which had been lower than he had expected, but the estate agent had told him something about a special offer because of the aftereffects of the recent pandemic's financial meltdown which had drowned the City for a while.

Jake wasn't convinced by the story but wouldn't argue because he was getting the offices for a bargain price.

"Hmm," said a voice," They look like pizzas hung on the wall." It was Bigsy appraising the corporate artwork supplied with the offices.

"Hi Jake, I thought I'd bring some of my electronics over, maybe give the place a quiet sweep," said Bigsy.

He was pushing a large black hard-shell suitcase until he had caught up with Jake.

"What have you brought?" asked Jake.

"A few bibs and bobs," explained Bigsy, "After I discovered those extra devices in the temporary offices, I thought we should look here too. I'm also replacing the wi-fi receivers with my own set. I can set the encryption and other general security settings. I just need to find the wiring closet…"

Bigsy disappeared off around a corner. Jake could hear him unscrewing something and realised that Bigsy could be happy for hours.

The Fool

Innocence
New Beginnings
Wonder
Foolishness

Hekla

Christina was back at her apartment. Her phone rang.

"Hello?" she said; she noticed the dialling code was +354 - Iceland.

"Hello? Agnes? Aggi? It's Hekla here."

"Hekla? Guð minn. Hvað í ósköpunum ertu að hringja í mig? What on earth?"

"Hæ Agnes, ég held að þú myndir helst vilja tala á ensku nú á dögum?"

"Yes, Hekla, it would be fine to talk in English. This is a remarkable moment for me! I have not seen you since my family left Kjalvegur for the airport and to another world."

"But how on earth have you tracked me down?"

"It's a long story - Oh this is so exciting! - I am a big music fan of 'Ian and the Annalists' - Well, imagine my surprise when Ian posted an Instagram from Stuttgart airport, where he said he'd just met up with you. He showed you and another pretty lady and him in the middle. He called you Christina Nott and said you'd played together on some recordings in Amsterdam."

"But you still couldn't recognise me from that picture? queried Christina.

"No," but I also know Kristján Sigurðursson, who is something of a muso in Reykjavik. He told me he had run into you after a council meeting once and that he had later introduced you to some people in the business. He also told me you were going around with the name Christina Nott. I checked you out on YouTube and Spotify and that's how the connection worked. Then I contacted Ian, from the band and he sent me your number."

For Christina, this was the second time in her life that Hekla had set off warning alarms. The first time was when she fell through the roof of the wool-store and discovered Pabbi's listening station. That was when the entire family had to move suddenly to Russia to avoid detection. Luckily, Pabbi was a well-honoured jet-fighter pilot as well as an embedded agent and so they had been moved to a very comfortable apartment in Arkhangelsk, which is where Christina had learned about becoming an agent.

This time, she was concerned that Hekla had somehow joined the dots all the way from Reykjavik to London. If she could, then maybe someone else could also follow her.

"So, where are you now?" Asked Christina

"Well, here's the thing, I've booked a short break to London - you know to see the sights, but when I realised that you lived in London, Agnes, I thought it would be great to meet up again!" replied Hekla.

"Wow," that would be great, " said Christina, carefully weighing up options, "When do you get into London and where are you staying?"

"I fly in on Saturday," said Hekla, "And I'm staying at a hotel by Tower Bridge. It's called the Citizen M, I think."

"Citizen M? I know that hotel, I even walk past it sometimes. It can be busy but I think the location is fine and I've heard that the rooms are good. Why don't I meet you there? We can go out to somewhere pleasant in the neighbourhood. Just let me know a time when you arrive."

Hekla could hardly contain her excitement. "There's so much to talk about," she said, "It'll be brilliant fun."

Hilton Brussels Grand Place

Chuck's cellphone chirped.

He looked across. He was in the Hilton Brussels Grand Place, and his room seemed to be in the roof space of the hotel but with excellent views in all directions.

He was adjacent to the train station where he'd arrived from London. He had travelled on his Canadian passport and the name Charles Desjardins, which fitted with the Québécois origin.

He picked up the cellphone.

"Hello?" he said.

"Chuck? This is your friend in London."

He realised it was Amanda but that she was being cautious.

"No need to tell me where you are," she added, "But I think you would like to know something."

"You have my full attention," he said, aware that Amanda was giving signals that the line might be monitored.

"You might remember a couple of tracers in London? An auk and a puffin? They are looking for you for bounty from Minerva. Let me know if I am making sense?"

"Yes, that makes scary sense, except for one part. The auk and puffin are of a nation than the main Minerva station?"

"That is correct, we are trying to work it out. Some of your friends are also looking at the same puzzle. Even the musician."

Chuck could work this out. He was pursued by the two Russians who had first appeared in London. The Minerva Listening station had put out an alert for him. Despite it being CIA, it seemed that two Russians were chasing him. The Triangle team had his back and even Christina Hyde was stepping in to help him.

"Thank you. I liked it here, but I suppose I will need to move again," answered Chuck.

"I liked it 'there' too," answered Amanda.

"So did I, very much" replied Chuck.

Chuck weighed up the odds. He was in a good hotel, on the top floor, in a huge room. It was already late, and he was in one of the most well-secured areas in Europe, so close to the European Parliament buildings.

He would stay tonight and then prepare a plan for the next few days. He hated being on the run and would rather face-off to these two low-level agents.

He decided to sleep. But he would keep a pistol nearby.

Go Bag

Three in the morning in the Brussels Hilton and Chuck thought he could hear something. It was a small scraping sound outside his room. He was at once alert. Someone was trying to break in.

He knew that the suite he was in was too large for easy containment. He would need to take down the lighting and so he stealthily moved around unscrewing the side lights and switching off the main lights. Why did any luxury suite in a hotel have so many separate light circuits?

He felt in his 'Go Bag' and found his Night Vision Goggles. Armasight NYX-7. Expensive lifesavers. He could flip them down in front of his eyes and see like in daylight. If anyone tripped a light-switch, they would cut their amplification right down. Then he reached for two stun grenades and a neck tube.

He held the P226 in his hand in a confident way. He had even had time to add the silencer.

Now he had got the advantage, even if they were trying to break into his room.

He listened longer. There was still a scraping sound. These people were slow. He'd have a door opened in around three seconds. A hotel room with a swipe card? Come on.

Then the door opened slowly. He admired the clump of clothing he had put on the bed. In the dark, it looked as if someone was sleeping.

Then he heard two clicks. He knew the sound - they were shooting at the bed. They thought he was asleep. Then a shout. A rapid-fire rattle. He looked towards the door. Someone was entering with extreme prejudice. He looked towards the face. It was Christina. Talk about archangel vengeance, she had been firing a submachinegun which was now smoking from the heat she had unleashed.

"Christina- Steady," he called - She acknowledged him with a raised index finger and walked carefully towards the two assassins.

Chuck noticed that the gun she carried was tiny.

"Hey Chuck, I thought you might need some help," said Christina powering down from her onslaught,"Those two people were trying to kill you. Look at the state of that bed."

He realised that Christina was still jacked on adrenaline and from the sounds of the last few seconds.

"Thank you, you were amazing," he eventually said.

Christina looked around. "I've made a mess in here," she said, "I hope you don't mind."

He noticed that Christina clicked small levers around the submachine gun but also that she loaded another magazine into it. He also noticed that she, too, was dressed in black. The two erstwhile assassins were dressed as if out for a walk around Brussels.

"It's going to smell awful in here, " she said, "do you want to come back to mine? I'm not sure how we are going to break this to the hotel management."

She led Chuck out of the room. He noticed that she kept the tiny submachine gun prepared under her dark coat as she walked to the elevator.

They were soon back at her room.

"I'll let you have the big fancy suites, I've picked a normal sized room for a regular guest," she said, "but it does have a minibar."

"So how on earth did you find me?" asked Chuck, "and how did you know all of that was about to happen?"

"I used my Russian intuition," said Christina, "First I went to a couple of Russian clubs in London. There's plenty around Belgravia and Chelsea. I found our two followers. They were not exactly low profile in London either. They had been given you as a mission but seemed to be enjoying the expenses that went with it. I soon found them and even got their real names. Then, it was a case of tracking them tracking you. To be honest, they were terrible. A couple of times I wanted to give them hints. But eventually they worked out that you were booked on a Eurostar to Brussels and they managed to catch the same train - as did I."

She continued, "I sat a row behind them and could hear them chattering away in Russian. They were planning how to get to you and I thought to myself at one point that they were making up a ridiculous plan because they had worked out I was listening. "

She shook her head, "But no, their plan was to follow you to your hotel, book in and then at around 3am to come to your room and shoot you in bed. Tap Tap."

Christina continued, "They didn't have night goggles, stun grenades, smoke or anything. They were just planning to break in and shoot you." She paused as if thinking, " Okay, they had silencers on their pistols - but that was it."

She smiled, "I thought there was no point in taking a penknife to a 'Chuck' fight so I brought along a sensible firearm. A Sig Sauer Submachine gun. An MPX Copperhead."

"Let me take a look," said Chuck, I've never seen one of these,"

"Maybe it's a bit of a girly-gun size-wise but its still got a 3.5 inch barrel with integrated muzzle brake, brilliant performance, great anti-recoil handling and is totally reliable. Oh, and it fits quite nicely into a medium sized Mulberry."

Chuck weighed it in his hand. "You know something, I'm gonna get me one of these. It's so compact yet devastatingly powerful."

They both looked at the gun. Then Christina said, "You were going to take them both with the P226 and the goggles? - Respect."

"Yes, I didn't have anything chunkier to hand, but I'd have managed it against those two."

"Look, what about tomorrow morning?" asked Christina. They'll notice a couple of bodies in your room and the bed shot to shreds."

"I suppose I'll have to put a 'no cleaning service' sign on the door for tomorrow, then buy an extra night and scarper," said Chuck, "Oh, by the way I'm Charles Desjardins here, over from Canada. And Christina - Thank You."

"Enchanté ," said Christina.

Galleria

Jake was trying to move the office to its new location before the end of the month. He hoped that they could save an entire month's charges if they were speedy. And anyway, the new office was nicer than the temporary one.

Across London, in the listening station, Pete Burr had set up new surveillance of the new office. It had been a mystery to him when the comms to the original office had suddenly cut out, although he had put it down to the intensive cleaning, which must have somehow dislodged the transmitter unit.

The new place had both microphones pre-embedded and an external circuit of CCTV, which meant he would finally get to see what these people looked like. He already felt he know some of them, but it would be good to see if his imagination was correct.

The CCTV was a boon too, and he didn't even need to use a clandestine link to get it. The cameras recorded a continuous feed to a cloud database and all he needed to do was monitor it. Fortunately, the cameras were also motion sensing, so he didn't have hours of dead airtime to scroll through.

Bigsy had been busy around the office too. He'd wired up the replacement wi-fi network and made a few other adjustments to the circuits. He did the universal signal for a pint of beer to Jake, who nodded and so they both walked towards the elevators.

"See what I mean?" said Bigsy, "Pizzas?" - he pointed to the artwork installed in the lift lobby.

"It's bright and cheerful," said Jake.

"I bet it costs a lot too," answered Bigsy.

"It's probably costed out by the square metre," ventured Jake.

They arrived at lobby level, waved to the security folk and were soon outside in the glass atrium of the Galleria.

They headed for one of the two adjacent pubs. It was already busy, but Jake staked out an outside table while Bigsy grabbed the beers. It would be very pleasant being able to pop out to sit along the river and watch the world go by.

"This is great," said Bigsy, returning with the two pints, "I think Louise the bartender is already starting to recognise me- she gave me the eye and poured these two pints despite all the tourists waiting."

At that moment there was a noise from the riverside and one of the large Thames Clippers appeared, getting ready to dock at the nearby pier.

"That'll be my commute," said Bigsy, "When I don't have to lug equipment around. I never thought I'd be going to work by boat."

"Look, I found a few things during my re-wiring. To begin with there's another collection of stealth microphones installed. This time they are per room and seemed to have been installed systematically. The ones at the last place were radio transmitters to that little box. These are a bit more sophisticated and are wired into the Local Area Network."

"So, we are being properly monitored?" asked Jake.

"Yes, that's right," said Bigsy, "And by the look of it by someone for whom no expense is too great."

"It points back towards Minerva, then?" asked Jake.

"That was exactly what I thought. Yes, they have added intelligent devices to our LAN this time. Not just the microphones, but also the CCTV cluster. It all records on movement and sound and send the recordings to the Cloud."

"What are we going to do about it? We can hardly have multiple cleaning accidents?" said Jake.

"It's lucky I was planning a few tweaks to the LAN, said Bigsy, and it is a case where their strength becomes a weakness. I brought a couple of spiders with me, in case I needed them for diagnostics."

"Nah, you've lost me," said Jake, "I know spiders can get through small holes and probably, like kittens, have something to do with the world-wide-web?"

"It's a little box we can plug into the LAN - You know, the wired Ethernet part. Then it gives us access to everything on the LAN. Intelligent boxes included. I wrote a script for the spider."

"What, Hamlet spouting spiders, whatever next!" laughed Jake.

"Yeah, it is a simple on-off switch. We can control all of the microphones and all of the cameras from a simple console. I'm going to add a couple of 'BigButtons' in the office."

"BigButtons?" queried Jake.

"Yes, they are what they seem. I'll have a BigButton to switch off all the microphones, another one for the cameras, and maybe a Blackout button, like they have in theatres, which will take everything offline. I just need to get back onto Amazon to find the products."

"That's brilliant," said Jake, "but it implies we can only control it from inside of the office?"

"I thought of that," said Bigsy, "I was planning to add OOBI to the network in any case as part of my Wifi update."

"Oobi-dooby-doo?" queried Jake.

"Yes, Out-of-Band Infrastructure management," replied Bigsy, "It's a simple idea. If you cannot get at the network because it is broken, then you can call it up over an 'out of band' service and fix the problem remotely. The most common service is 3.5G telecoms."

"3.5G doesn't sound very impressive, when everyone is talking about 5G and even 6G?" queried Jake.

"Yes, but that is the point, you don't need to be all fancy and high performance and just about every phone will work on a 3G link. So, a dumbed-down service is all you need to reboot - or as importantly to mute the network."

"Are you going to trust us with this?" asked Jake.

"I should think so," said Bigsy, "Just a case of remembering to switch off the microphones or cameras when something confidential is being discussed. I was even thinking of designating one of the rooms as a confidential room. If we do that, I can automate the shutdowns."

"Okay, and I assume the reason you are keeping the system online is to avoid suspicion?" asked Jake.

"Well, I looked at the costs of office space around here and looked at the tech they are providing, and I suddenly realised that there is no way we'd have been able to afford this location."

Bigsy looked at Jake, "It makes me think they've lured us here so they can keep an eye on us. I'll be exploring the rest of the wi-fi nodes running in the offices next to us, to see who our neighbours really are, " answered Bigsy.

Hierophant

Tradition
Legacy
Society
Organised Religion

Yacht

Sir Charles Frobisher was enjoying life here on a yacht in Monaco. He needed the sunshades and was surprised when Ray-Ban had approached the Lucky Two yacht with a whole choice of complementary sunglasses to wear and to distribute to others boarding. Gerhardt ensured the crew came equipped with the right entertainment credentials, so the next few days should be a delightful break.

Every so often he was getting flashbacks of his time here last year, when they all visited to watch the Grand Prix. Even Bernard Driscoll, who had died in the car accident.

Still, Sir Charles had new people to entertain, and he was sure that Gerhardt would serve them up in the right order.

Sir Charles was quietly pleased that Gerhardt had gone for a smaller yacht this time. The so-called yacht used last time was gigantic. 106.5 metres long yet with accommodation for just 16 people. The crew to run the yacht numbered 36 although Charles acknowledged they were selected for their looks.

But somehow when in such a large yacht, it felt more like being on a cruise ship. Only 8 cabins, yet about 6 floors. A waterfall for heaven's sake! A helipad to use up some space. That yacht sat 'on' the water and Sir Charles could tell the difference.

This time the yacht sat 'in' the water so that people on the quayside could look across. It felt better to flaunt one's wonderful fortune rather than hide away behind reflective darkened glass.

"Champagne, Sir," bobbed one of the crew.

"Thank you, my dear, that will be lovely," he glanced across to the shore where he could see several people noticing the pretty crew member serving him the champagne. Yes, Gerhardt had got this one right.

"I tried a smaller craft this year," said Gerhardt, "That yacht last time was a monster, and although it meant we could invite more people, it was something akin to crowd control keeping up with everyone. This time we can bring them on in batches, which gives the impact but also keeps us amused with an ever-changing cast."

"Anyone famous?" asked Sir Charles,

"It's a tricky one," said Gerhardt, "The stars look as if they own the yacht when they get on board. It can detract from what we are trying to do. It is different with the models. They can pose around the yacht as much as they like. And there's always room for them on the sunbathing decks."

"I'm glad to see you have some guiding principles for all of this," smiled Sir Charles. He had just been offered a back massage by one of the crew.

Then another crew member came along with a phone. Sir Charles realised it was a satellite phone. They always seemed to make a conversation seem more important.

"Sir Charles, someone for you."

"Hello, Charles Frobisher here, how can I help you?"

A Russian accent: "Hello, Sir Charles. This is Vassily Turgenev. I don't think we have met, but I am acquainted with your recent problem."

"Hello, No, we haven't met; where did you get this number?" Sir Charles shook from his tranquil and champagne-fuelled yacht relaxation.

The voice continued, "Regrettably, you ordered a shooting expedition which resulted in the loss of two of my people. I have heard they were discovered in a hotel room in Brussels. This puts us in a tough position. One that might require your help in the future. How can I put this? Without your co-operation, we could see some very unfortunate things happen. Accidents or even more prejudicial situations."

"I'm not sure what you are talking about?" asked Sir Charles.

"Well, you'd better ask your fixer - I'm sure he can explain things to you. I will not demand anything today, but you'd better be sure that if you hear from me or one of my representatives again, then you follow the instructions."

There was a click. The line went down. The little screen on the phone played an animated 'Iridium' logo.

Sir Charles looked stunned. He was not used to having circumstances running away from him. He was usually the one pulling the rug from under others' feet.

Gerhardt looked over, "Is everything okay?" he asked.

"Not really, I've just had a call from someone called Vassily Turgenev. He claims to know something about the Colonel Chuck Manners situation. He advised me to ask you."

Gerhardt grimaced, "I was waiting for the right time to tell you about this, " he answered, " I felt it could put a dampener over this time with the yacht."

"Not as much of a dampener as when I get a strange Russian calling me on my satellite phone, you'd better explain."

Gerhardt told Sir Charles about the discovery of the two FSB people in the Brussels Hilton. That they were found in the bedroom of a Charles Desjardins.

"Okay, but that's not Chuck Manners, " said Sir Charles.

"Yes, but it is," replied Gerhardt, "He has multiple passports, and this is another one that he uses - it's Canadian."

"But how is it that two FSB - Russian- agents are involved in this?" asked Sir Charles.

Gerhardt replied, "They were freelancers. To be honest, I am not sure how they were ordered to go after Chuck. It did not come from us. I thought Station Minerva had ordered it. I was happy to have 'plausible deniability' and not to ask too many questions, but now this Turgenev is calling I suppose we had better know what is happening. And come to that, to know who Vassily Turgenev is!?"

Gerhardt could see that Sir Charles was becoming increasingly annoyed.

"Look," said Sir Charles, "We - and by that, I mean you Gerhardt - specialise in a form of nuanced suasion - we even refer to it as Kompromat sometimes. Now, it seems as if in one fell swoop, I've been caught by the Russians in exactly the same way. You had better resolve this - and fast."

Gerhardt didn't look his usually suave, relaxed self.

Icelander

Christina had said goodbye to Chuck at the Brussels hotel. They would both be going their separate ways again. She had done a similar codeword exchange with Chuck so she could stay in contact if needed. She also said she would tell Amanda that everything was back to normal.

It would break Chuck's link to Amanda in case they had used it to track him down. Now Christina's high priority was to get back to London to meet Hekla.

...

Christina knew the hotel where Hekla stayed well, and it was only about a fifteen-minute walk from their new offices in Hay's Galleria. Christina was not sure whether she would reveal that location to Hekla, until after they had met.

She walked into the hotel lobby and found a quiet area around the back. There were several men with laptops and a family were buying food from the open kitchen area in the middle of the Lobby.

Christina thought this would not be a bad place to work as a freelancer, with tables, desks and coffee on tap. But then she remembered her new offices across the other side of the river. Just a stone's throw away.

She had texted Hekla that she had arrived and now waited until they could meet. She wondered if she would even recognise Hekla after all of this time. Although Christina had been back to Reykjavik in the intervening years, it had always seemed a sad and lengthy side visit to go back to the old farmstead where she and Hekla were near neighbours.

Christina wondered how Hekla had fared, considering she had stayed in Iceland all the intervening years.

Then she saw someone appear from the corridor leading towards the lifts. Strikingly blonde and with the unmistakable knit of an Icelandic jumper. The vivid white pattern went around the front and over the shoulders. Christina thought she looked like an exotic creature here in the streets of London.

"Hekla," she called, and the blonde's head turned.

"Ó guð minn þú ert ótvíræð" she said.

"Wow, and you are pretty stunning yourself," said Christina, "Iceland has obviously agreed with you!"

"I like to think I carry some of Iceland with me when I travel," said Hekla, reverting to English.

Christina noticed she had an American accent when she

spoke English.

"So how is it you decided to come to London?" asked Christina still thinking of Hekla as a country-girl.

"Well, a lot happens in these many years," she said, "But I realise that with my travelling I have only ever been through London, never stopped in it."

"Travelling?" asked Christina, intrigued.

"Yes, I know you have got around 'Christina Nott' - and well, so have I."

"Tell all," said Christina.

"Let's get a drink first," said Hekla, "We can charge them to my room."

"Okay, but I will want to show you London at some point!" said Christina.

They ordered two glasses of wine, chinked the glasses and said "skál."

"Right, well, a lot happened to me after you left 'forever' to go to Russia," said Hekla, "I must admit I was sad for several months after you had gone. But then Geir and Hanna moved in and I had some new playmates."

"Did you tell them about the wool-store?" asked Christina.

"Of course, it was big news to a small farm-girl. I elaborated the story and added some rockets and guns into the picture. Geir was most impressed. The strange thing was, we went to explore it, but it was empty. Just some wool bundles tied up in a heap."

"Ahah," smiled Cristina, "Have you heard of deep cover?"

"No, but seriously, was your father a spy?" asked Hekla, sipping at her wine.

"What do you think?" said Christina, "Sure he flew jet planes when he was younger and so there was always some gossip following him around. But think of it; he was running a farm. D'you remember, after you fell through the roof and we went to find him? What was he doing? Painting the water trough for the sheep. Now that's what a super spy would be doing, like James Bond."

Hekla smiled, and Christina noticed several of the men around the bar area look over to her. She had an ability to light up the room.

"What happened after the playmates?" asked Christina.

"Well, to cut a long story short, I discovered the Americans."

"Hekla!?"

"Well Geir became old enough to drive and would give me lifts into Reykjavik. We hung out around the Laugavegur and down by the Solfar - you know the Sun Voyager ship."

"Er - I haven't had my mind erased," said Christina, "although you sound like a *Lattelepjandi miðbæjarrotta!*"

Hekla laughed, " I see your grasp of gutter Icelandic hasn't diminished! Although we didn't think of ourselves as latte-sipping city centre rats, more as *fágun* - sophisticates!"

"It was easy to meet new people there too. The Americans would come off-base and their entire chat-up line consisted of "What are Icelandic women like?"

"They had all been given the same spiel about Icelandic women. You know the one about beautiful Icelandic women - there always seems to be quite a large number of foreign men that just hear the words 'beautiful Icelandic women', which they automatically translate to 'sexy Icelandic women' but don't seem to listen when words like 'strong, independent and feminist Icelandic women' come up."

"I became quite practiced at the art of men swatting. One of my friends around this time was an athlete. We'd sit together for a chat in a cafe and get hit on about a dozen times. She went in for the Olympics and for a laugh did Miss Iceland. It was incredible that no-one in the press and media picked up on her athletics. They all just focused on her beauty."

"Such difficult problems, being a hot female in Iceland!" smiled Christina.

"Well it was different with Icelandic men. Icelandic men are supportive and respectful. If something needs doing, they expect women to be able to do it just as well as them. Most men I know don't think about tasks as being male tasks or female tasks. It does mean that if you start dating an Icelandic man and you are out driving and the tyre goes flat, he'll probably expect you to know how to change it yourself. It can look rude when you have been elsewhere. Icelandic men don't go out of their way to hold doors open for women, or even to offer to pay for drinks - they normally expect women to be able to hold their own doors open, and pay for their own drinks."

"I've missed all of this by living in a very macho country through my formative years," smiled Christina.

"But hey, it seems that we've both turned out all right," said Hekla.

"So, what is this about Americans then?"

"Well, I finally succumbed to one of them. He was sitting alone in a cafe on Laugavegur - Sandholt's to be precise - he was reading a book and I had to sit at the table next to him. I could see the book was in English and that every time he got to the end of a page, he would look up at me before continuing. So, I asked him if it was any good.

"Well, that stopped him in his tracks. He mumbled something and then said he wasn't sure yet. He'd only read the first few pages and had not been properly concentrating.

"' Here it comes' I thought, He is going to lay down a line now."

"Well. He didn't. Instead I asked him why he looked so unhappy."

"He snapped around a bit when I said that, but then he admitted that he was new in town and it wasn't like he was expecting. He'd come over from Texas, which I thought of as all oil wells and - well - like that Dallas show on television - but he said he was from San Angelo and had been transferred from Goodfellow Air Force Base."

"It didn't mean anything to me, but he carried on anyway. He said most people thought of Texas with oil wells and cowboy hats and big shoulders, but the part he was from was a rural farming area. His family farmed sheep and goats.

"I was somewhat surprised by this. I had never even thought about Americans farming anything as small as sheep and goats. Especially in Big Texas. Buffalo, yes, horses and cattle, but sheep and lambs?"

"So, he was a sheep boy, then."

"Stop it. Anyway, he introduced himself as Daniel Williams, and said he was a pilot. He flew the little jets that the Americans use. F-15s I think they are called. He said that he had been transferred to either Iceland or England, but he thought England would be too intense for him. He was part of some kind of NATO swap."

"He doesn't sound like fly-boy material?" suggested Christina.

"Yes, that was the thing, I expected him to be all Tom Cruise in Top Gun, but he was much quieter."

"Well, that's how I got to know him some more. He didn't have a good chat-up line, seemed a bit depressed, but had some potential as a fighter pilot."

"In other words, a Project?" asked Christina, "I do and don't like the sound of this."

"Well, you might not know that the Americans moved out of Keflavik a few years ago, but then, after a few Russian submarines circled Iceland and some of their planes flew around, Iceland decided to invite America back, but as part of some kind of NATO deal. Danny had to go on 'patrol rotations' which seemed to cover an awfully large area."

"Let me guess…You took him to look around the farm and pet the animals?" asked Christina, smiling.

"Ooooh. You are so mean... still ...I love it!" laughed Hekla, "That is exactly what I did. He had a car and could drive me to and from Reykjavik, and -well- we sort of fell in love."

"Hekla! - Nooo. Is he 'The One'?"

Christina looked at Hekla's fingers. A few Icelandic rings, but no obvious sign of marriage. She asked, "What did your parents think? Your dad could be quite fierce."

"Yes, he was to begin with, but then Mamma could see that we were smitten with one another and helped persuade Pabbi."

"Oh, it's so good to hear certain words like Mamma and Pabbi again," said Christina.

"Yes, there were also some practical aspects to consider. Danny had been driving back and forth from Keflavik, but now he could stay over without Pabbi getting emotional about it."

"Scusi me, ladies, my fren' and I were wondering if we could join you at this table?" came an Italian accent.

"No," chorused both Christina and Hekla, and then Hekla went on to add, "We are waiting for our boyfriends."

"Perfect, man-swatting," said Hekla, "Just like in Laugavegur!"

"So, is he the one?" asked Christina persisting.

"It all went wrong about a year ago," answered Hekla.

"His tour of Iceland finished, and he was due to go back to the USA, to his home base. He asked me to come with him."

"I wasn't sure, if I'm honest, and the thought of an adventure in Texas was the biggest pull. Danny was up there in my thoughts, but I worried that he was too much focussed on flying to the exclusion of all else. It was like he had a manic state. Something that I'd seen in that very first encounter in Sandholt's."

"I met his family. They were not what I'd expected. They were very loud, warm and affectionate, not at all like Danny. They lived on the farm and had dozens of friends and neighbours. Despite the Texan distances, it wasn't like the solitude that we had around Sprengisandsleið. And it was very hot."

"Danny and I had arrived without a plan, although everyone expected that we were (a) engaged (b) would get married in a big showy ceremony and (c) start having lots of children.

" 'Danny introduce us to the little lady, will you,' was a common request. My mind was starting to explode.

"They had a gun culture too. Everyone had a gun. The women carried small Derringer pistols - they called them Texas Defenders and even the teenager girls had pink pistols. Imagine buying a Glock handgun in 'Prison Pink'? That's exactly what one of Danny's sisters did!

"They wanted me to shoot weapons too; they didn't know about us on the farm and what we used to get up to. Christina. I think you were the best shot, but I was pretty good too.

"They took me out to a range near to their homestead. The targets were static and laughably close. I borrowed one of the brother's hunting rifles, it was quite like one of ours, but made to look like a carbon fibre boy's toy. Then I shot a double."

"Two bullets through the same hole?" asked Christina.

"Yes," said Hekla, "Some skills don't go away."

"They didn't believe it of course, and thought I'd missed with the second shot. Then they looked at the target paper. Oval hole. Two grease rings. A confirmed double."

She sighed, "They called it beginner's luck, so I said I'd

try again. Remember this is over such short distances as well. Pause, listen to heart rate, breathe, Tak-Tak. I admit to certain relief when I realised I'd done it again."

The men didn't like it. Danny was different, but they saw it that a random foreigner had somehow done something that they all attempted unsuccessfully. And done it twice. I was now noted as a strong woman. I think Iceland has a history of strong women, since the women would have to stay at home while the men went out at sea and then the women had to completely take care of their farms on their own. Take care of the animals, do repairs, take care of the kids, clean, cook etc - and often their husbands and/or sons would die at sea, so they'd be left to continue on their own.

"Well, in Amer—i—cay, or in this part, the women may be strong, but they keep it to themselves. I kept getting referred to as 'my little lady' and 'ma'am' when I went out anywhere. No one meant anything by it, but it did stick in the claw.

"And the women folk had a lot of questions for me about children. Was I going to have a big family with Danny? They were questions I was not ready to answer.

"Danny's family were also Evangelical Protestants. I went to the church with Danny and his family one time at a place called Lakewood. It was like a weekend break. We drove for about six hours to stay in a motel, then went to the church. It was massive. Like some kind of rock stadium. I think it seated over 50,000 people - and that was every week.

"The guns, the church, the heat, the massive family. It was too much for me. I had to tell Danny and then leave him. To be honest, I think, when I did, that he was relieved. I don't think he'd thought any of it through and the pressures from home were cutting in on him. I sometimes think it improved his status there in Texas, bringing back a foreign girl-friend but then 'seeing the light' and picking someone else from local stock."

"And you know something, I was flooded with relief when I sat on the runway on the way back to Iceland. It was such a tangible feeling, like a whole episode had drained away and I could start to behave normally again.

"So I decided, all in all, it seems that Iceland is the best place in the world for women to live and work, and I can taste the difference in the air each time I come back to Iceland after having spent some time abroad."

Christina smiled, and Hekla continued, "I don't know exactly what it is, maybe it's the fact that there's no cat-calling on the streets, or that in the office where I work there's pretty much a 50/50 of men and women, or that it doesn't take more than 'no thank you' to shake off a guy that's hitting on you if you're not interested."

Hekla paused, sipped her wine and then continued, "I think it's all the little things. The fact that you go to a protest march and you see your little cousins there. And your friend's parents. Or that outside sport stadiums there are posters of female athletes as well as the male ones. Or that when the presidential elections take place, half of the candidates are female - and that fact isn't blown up. It just, is. And if you're walking down the street and some mother is breastfeeding her kid, nobody takes notice of it."

Christina smiled, Hekla was as intense and lovable as she

had been when they played together as small children. She'd found a few new causes and gained some worldview too, Christina had expected her to be a child of Iceland but she realised that Hekla was an Icelandic woman of the world.

"But hey, Christina, I can see you are toned like an athlete- the way you move is like a cat - you are as elegant as anyone in the room and clearly cosmopolitan. You'll have to tell me about your last few years!"

"You'd never believe it, " answered Christina and started to pour out her edited highlights.

Vassily Turgenev

Gerhardt was pleased that he had arranged for the yacht Lucky Two to be based locally in Monaco. It would go out for a cruise to Nice or across to Cap d'Antibes and then back. Everyone enjoyed it - not too long for anyone and plenty of time to pose around at whatever port they arrived in.

Now the short times at sea played to his advantage. He could get on with finding out more about the Russian who had threatened Sir Charles.

He used the satellite ship phone called one of his contacts back at the ISMC offices in Frankfurt. Felix Rossmann would know more about Vassily Turgenev.

Felix spoke up, "Turgenev: This is all about the business of corruption. We all know there is a pervasive culture of corruption in Russia that persists despite efforts by the government and opposition activists. Remember Russia was 137th out of 180 countries in the last Transparency International corruption index."

"Russia tries to introduce anti-corruption measures without any will to implement them, without understanding why they should be done," Felix said.

But is Vassily Turgenev dangerous?" asked Gerhardt, "He threatened Sir Charles,"

Felix continued, "Very Dangerous, despite the trimmings around his name. A quick search shows that Vassily is a Doctor - A physicist with a string of diplomas and memberships of august institutions. I guess that affords him some respectability."

Felix added, "But, the Russians also use academic corruption to jumpstart careers. Plagiarized works have emerged as a routine way for Russians to develop careers in politics, medicine, academia, and law.

Felix continued, "Some members of the state Duma have diplomas that are nothing more than a printout on some beautiful paper conferring a degree to them in the name of some non-existent academy of science or non-existent university,"

"Yes," said Gerhardt, "That's all very well, but it doesn't trace why Vassily would threaten Sir Charles?"

Well, it seems to link back to an incident in Brussels a brief time ago. A couple of Russians were killed. I'm guessing they were 'employees' of Turgenev."

Vassily Turgenev is a friend of Putin. Low in Putin's structure, but an enforcer for Kasharin Timur Maximovich, who is the Head of Russian Infrastructure.

"Maximovich?" asked Gerhardt. "He's involved with the

Celarus project."

Felix added, "You've got to remember that corruption has been commonplace in Russia for centuries and the labyrinthine Soviet bureaucracy and constant shortages has created a culture of kickbacks to get around the USSR's ubiquitous shortages of consumer goods - the infamous *blat*."

"Ah yes," Gerhardt nodded, "We are not the only ones to provoke moral suasion."

Felix continued, "Since Post-Soviet Russia we've seen the rise of oligarchs and 'wild-east capitalism' with few rules and threats of violence amid tumultuous political times."

Gerhardt asked, "So Maximovich, who we are talking to about Celarus has Vassily Turgenev, a friend of Putin, as an enforcer?"

Felix agreed, "Yes, and you can bet that Putin and Turgenev both go back to the same teams inside the KGB. Putin has kept long-term allies from those days and well into the FSB times."

"This corruption has found its way into President Vladimir Putin's Russia despite frequent pledges from Putin to tackle the issue. You'll have seen him wringing his hands on television, 'I, of course, feel responsible for this mess,' he says when asked about his role on corruption during a televised question-and-answer show with the public. And then he sheds a few crocodile tears and cranks it up to the next level."

Gerhardt summarised, "So here we have the perfect set-up. State-sanctioned skimming, under the watchful eye of Putin. Exercised by Maximovich and enforced by Turgenev.

"But Tima Maximovich has been a friend of Gavy Yegorin too. He's the Russian Freemason that the Kremlin is turning over at the moment."

Felix added, "Yes, but here's the thing - and why this is getting dangerous. If Maximovich falls out with Putin, he might also join the Yegorin statistics. There's around 40 prominent Russians who are victims of unsolved murders or suspicious deaths since the beginning of 2014, according to a list compiled by a well-known US newspaper in collaboration with a British journalist.

"For example, the list contains 10 high-profile critics of Russian President Vladimir Putin, seven diplomats, six associates of Kremlin power brokers who had a falling out — often over corruption — and 13 military or political leaders involved in the conflict in eastern Ukraine, including commanders of Russian-backed separatist forces."

"Two are connected to a dossier alleging connections between President Trump's campaign staff and Kremlin officials produced by a former British spy and shared with the FBI."

"I know you'll think I'm making this up but check it for yourself. Dig out the USA Today articles or run a search on Google. Twelve were shot, stabbed or beaten to death. Six were blown up. Ten died allegedly of natural causes. One died of mysterious head injuries, one reportedly slipped and hit his head in a public bath, one was hanged in his jail cell, and one died after drinking coffee. The cause of six deaths was reported as unknown.

"They have become so frequent, that a Russian TV cartoon show even put out an episode showing Putin disposing of the people - it's even on YouTube. You just don't want to be on the wrong end of Putin or former Prime Minister Dmitry Medvedev's pointing fingers."

Felix added, chillingly, "We should regard Vassily Turgenev as just as dangerous and now he is also pointing his finger towards us."

Eight of Wands

(Reversed)

Panic
Waiting
Slowing Down

Kompromat

The next day, Gerhardt could see the bubble of people as Sir Charles approached the yacht. He could tell that they were a fresh batch by their unbridled excitement at coming on board a luxury yacht for a trip around the bay. Gerhardt hoped that they would strike some useful deals in the process and even noticed that Nina, one of his earlier escorts in London was coming on board.

Sir Charles made a direct line for him when on board asking, "Gerhardt, so what have you managed to find out?"

"Sit down, Sir, I don't think you will like this," Gerhardt then explained what he had gleaned from Felix in the ISMC Offices in Frankfurt.

"This sounds outrageous, we are being played at our own game," said Sir Charles.

"Yes, and I think if our ultimate backer is Raven, theirs is probably The Kremlin," answered Gerhardt.

"Can we do anything?" asked Sir Charles, "I mean Vassily has not asked for anything yet."

"That seems to be the way it works. Kompromat. And strengthened because Vassily Turgenev thinks we have killed two of his operatives."

"Well, can we give him the name of the killer?" asked Sir Charles.

"Well, that's just it, we have a name, but we think it is false. Charles Desjardins, a Canadian. It looks as if he was packing some serious firepower too. Reports say that 22 rounds were fired in less than a minute."

"Blast, we have opened a Pandora's box, here," said Sir Charles, "You know what, I'm getting out of Monaco today. It will be safer for everyone if I've gone. I can say there's been a family emergency."

Gerhardt nodded, "Yes, Sir Charles," he realised he was left holding the whole situation.

"I'm going to catch a helicopter back to Nice," said Sir Charles, and then fly back to London."

Gerhardt was momentarily diverted by Nina, who came over and sat herself on his knee. She was prepared for sunbathing and felt quite delicious.

"Hello Gerhardt," she said, "We haven't met since that time in London; remember? The Freemason Ladies' Night?"

"How could I possibly forget?" said Gerhardt.

"Good," she said, "Then you remember that I work for Jennifer?"

She referred to the agency who brought many of Gerhardt's escorts to the variety of parties that he ran.

"Naturally, " he said.

"Well, this time I'm working for Vassily Turgenev. He asked me to deliver this message to you. I am to tell you that his men were sent away by Charles Desjardins and a Russian woman named Christina Hyde. He asked me to give you this photograph too."

She fiddled around with her phone and found a picture.

"It was taken by Vassily's third man, the one who waited outside for the other two to return."

"He says you will know what to do."

"Yes, you had better give me the picture," said Gerhardt. He looked at the woman in the picture and thought she looked somehow familiar, but couldn't think where he had seen her.

"I think the woman was at the same Raven function. She was wearing a beautiful blue gown," said Nina, "I met her briefly, and we said hello. She said she also worked for Jennifer."

Gerhardt remembered. He had held a lengthy conversation with her; she was there with another Freemason, someone called Antanov, who was high in the Masons. He remembered she wore a brooch denoting a top rank in the Rosicrucians.

Nina wriggled away from Gerhardt. She planted a soft kiss on his cheek. "Now you be very careful, playing with Vassily. He can be very rough," she said.

Gerhardt was pleased with this outcome. Now he had two names and could start the search for the people who had dispatched Turgenev's men.

Minerva

Gerhardt knew about Minerva, the London Listening Station. ISCM had been instrumental in the sale of Raven's Qube to make Brant which became the outsourcer to support Minerva.

Gerhardt could use some of the Minerva people to help him trace Charles Desjardins and Christina Hyde. He called up Brant to discuss an operation. Emily Karankawa was on the duty desk and took the call.

"We need to start full scale tracing for these two- Charles Desjardins - Canadian and Christina Hyde - Russian," he said, "Sir Charles will want this to be a top priority."

"Wait a minute, you want us to track a Canadian and a Russian, for no specific purposes?" asked Emily.

"There is a reason, but it's above your pay grade," said Gerhardt, pompously. He had always wanted to say that, and this was his big moment.

"No, I'm Duty Officer at the moment," said Emily, with a

sense of humour failure at Gerhardt's last remark. She would not be pushed around by some arrogant sleazebag spouting Sir Charles' name.

"Look," said Gerhardt, "I'm sending you over a picture of them both together. - It will be on the station feed from ISCM," said Gerhardt.

"No," said Emily, still annoyed at Gerhardt's aggressive impatience, "If you do that then the entire station will see it."

"Good," said Gerhardt, "And it's too late anyway, I've just sent it."

"Now see what you can do for me, honey, will you?"

Emily was deciding what level of action to take against this nauseous man, but he had already hung up.

...

The photo arrived and was the subject of much mirth around the station. "Now we are getting unsolicited requests to trace people? This is truly bizarre."

Pete Burr was one of the people that received the picture, now tagged with a whole string of witticisms. He noticed something at once. It was one of the occupants of the Triangle offices. He had been listening to them for so long and now he had the camera feed, he was almost certain he recognised her. Christina - although he thought they talked about her with a different last name.

Pete had to decide whether to action the request, which looked like a very unofficial request. He put it to Olivia, his CIA- field boss.

"Look, he said, this iffy request that has come through from ISCM. I think I can identify someone. She's one of the group I've been monitoring for the last few weeks. Christina Nott or Christina Hyde. She is part of that Triangle Office that we are asked to bug, the one that is in Hay's now."

Olivia was delighted with this news. Not only had she been able to elevate the profile of Chuck Manners when they dispatched the two agents to terminate him, now she had another suspect lined up.

"Wait, though where was this picture taken?" she asked Pete,

"Er, in Brussels, according to the GPS data with it, it comes from the Brussels Hilton."

Olivia froze. "Is this the aftermath of the Chuck Manners situation?" she asked.

"I don't know," said Pete, "It just came in over the generic email with a FIND request for both of them."

"What is it dated?" asked Olivia.

"What? when was it taken, or when did we receive it?" asked Pete.

"No, when was it taken?"

"Three days ago, in Brussels, in the Hilton Grand Place," repeated Pete, "Carrefour de l'Europe 3, 1000 Bruxelles, Belgium, to be precise."

"The man then, is Chuck Manners," said Olivia, "He got away from us the last time, and this woman Christina must have helped him."

"Okay, so it is a lucky result?" said Pete, "Or unlucky for them," added Olivia.

Mil-38

Sir Charles was making his way to the Monaco heliport. He had been picked up from Port Hercule by a smart black Mercedes and the coolness of the car's soft interior helped to sooth his jaded nerves.

Inside the heliport he noticed the row of helicopters lined up, six almost identical ones in red and white and then, at the end in the last bay, an all-red and somewhat larger helicopter.

"This one is ours," said the driver and he walked around to open the door of the limousine.

Charles walked across the tarmac and as he did so, he noticed that there were already a couple of people on the helicopter. He turned inside and saw a considerable number of seats, far greater than he was expecting.

"It's okay, we struck lucky today with a Mil-38, said one of the men, they can carry up to 30 passengers. The little guys in here can only take six."

An air-steward showed him to a seat near the back. "It is for load distribution during take-off," she said.

Sir Charles thought about this but could not raise a question. Instead he took a glass of gin and tonic and waited for the clearance for take-off for the short ride back to Nice Airport.

"We'll be flying out over the bay," announced the pilot, "You will get a beautiful view, but it is mainly to reduce noise pollution."

The blades started to spin and then the 'copter took off. Sir Charles was still fascinated with how quickly everything changed as they ascended into the air above Monaco. He looked towards the Monte-Carlo Casino and then down towards the dock where he had been on the yacht a fleeting time ago.

The helicopter headed out to sea and Sir Charles looked out of the window at the view. Maybe he would get out from this. He was sure that Gerhardt would come up with something.

He was aware of some movement in the cabin. A tall, lean gentleman sat in the seat opposite.

"I don't think we've been introduced?" he said, "My name is Vassily Turgenev."

Sir Charles felt all the blood drain from his face. He was now sitting opposite the man that had threatened him..

"Hello Vassily, I didn't expect you here."

"And neither did my men expect Chuck Manners to be

supported by a wild banshee with a submachine gun. You must have told him something or tipped him off that he was being followed. That work from that woman was terrifying."

"Now we need to make things even. My brother would not expect it any other way."

"Your brother?"

"Was one of the people killed. The woman with him was his wife as well as an agent."

"But don't worry, we have prepared something a little special for you. It's why we needed a larger helicopter."

He motioned to one of the other men sitting behind them in the helicopter. The man pulled out some cable ties.

"Always so useful, don't you think?" as the man pulled the cable ties around Sir Charles leg's and then two more around his arms.

Sir Charles had frozen. He was not resisting.

The man searched inside Sir Charles' jacket and brought out his phone, "Good, iPhone X, face recognition." He held it up to Sir Charles and the phone unlocked.

Sir Charles saw the man tapping some codes in, which he guessed disabled the security. He felt weak, knowing he was probably facing his execution.

"Didn't they teach you any self-defence in your role?" asked Vassily, "You makes it rather too easy."

"See what we has done? In a moment my men has to do some heavy lifting, The *Kabel'nyye styazhki are* attach to those rope and the other end of the rope has concrete blocks on them. You make excellent test to see how the *styazhki* can handle the pulling, although it says their breaking strain is over 2000 kilos. To be honest, I think your legs might break before the cable ties."

"Now, we only fly at around 2000 metres height, so you will take maybe 20 seconds to fall, by which time you'll be doing something like 700 kph. The sea does more than sting at such a speed."

Sir Charles was in shock, he looked as if he was about to have a heart attack. "So, thank you, please, to leave your phone behind and I'll say '*do svidaniya.*' "

Sir Charles was aware that the helicopter was now hovering. There was a sudden increase in noise as a door was opened and then he felt a sharp pull to his legs. Then he blacked out.

Inside the helicopter, one of the men closed the door. He looked down out of the window and after few seconds said, "*kosnut'sya zeml*"

"Yes - Touch Down," said Vassily, He was sending a short text to Gerhardt. Then he called to another of the men in Russian, "Make a copy of this phone and then throw it in the sea."

Shad Thames

Hekla looked at her watch. "Wow, is that the time? We have been chatting for hours!"

Christina grinned, "Yes, and just about everyone who was in here has changed since we sat down. We are in for the long haul."

She stared pointedly to a corner table where a slightly scruffy man was sitting working on his laptop. Dark-haired and crumpled clothes, he didn't have quite the 'expensive' look that many of the tourists or Londoners had that dropped into the hotel to do some work.

"Ha, you noticed him as well," said Hekla, "I get the feeling he has been staring at us for quite some while. I don't think it is about our looks either."

"We must find out some more about him," said Christina, "Call me suspicious, but I think he's here because of us."

"Agnes, you really meant it about being a secret agent?" asked Hekla, "Or is this just a wind-up?"

"Well, let's just see what happens." Christina stood up and walked to the kitchen area in the middle of the hotel lobby. She selected some kind of rice curry dish. Then she wandered back towards the man with the laptop.

"Oh, excuse me," she said, "Could you hold this for me for a couple of seconds. I need to adjust my clothing. I'm really sorry."

She held out the tray with the curry and surprised, the man held out his hands. Then she pulled in her belt by one notch. "Thank, you," she said as she took back the food. The man smiled, not certain what had just happened. She walked towards Hekla.

"He is following us," she said, "Or at least following me. I could see his laptop screen. The emails were in Russian. I'm not sure what he wants."

Hekla looked fidgety. "Shall we leave this area then?" she asked, " I know I'm staying here, but it might be better for me to look as if I am going somewhere else."

"Sure," said Christina, "But I'll see you back to here later. Look, I'll show you London properly tomorrow, but why don't we go to Shad Thames now, where I can show you some of 'Old London' that is right near to your door step?"

"This is your city, *elskan*," said Hekla.

"Babe!?" laughed Christina, "I haven't been called that in a while!"

"Let's go!" she placed the tray unceremoniously in the

middle of their table and they both made for the exit.

As they walked outside, Christina could see that the untidy man was packing up his laptop.

Christina linked arms with Hekla, and they set off at a brisk pace.

"This is a great area, you know, over there is The Tower of London, which is where they keep the Crown Jewels. In the late 15th century, it was the prison of the Princes in the Tower. Under the Tudors, the Tower became used less as a royal residence, because it could not withstand artillery.

"Then it became a prison in the 16th and 17th Century when many figures who had fallen into disgrace, such as Elizabeth I before she became queen and Sir Walter Raleigh were held within its walls. Right now, we are in the notorious Tower Hill which is where more than 100 executions took place.

Hekla asked, "What is that glass bubble on the river side?

"Oh, that's the town hall for London. The built a new one on the riverbank to replace the one up by Parliament."

"Now we'll be going over Tower Bridge, which is one of the most famous landmarks in the world. We'll get a picture right in the middle for your friends on Instagram. If you look back from her you get a splendid view of the tall buildings around the City of London.

"And I guess that one is The Gherkin?" asked Hekla.

"Yes, you are right, and on the other bank, in the distant

- that big spike is called The Shard," answered Christina. She had avoided pointing out where their new office was located, although the area could be plainly seen from where they were walking.

"Then we can hang a left down into Shad Thames, which is such an interesting area of old London." Said Christina.

They climbed down some stairs.

"Wow," said Hekla, "This is like one of those TV shows about Charles Dickens!"

Hekla looked around. The area was filled with picturesque converted Victorian warehouses and had cobblestones underfoot. Above were overhead gantries connecting the converted warehouses. Many of the ground level buildings were converted into what Hekla assumed were high-end shops.

"The street's warehouses were used to store grain, fruit, sugar, coffee, tea, and spices from all over the world," continued Christina. She looked back over her shoulder and could see the untidy man was still following them.

"Yes, and the overheard walkways were used to roll barrels from one warehouse to another. The area used to have the nickname 'the larder of London'. "

There was a puff of brick which exploded above Christina's head.

"Get down," she said to Hekla, "It's the scruffy man from the hotel - he is shooting at us. Get flat to the ground."

A couple of tourists looked around as Hekla laid down

flat on the pavement and Christina walked around in front of her. They were expecting it to be the start of some kind of impromptu London show.

There was another puff and more brickwork dislodged. Christina estimated the second shot had been closer, but then the man was using a handgun - maybe just a 9mm, so the accuracy was limited to around 50 metres.

She pulled into her handbag and Hekla gasped as Christina revealed the Sig submachine gun and quietly clipped in a 30 round magazine.

"Stay here," she said, "Do not move anywhere whatever happens until I get back. Squeeze more fully into that corner."

Christina ran off, leaving the Mulberry scattered on the ground.

Hekla noticed Christina really did move like a cat - even in heels.

Then she heard a noise like a ruler scraped along railings. Some tiny sound like nails being dropped.

And silence. No other tourists.

Then footsteps.

Christina had returned. She was breathing normally despite having just run around a 200-metre loop. No shoes though.

"He's gone, fell in the river actually." said Christina, "We are safe now. And Hekla, my dear, you are safe as well."

Hekla noticed that Christina's gun was still smoking. Then she saw Christina unclip the magazine and replace it with a shorter one.

Christina put the whole gun back into the Mulberry.

"Bayswater tote," she said, "It's a Mulberry icon. You can get a lot into it."

"Okay," said Hekla, "I'd almost forgotten what it's like to be around you, Agnes. Why I always had so many scrapes and bruises when we played around in the fields. Are you a bank-robber or something?"

"No," said Christina, "There were some people were after a friend of mine, over in Brussels. This man must have been a relative or something. He's gone now, though."

Hekla could hear police sirens in the distance coming across Tower Bridge.

"I guess some tourists saw what happened and dialled 999, said Christina. This area has seen its share of violence, what with nearby bombers and other terrorists. I'm sorry to have contributed to it. Come on, let's carry on with our walk."

Hekla looked a little shaken by what had occurred.

"You know something, Aggi, you have turned out even more bad-ass than I expected - I wasn't sure whether to believe you being an agent, but now I do. And, by the way, how did you get that gun into the UK?"

"You have to know the wrong people," said Christina.

Lucky Two

Gerhardt looked towards his phone. A text had just arrived from Sir Charles.

It said "zu wenig zu spät," Gerhardt was confused, he knew that Sir Charles didn't speak German and would therefore be unlikely to send him a message like "Too little too late" in German.

Sir Charles was all over ancient Greek. He wondered what Sir Charles had meant by this. He had heard Sir Charles say 'Either with your shield or on it' in the past, about the need for courage in their endeavours, but never this phase and never in German.

He called Sir Charles. It rang through to voice mail. He decided not to leave a message. He would see Sir Charles soon enough in London.

He looked at his watch. It was already getting late, time to turn in. He could hear the partying going on about the yacht, but he just wasn't in the mood. Nina's move on him had been tempting, but he knew he has a busy couple of days and needed to be sharp. With Nina it could easily turn into an all-night session and he was sure she would have brought drugs on board.

No. Self-discipline. Tomorrow they would make a quick sprint across to Nice, enjoying breakfast on board the yacht. Then back for a scenic arrival in Monaco and then he'd make his excuses and leave the yacht.

He settled down in his cabin for the evening. Outside he could hear the water lapping and the hubbub from the revellers on board. Apparently, they had just discovered another yacht with a party and were now combining to make something memorable.

He felt a bang to his head and awoke. No, he'd imagined the bang. He was just having a restless night. Too much coffee and booze in the day, probably. Then he heard another bump along the side of the hull. It could only be the yacht hitting the jetty. He dozed off again.

Bright sunlight. Morning. A hint of buttery croissants and black coffee. People moving around on deck. He emerged just as Nina was walking past his cabin. She smiled to him and quietly kissed him. He noticed she was already in her bikini but draped with a towel.

"I've been called away," she said, "Another party, you can come along if you like?" she kissed him softly.

"No, they have left me in charge of this group whilst Sir Charles goes back to London."

Nina looked at him darkly, "You'll regret it," she said, " I promise you'll have more fun with me, than stuck on this yacht."

Gerhardt patted her, "Be gone, oh Temptress!" he said, and she skipped off playfully toward the gangway back to the dock.

"Le capitaine appelle, dernière chance de partir pour le rivage. Captain calling, last chance to leave for shore,"

Gerhardt could hear the engines start. They called it a yacht, but it still had four motor engines.

With a whirr, they had left the dock and were pottering to the edge of the harbour, past the other huge luxury yachts. Anywhere else this yacht would be a head turner, but here it was lost in the mix.

Then as they pulled away from the harbour protection and the speed restrictions, the Captain opened the engines. This yacht could really move, leaving four white trails behind in the water. Gerhardt watched as Monaco became smaller. He was aware of a whistling sound, he looked over the side of the yacht and could see an orange bulge on the rear of the hull. It would be in line with his cabin. He wondered whether it was some kind of listening device. It was sure making a noise.

The yacht became an explosive yellow fireball, with fragments spinning away from the burning hull. The orange magnetically attached mine had done its duty. A MILA smart limpet mine, attached to the outside of the hull by a Special Forces hybrid Swimmer Delivery Vehicle. It was the type of computer-controlled mine used by US Navy Seals.

The mine was used in demolition. Those on neighbouring yachts could see why.

From his own yacht, Vassily Turgenev looked through his Zeiss image stabilised binoculars.

"Magnificent," he said, "So good of Sir Charles to put on a display for us."

Ace of Wands

Creation
Willpower
Inspiration
Desire

Frosted walls

Jake was sitting in the office in Hay's Galleria. He could hear the lift ping and then saw Christina and another woman get out.

They both looked slightly shaken and Jake walked across the main office space to greet them.

"Hello Christina, and hello 'Christina's friend'" he said.

"My name is Hekla, I've known Christina since she was Agnes, " answered Hekla.

"That must be a very long time ago, then, said Jake. "I've never heard Christina called Agnes. Katarina, yes, but Agnes? - Was this in Russia?"

"No, even before that, in Iceland," answered Hekla.

Christina looked worried.

"It's okay, I've pushed Bigsy's BigButton. There's no

sound or vision at the moment. I still think we'd be better to go into the quiet room though."

Christina nodded and Hekla followed Jake into a glass-walled meeting room. Jake pressed a button and the walls frosted.

"You have a very smart office," said Hekla, "and it is in an ideal part of London."

"We have just been followed," said Christina to Jake, "It was a bad job. A bodged single operative with a handgun. 9 mm at best and at a stupid range."

"Where are they?" asked Jake.

"Gone," said Christina, "In the Thames. He fell in, with some encouragement from me. I think he was working alone."

"You must be one of Christina's friends," said Jake, "How much do you think you know about her,"

"Oh, I know everything about 'Christina' when she was young, well very young. Right up to when she left the farm and went to Russia. Then nothing for many years, until I discovered her because she had renamed as Christina Nott. Reykjavik is a small place. Everyone knows everyone else in Iceland."

"Are you in Christina's line of work?" Asked Jake. "Oh, no, I'm a journalist and freelance translator," answered Hekla.

"I was a journalist, I worked for the Street magazine, here in London," answered Jake, expecting a response.

"No, I don't know it, but then if I told you my magazines I don't think you would know them either. Okay, maybe The Manhattanite," said Hekla.

"I should think so, what do you write about?" answered Jake. Christina looked intrigued too.

"Well, I started writing about daily farming and the rural stories; it wasn't the main emphasis of The Manhattanite, but they liked to include some as feel-good factor moments in the magazine. I was originally based on a farm out in Texas, so it gave an intriguing off-beat story every week."

"What about cattle, cowboys and oil wells?" asked Jake.

"You'd be surprised," answered Hekla, "Then, because of my writing style, they asked me to do some sections for their on-line magazine. That's where I've stayed right up to now. It's part of the reason that I'm in London. Getting some colour to include in a piece about the President."

"Okay, so will you be discreet?" Asked Jake, " Look, I had to not tell anyone about Aggi's back-garden missile silo for years, " said Hekla, "So I think I can be trusted with this."

"Aggi!" exclaimed Jake, "There's a first."

"Yes," said Christina, "Quite a lot is coming out since Hekla arrived,"

"Okay, and the missile silo?" asked Jake.

"Hekla is making that up," said Christina, "We'll need to

watch her!"

"Sorry," said Hekla, "I couldn't resist."

"Okay, Let's try to work this out."

There was a ping. They looked towards the elevators. Clare and Bigsy had just arrived.

"Oooh - secret squirrel," said Clare, then noticing Hekla, said, "Hello I'm Clare - you must be the friend of Christina?"

Hekla smiled, "Yes, 'Christina' - that is Agnes and I go back a long way - all the way to Iceland. We've just been in a scrape together. Just like when we were little. Only, I'd say the stakes were higher this time."

Christina turned to them all and said, "Yes, Chuck was fired upon in Brussels the other day and now I was shot at in London. I'm certain the two events are linked."

"What happened?" asked Bigsy, "Are you all right?"

"Yes, both Hekla and I are fine, although I've messed up some really good shoes and Hekla's coat is in a bit of a state. The gunman was terrible. Too feeble a gun and too much distance. Luckily I was carrying my little sub with me."

"Sub?" asked Clare,

"Submachine-gun," answered Christina.

"Of course," said Bigsy, " never be without one."

"I'm going to teach you all some self-protection," said Christina, "Not like the stuff you see on the television; the serious short-range stuff that works. Not now, obviously, but soon."

"So, do we know who set up these attempts?" asked Jake.

"We think the last person was a Russian," said Hekla, remembering what had happened in the hotel.

"I don't know about the ones in Brussels," said Christina, "They didn't say anything, and I was more concerned with getting Chuck away. I'm certain that these events were all triggered because of our visit to the CIA Listening Station - Minerva."

Hekla looked surprised at this latest turn of events, "CIA? It doesn't make any sense," she said.

Wild Child

"Okay," said Clare, " So we need to piece this together."

"We first found out about Minerva station when Christina and I met with Anne-Marie along at their building. Then they traced us and we think they torched the office.

"Somehow they have found out about Chuck and now they are chasing down Christina and Chuck, with extreme menace."

"The strange thing is that they seem to be Russian."

"I think the Russian influence comes from Brant," said Christina. "The CIA have outsourced their operation both here in the UK and over in Celarus. It's ironic that the Americans are once more being run by Kremlin-supported oligarchs."

"What like the President?" asked Bigsy.
  "Allegedly," answered Jake.

"What about other links that we have?" asked Christina, "We had a way to get to Raven via the Masons and also through that separate company ISMC? - You remember - Sir Charles Frobisher and Gerhardt Schmidt. I met them both at the Ladies' Night occasion at Raven's building in London."

"Well, there's some news about Schmidt," said Bigsy, " I don't know how to tell you this, but he was on a yacht that caught fire in the Mediterranean."

"Caught Fire?" said Christina, "Or was torched?"

"I've only got this Associated Press report. It seems it was just leaving Monaco (as one does!) and then was on its way to Nice, when it caught fire. No survivors."

Christina looked at the article. "Let's dial it up on something French instead," she said as she typed 'Libération' into Bigsy's computer.

"See a more colourful French paper," with pictures, she said, " Look here is an article about the Lucky Two yacht. It says, according to eyewitnesses that the yacht exploded in a yellow fireball, while travelling at speed. This man was interviewed and said it reminded him of a missile strike, although there were no planes around. In other words, the actual damage to the boat was far more forceful than implied in the English language press clippings."

Christina continued, "Let me try a straight-laced French paper... Here we are, Le Monde. I will see if I can find the article... Yes, here. Same story as Libération, but an interview with a different yacht's captain... This one says the police are investigating what might be a multiple homicide. The captain says he knew the captain of the yacht too and would always describe him as a 'quelqu'un de sûr' - someone sure - hmm - it's like a safe pair of hands. "

Hekla spoke, "Are you sure you should be messing with these people? They sound like hardened criminals. I mean, we've been shot at and then a boat carrying others has been blown up! Christina, this is strong stuff even for the wild child."

Christina grinned, "Huh - *Villt barn*! I'd forgotten that nickname. Hekla, you keep reminding me of life on the farm!"

"It was never like this," said Hekla, "You know something, I'm going to call my foreign desk at the magazine, see if I can get something useful. Don't panic, I'm not going to print any of this, but my friend Irina Barnaby might be able to help us."

"Irina Barnaby?" asked Christina, "An unusual name."

"She's married to someone from Yorkshire," explained Hekla, "I think her name was Irina Koval before she got married."

"Is she Polish?" Asked Christina.

"Not exactly, I think she is from the Ukraine, actually, but she knows her Russian stuff too - especially about Putin and his cronies." answered Hekla, "Here; let me try her," she fiddled with her phone.

"Hi Irina, Yes I've got here- London. I will be able to see you in a couple of days. The flight was fine, and I am staying by Tower Bridge. Yes… No, I said I was going to look up an old friend first. We've already met and I'm with her right now."

"To be honest, I wanted to pick your brain, she has asked me about some Russian things, and I knew you'd be the best person to answer! Well, it is a bit complicated. How about we bring forward our meeting to tomorrow? I think it has a great tie-in for that side book you are writing, you know, the one about Russian Mafia corruption. Yes. Do you know ", she looked at Jake, "What is this place called?"

"Hay's Galleria," answered Jake.

"Hay's Galleria?" asked Hekla, "You do- that's brilliant, can we meet here tomorrow? I'll have my friend Christina with me, and maybe a couple of her colleagues."

"Yes, if you come into the Galleria, say 10 o' clock. There is a big metal sculpture of a ship. If we can meet there, I'll show you to a meeting spot. It'll be great to see you again. Sorry this is like work, but I promise you it is interesting."

Hekla clicked off her phone.

"Yes, Irina will meet us tomorrow, right here. She said she knew the area well, and that it is not even far from her offices."

Irina

At shortly before ten a.m., Irina arrived in Hays. She walked directly to the ship sculpture and Hekla could see her striding towards them. Inky hair arranged in raggedy looking cut, but entirely London fashion of the moment. A plain white tee shirt and dark jeans. A short colourful shawl draped around her neck. Christina recognised it as a nod towards a Russian shawl.

Christina smiled at her, and they introduced themselves. Christina spoke English, despite knowing that Irina would speak very good Russian.

"Hello Irina, I love that shawl, is it Russian?" she asked.

"Pavlovo Posad," she replied, "They make such happy, bright things."

Do you work around here?" asked Irina.

"Only just," answered Christina, "We move here a few days ago from near Hoxton."

"I see, staying with the hip crowd?" smiled Irina.

Hekla began, "Christina and I go back many years. To be honest I didn't think I'd see her again, but now, in these couple of days it is like we were never apart."

Irina looked intrigued, "How did you get to know one

another?"

"We lived on adjacent farms in Iceland - then Christina moved away, " answered Hekla.

"Wow - it is so unusual to find old friends like that!" said Irina, "But I'm intrigued, what is it you wanted to know from me?"

"Can we show you to our office?" asked Christina. Irina nodded and the crossed the concourse in the Galleria to the entrance to the offices.

"Nice building," said Irina, "I'm over by London Bridge in the mini-Shard complex. "

Punching at smoke

"What do we know, then?" asked Christina to Irina, "About the structure of the way the Russians operate - Putin down?"

Irina began, "Well, to begin with, Putin's system of rule is still often described as a monolithic pyramid. In the eyes of society, Putin presents himself as an irreplaceable leader-statesman- the west call him a tsar-. It is him solely making key decisions."

"Yes, the big boss without whose agreement no decision can be made?" asked Jake.

"Precisely, Jake, it's what they want the western press to think, but I think such an understanding of ruling processes in Russia is one of the main mistakes which prevents the west from obtaining a deeper insight into the regime's origins and foundations."

"Oops so I'm wrong then?" asked Jake, smiling.

Irina continued, "Forgive me if I seem sharp-tongued, but the Russian authorities do not comprise a strict vertical structure, ruled by one person. The vertical image is nothing more than a propaganda cliché."

"The Russian authorities are a conglomerate of clans and groups which compete with one another for resources and power. Putin's role in this system remains the same—that of an arbiter and moderator."

Irina continued, "The clan structure is a key to understanding how the system works, and how it can have its finger in so many pies.

"You have to think of it now as Politburo 2.0 and the style of making political decisions has been shifting towards that of the USSR's Politburo. That would be at the hand of Putin, who you must remember was an unexceptional member of the KGB who has risen through the ranks.

"The result is something of an expert's class in influence strategy. There's the creation of national corporations in politics and economy coupled with one of the 'Politburo 2.0' specifics is that its members almost never hold joint sessions."

"Deniability?" asked Bigsy.

"Straightforward shady behaviour," said Irina, "Any investigation will always be punching at smoke."

Irina continued, "Then, like a form of Masonic lodge, the formal status of its members does not always reflect their actual influence when making decisions. And in terms of sheer influence, the 'Politburo 2.0' has amassed a number of elite groups which, to some extent, can be divided into 'power', 'political, 'technical' and 'businessmen'."

"Ah yes," said Jake, "Value solutions: Got a problem?

Find access to a solution, define the corporate and personal value of that solution, gain access to power and make a plan for how to deploy. If Politburo has access to all the types you describe no-wonder it is unstoppable."

"Well, the little extra spice in this is the access to tactics, which could easily become strong arm," answered Irina, "and that is part of the challenge for even Putin. The groups support the 'Politburo 2.0', yet they constantly fight among themselves for influence and try get their members inside it," answered Irina.

Christina chipped in, "That's why they call it 'collective Putin'; he has to be the focus for many factions."

Irina nodded, "Putin is a symbol of this ruling system though he hasn't lost his role as an arbiter and moderator. There's a continuous struggle for power inside the Russian authorities which determines the outcome of decisions while Putin is constantly struggling to balance the powers."

Christina nodded, "Yes, the *siloviks* - that is representatives of power structures - and the 'liberals' in Russia are at loggerheads."

Irina agreed, "Yes and make no mistake that the siloviks are quite ruthless."

"I think some of those liberals are also not what they seem," said Christina.

"So, have we unleashed this somehow in the Raven and Brant situation?" asked Bigsy, "I mean, look at the increasing number of incidents. There was our building catching fire, then there was Bernard Driscoll's car crash.

Then they shoot at Chuck and now they've shot at Christina and Hekla."

Irina looked at Bigsy, "Incidents! I'd call that all out warfare!" she said.

Bigsy said, "Keep talking, I'll bring us some coffees." He disappeared off to their new kitchen area.

Christina replied, "Ha - Yes, Dmitry Medvedev, self-styled leader of the 'liberals' - he still behaves like a clan leader, except his clan is the Liberals. He criticised Russia's foreign policy only because it 'cost too much to the country'. And he received the support of another famous 'liberal', Alexei Kudrin, who said that soon foreign policy goals should be adjusted, but only to ensure stable investment."

Jake asked, "So who are the dominant clans controlling Russia?"

Irina answered, "In Russia, the most influential clan is that of Igor Sechin, Head of Rosneft and factual curator of the country's energy. Energy rights are a particular source of income for clan members and so the tie-in with Celarus has to be investigated."

Jake cut in, "So what we can see is that Celarus discovered plenty of oil - enough to disrupt the Russian supplies to Europe."

Bigsy returned, "Here we are, coffee for all plus milk, creamer and sugar - help yourselves."

Jake took a black coffee and took a sip, "Then Celarus made friends with the USA who 'helped' it by putting some small defensive platforms in country. An airstrip filled with F-15s and a couple of military bases filled with soldiers."

He looked at Irina and realised that she was not so aware of these recent developments.

Bigsy added, "Except the US DoD subcontracted out the building of the new airstrip, the barracks - complete with its own US-style shopping mall - and several defensive missile emplacements along the Celarus border."

Jake again, "And who did it sub-contract to?"

Bigsy replied, "Brant - i.e. Raven. Now we've seen that Brant is ostensibly American but seems to have an awful lot of Russian influence within it."

Clare carefully poured a small amount of milk into her coffee, "So we see a game of Russian dolls. Dolls within dolls manipulating events."

Bigsy nodded, "Yes because we know that Celarus wants to build a pipeline across into Europe. That would be might inconvenient for Russia, although a big ker-ching for Brant and Raven."

Irina agreed, " Yes, That's a fairly typical set of moves. It is hard to follow because the clan structure gets in the way. It means there are many self-interested moving parts. Probably still only Putin, Medvedev and Sechin really know what is happening."

"One of the factors in the Brant case was the introductions via the Freemasons," said Jake, "Christina and Antanov were first introduced into all of this via Sir

Charles Frobisher at a Masonic meeting in London."

"That would have been the opportunity for a lure," said Irina, "A honey trap probably. Entice the unwary into a trap, compromise them and then force them to play along."

Hekla nodded, "I'm afraid one of the magazines I freelance for specialises in that kind of gossip."

Jake smiled, "Yes, when I worked for 'Street' it was about half the publication."

"The honey trap," said Christina, "That was the MP and government minister Bernard Driscoll, who pushed through the agreement for divestment of Brant- it had to go to Parliament because of its implications - and then Driscoll walked it through."

Christina continued, "We also know that Driscoll's, 'lure' was probably a woman known as Marion Charlotte."

"Not THE Marion Charlotte?" asked Irina, "She's all over the tabloids at the moment in some kind of Cabinet Minister scandal."

"Sounds like it," said Christina, "Although I must admit I've not seen it."

Irina sipped her coffee, "You will have to tread carefully with this. The siloviks will go in with all guns blazing - literally. The liberals are as dangerous, though possibly more subtle - think hypodermics instead of bullets. It is far more difficult to identify the leaders of the so-called 'liberal' clans."

Hekla noticed Christina frowning as she heard this.

Christina added, "The liberal clans don't lack competition, but avoid open fights as much as possible. That is why it is difficult to define their borders. All groups often act as allies rather than reckless opponents. This clear unity is the reason they are simply called the 'liberals'."

Irina looked into her coffee cup, "Overall, Russia's biggest businessmen act very differently – some are related to specific groups and are using their protection and lobbyism, while others successfully manoeuvre between numerous groups."

Irina sipped her coffee again, "But even most influential power centres in Russia show that Putin is constantly playing the role of an arbiter and manoeuvring to maintain his power. The contradictory system of rule he has created guarantees this."

Irina added, "Contradictions have become the source of Putin's power. They allow him to act in several political areas at the same time and maintain reliability despite dubious reasons for doing so."

"This has been brilliant!" said Jake, Bigsy and Clare nodded their agreement.

"So you, Irina, are planning to show Hekla around London in a couple of days?" asked Christina.

"Yes, that was our plan - a simple tourist jaunt to see some of the sights."

"Well, I was planning a similar trip with Hekla

tomorrow," said Christina, "You know, we could combine and have one 'girls tour' of London. What do you think?"

"You know something, I was thinking just the same thing," Said Hekla.

"So how would you be fixed tomorrow?" asked Christina to Irina.

"That can work for me," said Irina, " We could meet here somewhere on the South Bank. My tube stop is London Bridge, anyway."

"This could be excellent!" said Hekla smiling, "Christina - will you be bringing your Mulberry?"

"You bet, " said Christina, "At the moment I won't go anywhere without it!"

Two of Cups

Unity
Partnership
Connection

Christina Hunt

Christina was back at her apartment asleep. Her phone rang. It was Antanov.

"Hey Antanov, how are you?" said Christina.

"Ha, I'm good, kotyonok, just a little worried for you!" said Antanov, "Look, I've been hearing some things. I thought you'd better know."

"Kitten? Your poor wife," queried Christina.

Antanov continued, "I've been told that you were being hunted by freelancers. That they work for Brant. Brant is being run by one of the clans - However, the FSB found out about the situation and have ordered an immediate cease. It turns out that someone higher up and more important has got your back."

"But that's not all, the Roslavl Bratva clan that have been arranging this are being run by Tima Maximovich. He also runs Gasneft, which is one of the largest gas exploration and production companies in the world. He wants to intervene in the planned oil extraction and pipeline creation from Celarus.

"Roslavl Brotherhood? Roslavl - That's close to Celarus too, isn't it?" asked Christina.

"Yes, so maybe that's why his clan ordered a couple of other things too. One was the assassination of Bernard Driscoll. They issued a kill for him, then staged a car accident. I heard they set up a roadside stinger (you know those things with spikes) to puncture his tyres, cause him to crash off the road and they then calmly fitted two replacement tyres to his car before they drove off.

"That was not the only thing, though. They have been burning the evidence trail linking Roslavl to the original Raven deal when it sold off Qube and formed Brant. Sir Charles Frobisher was heavily involved in that situation and was targeted. He's not been seen for several days and the rumours are that he is in the bottom of the Mediterranean off Nice."

"It doesn't even end there - they went after Frobisher's fixer Gerhardt Schmidt and blew him up in a yacht close to Monaco. That made the news but seems to have been reported as an unfortunate fire."

"Yes, and they have also chased down Chuck Manners and me - with guns," said Christina, "but it didn't end well for them."

"Yes - I'd expect no less, but now you've been given a blanket immunity by the FSB you should be out of trouble. That doesn't affect Chuck Manners though - I hear they are about to plant evidence to bring him down."

"Do you know what kind?" asked Christina.

"No," said Antanov, "Except it sounded big. I think they must be really pissed off with him."

"Antanov, thank you, " said Christina.

"Hey, stay safe, zvezda moya," said Antanov.

"Don't let your wife hear you calling me 'my star'," laughed Christina, But what about you? You are okay and distant enough from all of this?"

"Yes, when I flew back to Brussels, I decided to take a roundabout route stopping in Amsterdam and catching a train for the last part. It's covered my tracks enough to show that I've never even seen you this time," answered Antanov, "Hey Christina - stay safe."

The line clicked. Antanov was gone.

Clare remembers something

Jake and Bigsy were sitting around a conference table. Clare was typing something into a laptop.

Christina walked in; she was wearing sunglasses.

"Hey babe," said Clare, "Was it a good girls' day and night out yesterday?"

"Oh yes," answered Christina, "Irina knows some amazing clubs too. We started with regular tourist things like a Clipper trip along the Thames. Then the walk around the South Bank. Hekla wanted to see some other main sights too, so we did some of it by taxi - around Westminster, Buckingham Palace for an Instagram moment, Trafalgar Square, Downing Street and then back along to the Tate Modern and across on the boingy bridge. Then a Clipper up to Battersea and had a look around the shops at Chelsea Bridge by the power station. Another taxi down to Sloane Square and a look inside some of the high-end shops around the Square and a stroll along Kings Road. We got papped there. Someone thought we were a girl band."

"Did you 'do' Oxford Street and the West End?" asked Jake.

"You know what, we skipped most of it because both Irina and I thought it was too touristy. We went into Soho though, and that's when Irina's knowledge of the clubs really paid off. We avoided the nasty places and went into those where you walk up to a normal looking front door to someone's house, only inside it's a great club."

"We did the last part until around 2 am, but by then Hekla was flagging, so we bundled her into a taxi back to her hotel. We both came along to see she was okay and then I offered Irina a stopover at mine instead of going back home."

"It sounds full-on, " said Bigsy.

"I just wish we'd had a little more food to balance the alcohol. I'm a little frayed around the edges this morning, Irina can pack away the *wodka*," said Christina.

"It's nearly this afternoon," said Jake, smiling.

"See, I'm losing my grip on reality, "said Christina, "But I need to tell you all some things I found out from Antanov - he called me."

Bigsy hit the BigButton to mute the room's hidden microphones and cameras.

Christina began to explain what she had heard from Antanov.

"We'd better warn Chuck," said Bigsy.

"How will we get in contact - have you got a way, Jake?" asked Clare.

"Only that emergency thing where we put something onto the Triangle website and wait for him to call in," said Jake.

Bigsy nodded, "I can do that."

"Or we could ask Amanda Miller?" suggested Clare, "I think she and Chuck have been 'together'."

"I knew it," said Jake, " When Chuck was staying in London at that hotel - The Mondrian."

"Yes," said Clare, "I only inferred it, but Chuck looked suitably rumbled."

"Okay Jake, you have the most track record with Amanda…Can you give her a call?" asked Clare.

"Sure, " said Jake, "let me go to the quiet room to make the call," He walked across to another room.

"So, go on…. Last night… spill the beans, Christina, where did you go and what did you do?" asked Bigsy…

Roslavl Bratva Chatter

Eventually, Jake returned from his call with Amanda.

"Yes, she knows where Chuck is…He's moved out to Germany. He left the UK for Belgium and has then worked his way south. He's in a military barracks! Hiding in plain sight."

"According to Amanda, one of the Russian clans, the Roslavl Bratva run by Tima Maximovich are planning something. They want to put the finger on Chuck Manners and are about to frame him in some kind of terrorist incident."

Jake continued, "Amanda says she knows the Americans won't believe it and neither will SI6, but there will be such a high-profile news scoop that neither of the secret services will contain it."

"Do we know what kind of incident? Is there any way we could stop it?" asked Christina.

"No, we don't know either. Amanda has picked up the

chatter from the Roslavl Bratva and says there has also been some significant buying of shares in Gasneft over the last few days. It has Maximovich's fingerprints all over it and Amanda thinks the event implicating Chuck will be utterly ruthless. "

Jake continued, "Amanda told me that Maximovich has considerable influence over the news media. The best example is through his wife, Natalia Maximovich, who still controls somewhat liberal and influential media outlets: notably the news agency Lavlbalt and the Saint Petersburg newspaper Peterburgskij Komsomolets."

"I told Amanda about Irina, and said she works partly for The Manhattanite. I said it could be a useful aspect when this needed to be publicised for what it is."

Jake looked down to his small black Moleskine, where he had been taking notes from the call with Amanda, "Lavlbalt and Peterburgskij Komsomolets can feed direct news from Russia into the western press machine, where it gets syndicated everywhere throughout the west. I can remember using Lavlbalt when I was researching stories about Russians owning football clubs in England."

Jake looked back at his black notebook, "Lavlbalt was almost shut down last year."

Jake looked around the room, "The agency was accused of violations and the court revoked its license. But after the aggression in Crimea, when a new wave of media oppression began in Russia, the Russian Supreme Court repealed the decrees of lower courts and reinstated Lavlbalt's licence."

Jake flipped a page, "Amanda also said that Maximovich

became a representative of the Communist Party in the Parliament. It shows that in the Russian ruling system the most important role goes not to what party you are in (opposition vs. the ruling party) but what clan you belong to."

Clare nodded, "This ties in with what Antanov was saying yesterday. It shows the build-up of power through vice and then media messaging. An object lesson in corruption."

Christina asked Jake, "Barracks, you said. Do you know which one?"

"Hmm, said Jake, looking through his notes, "Not sure - Ah yes, here we are - 'Panzer Kaserne'."

Christina smiled, "Typical Chuck- you know what Panzer Kaserne means? Tank Barracks. At least he is well-fortified."

 Bigsy googled it, immediately, "Unbelievable, it's in the same part of Germany that Christina and Clare visited recently. Where you met Oskar. And the Barracks might sound German, but it's an American base, taken over by the Americans from the Germans years ago."

Brussels

Christina had called ahead to Antanov. Now she was on the Eurostar again, still on tasks related to Chuck Manners. It would be strange asking Antanov to spy on the Russians on her behalf, to find out something which could only benefit SI6 and the CIA.

She knew that Antanov would be careful and was now intrigued that she would meet his family.

She climbed out of the train and onto the platform in Brussels. As she approached the gate she could see Antanov waiting there.

"Hey Antanov! I wasn't expecting this!" she said, "Being met at the gate, truly an honour."

"Yes *kotyonok*," said Antanov, "I thought we'd better establish some ground rules before you meet Camille. Remember we are old acquaintances who worked in the same office in Arkhangelsk and that's it. We haven't seen one another in fifteen years, but as you were passing through Brussels you thought you'd say 'Hi'. Oh yes, and it is okay to be asking me some Freemason questions too."

"You'd better not call me 'kitten' then," said Christina.

"Fair point," said Antanov.

"Don't worry - if you do, I'll say it was my nickname around the office."

They walked out towards the busy taxi area at the station.

"No, we don't want here," said Antanov. "Let me show you around to the nearest hotel with a separate cab rank."

Christina smiled as he showed her to the Hilton. It was exactly the hotel that she had stayed in with Chuck a few days earlier.

They ordered a cab to Christina's hotel, which was confusingly called The Hotel, and turned out to be a modern skyscraper in the centre of Brussels.

"I've never been in this hotel before," said Antanov, "But it looks pretty good."

"Do you mind if I drop off my luggage before we talk?" asked Christina.

"Sure, I'll be in the bar," said Antanov.

Christina tapped the floor into the lift and was soon in her 12th floor room. It was light and airy, with fantastic views across Brussels. She placed her small travel bag on the bed, picked up her handbag and was soon back downstairs, where Antanov was staring into a long, cool-looking drink.

"So, what is all this about? Not still Chuck, by any chance?" asked Antanov.

"You are good," smiled Christina, "Yes he's being set up at the moment, we think it is by one of our very own Russian *blatnoy*."

"And who would that be?" asked Antanov.

"Kasharin Timur Maximovich of the Roslavl Bratva, " answered Christina.

"I think I told you about Tima when we had that phone call, " said Antanov, "Head of Gasneft - and guess what, he's a Freemason too! It is one of the ways he got such a rapid spread of influence in western Russia. As a matter of fact, it is quite big news at the moment, because Maximovich is trying to establish the twelfth lodge of the UGLR - That's the United Grand Lodges of Russia. He's been arguing that such a lodge would fit right in, being between Moscow and Sankt-Peterburg."

"Well, it would be good to find out what he has been planning for my friend Chuck. There's some kind of plot out now."

"I can quietly ask around, " said Antanov, "Like I've said before though, I'm embedded here in Brussels now, have a good job with the EU and a wife and family, so I'm not looking for your high speed thrills."

"Scream if you want to go faster," said Christina.

"I'm not screaming," replied Antanov, "But I will look around for you. It could take me a couple of days. You can enjoy yourself having a look around Brussels. There's the Grand Place - which is a big tourist square, the Mannikin Pis - a statue of a little boy pee-ing, some cathedrals, a few old residences and my favourite - The Belgian Comic Strip Centre which features Tin-Tin and The Smurfs. And if you feel like taking the tram, you could visit the Atomium; oh yes and a few brown bars too."

"I can't wait," said Christina, "No wonder those diplomats have such a good time here."

"And come around for dinner, Camille would love to meet you. How about tomorrow night?"

"Lovely," answered Christina.

The whale sorcerer

The next evening, Christina was preparing to visit Antanov. She had casually tuned the TV into a news channel and was vaguely aware of smoke shown curling upward.

She listened to the news reporter. It was some kind of research institute outside of Rudnya, in Celarus. The reports were of a large complex which had suffered an explosion, putting a chemical haze blowing from Celarus towards the Russian border. There were rumours that the institute had been working on synthesised coronavirus vaccines, which were less essential since the outbreak of the one-time global pandemic had been contained, but were still, nonetheless, important products.

Reports said the laboratory that had exploded held both the vaccine but also the original virus. A full-scale lock-down of the area had ensued, both in Celarus and across the border in Russia.

Christina noticed that it was the area of Russia where

Kasharin Maximovich and his Roslavl Bratva operated. The distance to Rudnya was around 200 kilometres.

She walked downstairs and asked a cab to take her to Antanov's apartment in Brussels. The apartment was in the Européen Quarter and in a smart block.

Camille came to the door and greeted Christina and said, "Come in, come in, and welcome to Belgium! We don't get too many pop-stars coming around to visit!"

Christina proffered a hastily bought bottle of wine to her host and then saw Antanov with his daughter in the next room. It was a bright joint kitchen and living space and Christina noticed along one edge of it were a couple of laptop computers. She could just see into another room which looked as if it had been set up as an office.

"Hey Christina, welcome and let's have a drink, what would you like, a gin and tonic maybe? Or a vodka?"

Camille said, "Yes, I'll have a white wine please," and Christina nodded agreement," That sounds like a great idea."

"Look what Christina has brought us," said Camille," A lovely bottle of Chateau Le Prieure, Pomerol."

"Sounds delicious," said Antanov. What do you think, Lucy?"

"Daddy, I'm too young to know about wines. I'm only six. You have to be at least eight to know about wines," answered Lucy in very good English.

"That's right, now you show Christina your bedroom,

and then show her how quietly you can read."

Lucy grabbed Christina's hand and pulled her towards the corridor and then into a bedroom swathed in pink and decorated with unicorns. "Okay, this is my room, but when an adult comes in it, the only way they can escape is to tell me a story…" asked Lucy.

Christina thought for a moment, "You know, I'm from the land of ice and snow, and we have some good stories there. Let me tell you one."

"What, like in Frozen?" asked Lucy.

"No - these stories are from before Elsa and Anna were even born."

Lucy snuggled into her bed and looked intently towards Christina.

"There once was a fearsome King Harald Bluetooth who intended to invade poor, vulnerable Iceland and so he called for his sorcerer to help.

"His sorcerer had a good idea.

"He said he would change into a whale to find the island of Iceland's weak spots."

"What was the sorcerer's name?" asked Lucy.

"Oh - Øyvind Kjelda hvalrekinn," answered Christina, We can call him Walter, for short."

"And then each time Walter the whale-sorcerer tried to land, a *landvættir*, or "land wight," fought him off, thus creating the four guardians of Iceland."

"A wight in the form of a dragon protected Iceland's Eastfjords,

"In North Iceland there was an eagle ready for a fight.

"In the Westfjords, a bull was ready to fight the whale
"

and finally, in South Iceland, there was a giant ready to finish the job.

"Nowadays images of these wights are all over my country, Iceland, adorning the Icelandic coat of arms, certain coins and buildings."

"And the moral of the story?", asked Lucy.

"Good question - 'never forget where you are from'," said Christina.

"I like it, so show me Iceland on my globe…" asked Lucy.

She pointed to the illuminated globe in the corner of the room.

"Why it's here," said Christina, pointing to Iceland on the map.

"That's a long way from Belgium," said Lucy.

"It is, but I think the wights will also keep an eye on you here," said Christina.

"Are you keeping Christina locked away?" asked Camille, who had just entered the room, "I guess you have told a story already?"

"Oh yes," said Christina, and we've checked out where Iceland is on the globe."

"Goodnight Lucy," said Camille, kissing the child on the forehead.

"Bonne nuit maman," said Lucy.

They walked back to Antanov, who was uncorking a bottle of wine.

"I thought we'd save your one, Christina, but I hope you'll like this one," he smiled.

Camille said, "You'll have to tell me something about yourself, Christina, Antanov says you met in an office somewhere?"

Christina proceeded to tell her backstory, suitably edited to incorporate Antanov.

"But I guess you wanted to talk to Antanov about something to do with his Freemason friends?" asked Camille, " He knows I think it is all a bit like boys and their toys, when they go off into secret huddles with leather aprons and chisels."

Christina laughed, she could see that Camille and her shared some opinions about the Freemasons.

"Yes, but it can bring great insights into the actions of others," said Antanov.

"I was particularly interested in the moves that the Roslavl Bratva might make under the guise of the Freemasons," said Christina.

"What? Do you think that the masons are mixed up in that explosion in west Russia?" asked Antanov.

"It was in Celarus actually, " said Christina, "Close to the Russian Border."

"I heard something about it," said Antanov, "that Tima Maximovich sounds as if he could be implicated. They are trying to create a situation similar to the ones that the Americans sometimes create, close to a war zone."

"What is that?" asked Camille.

"Create disruptions to justify keeping troops in the area. If necessary, create a brand name for the peacekeeping initiative and then flood it with resources."

Camille said, "It all sounds a little calculated and quite disreputable. I hope your Freemason friends don't get up to those kind of tricks?"

"Not at all," said Antanov, "but unfortunately there are members of our team who are not as altruistic about the masons as I am and most of us are. They are trying to bend it to support their less-than-ideal behaviours. That Kasharin Maximovich would certainly not think twice about subverting the cause to meet his ends. Did you see the press conference?"

Christina shook her head.

"Well he is now alleging that the explosion was caused by a CIA-inspired Black Op, led by none other than your friend Colonel Chuck Manners. It will certainly have raised the hunt for him," said Antanov.

"It is what we predicted, yet I can't think why they would be so angry with Chuck," said Christina, "You know something, I was with Chuck here a few days ago, when they were shooting at him."

"Brussels is a strange town, what with all of the diplomatic incidents that occur here," said Camille, sipping the wine, "But I don't think I've heard of too many shooting incidents?"

"Are you involved with the EU?" Asked Christina.

"Yes, I've a role in the anti-corruption unit," answered Camille, "To be honest, most people think of things like cigarettes, fake medicine and some occasional smuggling of trademarked items. But we do look at embezzlement, bribes, corruption and so on, although it doesn't make for such good photos as piles of cigarette cartons or fake COVID-19 testing kits."

Camille continued, "Russia is a great case in point, I think the estimates of the level of corruption in Russia are around $2.5 bn from 2014- 2107. Instead of the money going to the government, it goes to representatives from the government and other people in positions of power.

"Putin may have presided over Russia for more than 20 years, but the 'anti-corruption' measures are often the settlement of political scores, rather than a realistic pledge to end the corruption."

"In Russia, the bagman hasn't gone. There are still bags of currency routinely moved around." said Camille.

"What about the FBK?" asked Christina, referring to the Russian Anti-Corruption Foundation.

Camilla continued, "Yes, the Anti-Corruption Foundation, run by Russian opposition leader Alexey Navalny has skewered Kremlin insiders and ministry officials through their illicit and often exorbitant holdings."

Antanov added, "A real fight against corruption is impossible under Putin. His whole system is built around it. Every attempt to really take on corrupt officials has ended in nothing,"

Camille nodded, and looked thoughtfully towards her wine glass, "Secret European villas, mansions, luxury yachts, stored artworks, wealthy relatives, and private planes ferrying pet dogs to international dog shows have all been subjects of the foundation's investigations in recent years."

"Say Christina, would you like some more wine? And I'm sorry that Antanov has tricked us into 'talking shop' for the last half hour. I want to hear about your time as a pop singer - and get some of the inside gossip."

Antanov added, "Yes, but before we finish this conversation, we should also flag the alleged secret wealth of former Prime Minister Dmitry Medvedev. And then that FBK was quick to note that Medvedev's replacement Mikhail Mishustin has family holdings that far outstrip his past government salary as Russia's chief tax officer. "

Camille added, "If your friend Chuck has been picking at this, then I would not be surprised if they seek retribution. Predictably, the Kremlin has launched raids and criminal investigations against FBK, moves widely seen as revenge for the organisations investigations and calls for democratic change. It seems to me that they have singled out your friend in a similar way."

"Now, what was it like being on the road? Was it glamorous or just a succession of hotels in different towns?"

Part Two – Tournament of lies

It's the end of the world as we know it

A government for hire and a combat site
Left of west and coming in a hurry
With the Furies breathing down your neck
Team by team, reporters baffled, trumped, tethered, cropped

Look at that low plane, fine, then
Uh oh, overflow, population, common food
But it'll do, save yourself, serve yourself.
World serves its own needs, listen to your heart bleed

Six o'clock, TV hour, don't get caught in foreign tower
Slash and burn, return, listen to yourself churn
Lock him in uniform, book burning, blood letting
Every motive escalate, automotive incinerate

Light a candle, light a votive, step down, step down
Watch your heel crush, crushed, uh-oh
This means no fear, cavalier renegade and steering clear
A tournament, a tournament, a tournament of lies
Offer me solutions, offer me alternatives, and I decline

It's the end of the world as we know it
It's time I had some time alone
And I feel fine

Mike Mills, Michael Stipe, Peter Buck & Bill Berry, 1987, Nashville, Tennessee

Ten of Swords

Failure
Collapse
Defeat
Backstabbing

Institute

Amanda Miller had seen the SPA report of the Institute explosion in Rudnya, Celarus. She knew that Colonel Charles (Chuck) Manners was described as the suspect and that it had turned into an international search.

She asked for the satellite scans over the area, which she received from GCHQ.

She was in a briefing room with Jim Cavendish, whom she had worked with for years.

"It doesn't look right," he said, "This has all the hallmarks of a stitch-up."

"I'm not even sure that there was actually an explosion at the site."

He zoomed into the satellite image, which fragmented as he went in for a close-up.

"There's not enough resolution to be sure," he said.

"Can we run proof of life?" asked Amanda.

"We are ahead of you," said Jim, "None of this adds up. Let's start with cellphone location data. The SPA - That's *Sankt-Peterburgskaya Analitika* report says there was no cellphone activity in a high-security portion of the Rudnyanskiy Institut Virusologii across the 'explosion' dates and that there may have been a 'hazardous event' during that period.

Jim sipped water from a glass, "Our analysis shows no direct evidence of a shutdown, or any proof for the theory that anything emerged accidentally from the lab."

"So, it could all be fake news?" asked Amanda.

"Yes, staged to make it look incriminating. Although it would need quite some influence for this to work," answered Jim, "If such a shutdown, it could be seen as evidence of a possibility being examined by U.S. intelligence agencies and alluded to by US administration officials, including the president — that a rogue US marine blew up a pathogen lab. From what I've heard about Chuck Manners this seems incredibly unlikely."

"So who could have orchestrated this?" asked Amanda.

"I can't say - officially, but I'd put the chances very high that it was local *blatnoy* Kasharin Maximovich. Consider that crime-lord Maximovich is active in the region. Then that the report was released by *Lavlbalt* and *Peterburgskij Komsomolets*, which are the two media outlets owned by his wife. The analysis seems to account for only a tiny fraction of the cell phones that would be expected in a facility that employs hundreds of people."

Jim continued, "Now what is interesting is that a different document from Lavlbalt obtained by NBC News says that an annual international conference entitled 'Genomic population structures of microbial pathogens' planned in the same lower-security portion of the RIV appears to have been 'cancelled and never took place'."

"It's tosh. The conference went forward as planned. There is even a YouTube screening from a couple of the sessions. The cameraman kindly swings the camera around before the session showing just how full the conference facility was."

"It makes us highly sceptical of the analysis, which is based on commercially available cell phone location data."

"Our own analysts in Cheltenham saw the document and said the data 'looks weak and some conclusions don't make sense.' "

"Earlier, U.S. intelligence agencies received reports based on publicly available cell phone and satellite data suggesting a shutdown at the lab, two U.S. officials familiar with the matter say. But after examining overhead imagery and their own data, the agencies could not confirm any shutdown, and considered the reports 'inconclusive.' "

"It seems this really is a case of smoke without fire. A staged explosion, pointing the finger to Manners, but no evidence. Someone could have burned some truck tyres on the roof of the Institute."

"And here's the thing. The RIV is a high-security facility next to an adversary nation and studying dangerous pathogens. It is a collection target for several U.S.

intelligence agencies. Data gathered would include mobile phone signals, communications intercepts and overhead satellite imagery.

"Analysts are now examining what was collected in October and November for clues suggesting any anomalies. There's none. Normal traffic patterns on the roads. No exclusion zone. No emergency buildings erected. Nothing."

Jim continued, "So here's my more pragmatic view. First look at routine telemetry data around the facility. If it shows dramatic drop off in activity compared to previous 18 months, it would be a strong indication of an incident at lab and of when it happened. But it doesn't. Life goes on as normal."

"So, it's all a fake?" asked Amanda.

"Looks like it," said Jim.

"To be honest, the report we intercepted that contains much of this evidence has several things wrong with it. There's badging showing the source consultancy *Sankt-Peterburgskaya Analitika* that provided the analytics. It looks to us like the bedroom company of a freelancer. Even the logo is suspect. We re-mapped it over a commonly available clipart from Star Wars and it has a greater than 90% match to a Darth Vader graphic, albeit with some recolouring.

"Profiling by us says the report was written by a precocious teenage gamer, who legitimised it by copying the style from - wait for it- Cambridge Analytica."

Amanda laughed out loud, "Sorry - it gets more

preposterous by the minute," she said, letting her relief that it wasn't Chuck escape.

Jim added, "Then the Americans kindly dropped a Scan Eagle drone into the area, admittedly on a short sweep. It showed workers going about their business in normal clothing. No airlock tent or other devices have been installed.

"Air surveillance of the car parks indicate they are as full after the event as they were before it.

"There's been no traffic re-routing around the site and no excessive amount of emergency vehicles clustered nearby. In fact, a confectionery factory fire about 100 kilometres to the south east received significantly more emergency traffic than this facility after the alleged attack."

"So, you are saying it's a made-up event?" asked Amanda.

"It sure looks that way," answered Jim, "And I've cross checked with our cousins in the US and they seem to think the same thing."

"So how do we get the event back into the news?" asked Amanda, "To show it is made-up?"

"Yes, - a real example of fake news, but all the more difficult to deal with. Ironically we will need to provide our report to a media feed interested in media manipulation." Answered Jim.

"I may have just such a contact," said Amanda.

209

Framed

Amanda called Jake, "Look, this is as far off the record as it gets."

"You were right to warn that Chuck was being framed. He is, and it is for that explosion in Celarus. We think it is the local clan there, but we've also got evidence that it is framing. There's the report that shows the explosion, which is being used as a basis for hunting Chuck.

"Then there's our report, done in collaboration with the CIA, and it shows that there's been no disruption to routine around the facility. That the explosion was Fake News. They even ran a conference there just after the explosions was alleged to have happened.

"I'm getting the reports cleaned up so you can have a copy. The Americans sent in a drone to cross check and found nothing. Our theory about the smoke is that some tyres were burned on the roof of the building. It was a really shoddy operation.

"I'm hoping you still have contacts in the press that can filter this out. We can do so from here but it will have SI6 fingerprints all over it by the time the report reaches daylight.

Jake spoke, "We didn't think Chuck could be up to no good. I've also got a contact from The Manhattanite who can help get this out. She'll be such a random source that no-one will be able to piece it together."

"Okay, best you don't tell me any more - plausible deniability and all that. Expect an email from me tomorrow! And take care!

The phone clicked - Amanda was gone.

Irina visits Raven

Irina had decided there was a story in the situation she had discovered with Hekla and Christina. She had left Christina's apartment early, found a coffee shop and shaken the mental devastation of the last night from her head.

Then she had walked into a nearby Marks, bought a new outfit and changed to be fresh for the new day. She'd read an article in Manhattanite about 'After date clothes' and now she was living it.

Now she had an interesting situation from across the pond, complete with a US-angle. She called and arranged to meet the Raven Press Office for a brief conversation about Raven, as part of a positive profile piece to cover Raven, Qube and Brant. She had explained it was for The Manhattanite market and to position Raven as a success story of a US company operating from London and spreading into Europe.

By afternoon she approached the Raven offices near to

Heron Quays, in Bank Street, just along from Morgan Stanley and JP Morgan's two huge plate glass buildings.

Irina was frequently around the area although still realised that she could easily get lost if she took to the tunnels and shopping malls which threaded their way around most of the lower floors.

It reminded her of Seattle, Calgary or even Toronto, with an entire infrastructure of fairly high-end shops, cafes, restaurants and bars in the labyrinth layers of the construction. The captive audience of thousands of office workers meant that the mall levels teemed busy with shoppers, yet it was like a secret zone, rather than destination shopping for anyone. No, if you worked here, you shopped here, men bought fancy shirts and suits here. Women found the latest fashions and high-end shoe-porn.

Irina entered the lobby of Raven, tiled in a vivid black and white diagonal pattern. She was at once impressed by the huge golden raven in the centre of the lobby, inside a circle of gold. The sort of thing an Embassy would position, but less usual for a corporation. Then she noticed the two rows of flags, to the left and right of the auditorium. She soon spotted the American flag, a British one and also an EU ring of stars, but she was more lost with some of the others. French, German, Belgian, Netherlands, Russia, but there were a few with added symbols that she didn't recognise.

Then she looked up towards the ceiling. It had been painted a deep blue and showed small stars twinkling in it. In the centre a sunburst and at either end of the atrium a rising and setting star.

Irina was also intrigued to see a large 'G' in the middle of the starburst, and seven extra-long strands radiating to the edges of the ceiling.

Then she looked back to the raven. She realised that the circle was not a simple ring. It was a serpent or some similar creature with its tail in its mouth. She remembered she had once owned a ring with a similar depiction, which she had received as a present from Egypt.

"Hello," said an attractive woman with spiky blonde hair and wearing a dark business suit, "I'm Isabelle Eastwood, from Raven PR."

"Oh, how did you recognise me?" asked Irina.

"Not so difficult when you are wearing a visitor pass and staring towards the ceiling," answered Isabelle.

"It's themed to look like our Head Office in Central London, which is, in turn, supposed to resemble a Freemason Hall. It turns out our head office is slap bang in the middle of the Freemason area of London."

"So is the Raven organisation Masonic in any way?" asked Irina.

"Not so's one would notice, but it's like all of these Head Office traditions. I had to visit a finance house recently. It was in a grandiose hall, complete with marble pillars. It turned out the finance house had been a bank and had taken the marble and pillars as some sort of forfeiture from another bank out in Milan or somewhere. It's incredible how these traditions seep through London."

"Even, it would seem, quite modern areas like your

building here?"

"Yes, this building was part of the Heron Quays development and I think was finished in around 2003. So, it is somewhat more modern than the old buildings in the City."

"I'm told our building there was built around the same time as the Freemason Hall, which means only built around 1930. Although the London masons go back much further to the late 1700s."

"You seem to know a lot about it, " said Irina.

"Want to know my secret?" smiled Isabelle, "I'm usually asked about it by visitors so I've accumulated my knowledge. I reckon I can talk about the building all the way from the lobby to the meeting room!"

Irina smiled, "That's brilliant, and you know all about my magazine The Manhattanite? I have to do a similar spiel about it to many Public Relations people."

Isabelle confessed, "Yes, actually, I'll admit I usually 'borrow' the latest edition from our press pile in the office. I enjoy reading it and many of the articles seem to come from well-known writers. It is surprisingly cutting at times too, mixing its comic-book humour with quite dark articles about the state we're in. Yes, I'm quite a fan!"

Irina started, "I've been based in London for some time. I'm usually asked to do pro-American stories from across the Pond here. Right now I'm interested in how Raven is pushing American business into Europe from Britain, almost despite Brexit."

Isabelle smiled, "That'll make a great story, let's get a few ground rules straight about quotes policy and so on, then we can begin. I've got a couple of pre-prepared quotes here too, from a couple of the big bosses."

They were inside a main meeting room on a high floor. Irina recognised she was being given the five-star treatment because this would be a good PR scoop for Raven. Featured in The Manhattanite, with a positive piece about their business development.

Isabelle proceeded to show Irina paperwork about policy on quotes and publicity, and Irina listened. Isabelle was clearly proficient because she had brought several quotes and a couple of good backgrounder pieces with potential to be woven into the main article.

"This is all great," said Irina, "But I was hoping meet one of the head folk here too, to ask a couple of direct questions. Will that be possible?"

"You know how tricky that is," answered Isabelle, "And it tends to skew the piece too. It will be more about the individual than about Raven. It tends to make it into an 'About Mr X' instead of about the whole company."

Irina realised that Isabelle was a professional and a strong gatekeeper too. She would not be able to get past Isabelle without pushing more of her magazine's leverage. And the truth was that she was acting independently, so the leverage would not be forthcoming.

"Okay, well, I'll say 'Thank You' then," she said to Isabelle.

"I hope we've provided you with enough to create an interesting article," said Isabelle standing as if ready to leave the meeting.

"Yes, that's great," answered Irina, walking to the door.

In the corridor she could see a couple of men chatting. They were speaking in Russian, and Irina could hear their conversation.

"Yes, Vassily Turgenev is meeting with Tima right now. They are to see Miller McDonald at 2 pm. He wants to understand what has been happening"

Irina was now out of earshot and standing by the elevators. Isabelle pressed the down button.

"Yes - I have to accompany you whilst you are in the office areas," said Isabelle, "You've got one of those Visitor passes."

"It's okay," said Irina, "I'm used to it, and I always look for the restrooms in the lobby!"

Isabella smiled, "Yes and they do make the ones here pretty fancy to impress visitors! Check out the sofas and the makeup area"

They were back at ground level. Irina said her thank yous and prepared to leave the building. But maybe she'd just take a look at these facilities before she left.

Ball's Brothers

Irina decided she would call Hekla.

"Hey Hekla, how are you doing after our epic night? You had to cave around 2 am, but we couldn't keep going much longer."

Hekla replied, "Yes, you and Christina showed me every side of London in less than 24 hours. My head was reeling when I woke up - Oh and that library where we had to go through the bookcase into the Speakeasy! Brilliant. Oh - I already thanked Christina - I should have thanked you too!

"No problem. Look - your other friends are mixed up in something with that Raven company. Guess where I've been today? - Only along to their headquarters. I was thinking I could tell you and Christina about it, but wasn't sure where we could all meet."

"How about back in Hay's Galleria? It is close to my hotel and also close to where you work. If we met there we could link up with the others? And there's a good underground wine bar too. What time?"

How about an hour from now? We can meet in Ball's Brothers?" replied Irina.

"Okay, I'll call Christina and tell her the plan!"

…

An hour later, Hekla was walking into Ball's Brother, down some steps and into a series of vaults. Across the room was a smart-looking bar and a large selection of wine.

"Er - I'm not sure?" Said Hekla.

"Try this," said the barman smiling, "It's our house red but pretty good. Are you expecting anyone? If so, may I suggest taking a bottle."

"Great," said Irina, "Yes please, a bottle then, and three glasses to start."

The barman carried the glasses and bottle to a table and Hekla sat down to wait. A few moments later Christina and Irina arrived together.

"Hey Hekla, we saw one another upstairs! I see you already have the wine. Excellent."

"Is this going to be like last time?" asked Hekla, "In which case I think I'd better know now."

"Em, no, we both have to work tomorrow, so we can't get too crazy," said Irina - looking knowingly at Christina.

"Okay, let's admit it - we all had a great evening! - Even

if it took a long time to recover."

"I've asked the others to join us," said Christina, "I hope that's okay?"

"Sure," said Irina, "The more heads to think about this the better"

At that moment Jake, Bigsy and Clare appeared. Bigsy noticed the bottle on the table, "I'll get some more glasses and another bottle," he said and walked across to the bar. Jake and Clare sat down.

There was a moment's silence, then Jake said, "The triple threat is back in town!" and everyone laughed.

"Hekla - you need protection from these other two," laughed Jake.

"It has always been that way around Christina. Minor bumps and grazes - now they just get bigger."

Christina smiled, "Well we all did very well, even Hekla singing that Björk song in the karaoke bar."

"Oh yes, said Irina, "I'd almost forgotten…'*Declare Independence! Don't let them do that to you!*' You had half the bar marching around in a column! Madness."

Bigsy returned, "So what's this all about?" he asked.

Irina proceeded to describe her visit to Raven. She described the inside of the building.

"Another Masonic building!" said Clare. The others nodded. Then Irina explained about the meeting but in particular about the two Russians she had overheard.

"They were clearly saying that Vassily Turgenev was meeting with Tima right now and then that they were due to see Miller McDonald at 2 pm."

"Tima - that's Timur Maximovich - the head of Gasneft and a leader of the Roslavl Brotherhood," said Christina, "Antanov told me about him when we spoke by phone the other day."

"So why would Turgenev, Maximovich and McDonald be meeting together?" asked Jake.

"Think about it," said Christina, "We've got Vassily Turgenev - who is Tima Maximovich's enforcer and the two of them are meeting with Miller McDonald. It can only be for some kind of strong arm tactic."

"Yes, and I've heard from Amanda Miller now," said Jake, "She says that there's some kind of alert out for Chuck. It is to do with blowing up a research institute, in Celarus. But all fake. Amanda has various items that prove it. She was hoping that someone could bring it into circulation. It would be a world scoop." He looked pointedly towards Irina.

Irina looked interested, "Okay, she said, I'm on the hook, let me see the material,"

"Sure thing," said Jake, "Amanda is getting it cleaned so that we can have it. I can let you have it by tomorrow."

"So, we can see it laid out," said Christina, "Raven must want some disruption in Celarus - it's good for Brant business. Who are you gonna call? The local hoodlums. That's the Roslavl clan, which is run by Tima

Maximovich. So perhaps the meeting today between McDonald and Maximovich was to receive payment?"

"It's clever really, create disruption in Celarus, which only reinforces the US presence - and indirectly the Brant presence. In return get Chuck Manners framed for the disruption," said Jake.

223

Chariot

Self Control
Discipline
Inner Strength

Plain Sight

Chuck had hidden in plain sight while the search for him continued. He'd left Christina in Brussels and taken trains across Belgium and then Germany until he could reach a US Army base in Southern Germany.

He knew he could lie low for a while and would be in little danger of being captured by anyone.

He'd selected Panzer Kaserne and the nearby Patch Barracks, mainly because he was on good terms with the Patch Commander. The Barracks were constructed in 1938 for the German Army and the two bases were linked by a tank trail. The Americans took it over in 1945 and had developed the base ever since. Throughout the Cold War, it represented a forward position, close enough to the East Germany and consequently the Russian border.

Just as importantly for Chuck, Panzer Kaserne was directly served by the regular Stuttgart Bus service and two nearby light rail stops in nearby Böblingen. It meant it was straightforward to enter and exit.

Since the formal end of the Cold War, the US Army ran U.S. European Command (EUCOM) at Patch Barracks and United States Africa Command (AFRICOM) at adjacent Kelley Barracks located in Stuttgart. With the long history of American occupation, a whole subsystem of Americana had built up around the base, including schools and a vast US Military Exchange shopping mall, which traded in dollars.

In it, the Panzer Food court was a home-from-home for American soldiers with a Popeye's Chicken, Starbucks, Burger King, Pizza Hut, Charlie's Subs and a Bun-D. There was also a huge Auto Center and Auto rental adjacent to the mall.

Chuck knew that because of its geographic location, Germany was of particular strategic importance for the American Armed Forces.

Despite this, the number of U.S. troops in Germany had been falling and several bases closed. One reason for this was the shift in the United States' security policy, which increasingly focused on the Asia-Pacific region. The egotistical US President had cut European operations because of NATO spending grievances. Russia could hardly believe its luck.

By having his military identity card, Chuck was able to re-equip himself with a complete uniform. Consequently, he was able to wander easily around the base. The same identity card gave him access to accommodation and other facilities.

Chuck was prepared for the worst. He knew it would only be a matter of time before the people who had been chasing him in Brussels re-appeared. He'd also seen the television reports, which implied he had taken a role in the destruction of a research lab. He knew what they were doing. By framing him they were just ensuring that more people could legitimately come after him. It was only a matter of time before the US military would awaken.

A Black Hawk and an Apache

Christina was back at her apartment. The phone rang.

"Hello is that Katarina?" asked a voice.

"Hello Blackbird," she replied, "Why do you call me by old aliases? What's wrong with my code name?"

"I have intelligence for you," answered Blackbird. "I know you have been talking to Antanov. He's told me about the Roslavl Bratva thing, in Celarus. We directly threatened Maximovich as a result. He's been getting too big for his boots and it has even come onto Putin's radar. We had to ask him to call off Vassily Turgenev from the direct hunting of you. I think he was relieved to have an excuse actually, you seemed to be terminating too many of his little gang.

"However, we heard that Turgenev has decided to still go after Colonel Manners as retribution for his brother who was killed in Manner's hotel room in Brussels a few days ago.

"Turgenev has discovered that Manners is on a US base in Germany. We've been told he wanted to send a helicopter with several of his men on it to hunt down Manners. The pretext is that Manners is wanted as a terrorist for destroying an Institute in Celarus."

Do you know when this will happen?" asked Christina.

"Not exactly, but they have only just got the military helicopter. To fly it into the base it needs to be American or European. I have the registration and can send it to you."

"Did you provide the chopper?" asked Christina, "Was it some kind of deal?"

"Yes - we said we'd provide it in exchange for Turgenev calling off the chase for you,"

"Nice to know I'm worth a helicopter!" smiled Christina.

"Well its a $6 million to $10 million helicopter, after all."

"And it took us a long time to provision it. We were looking for two helicopters in case you needed one. I found you a pilot too - your good friend Antanov Chekeryn. And you know something, Vassily Turgenev is getting a high mileage empty US Army painted Sikorsky UH-60A Black Hawk and you get a fully armed AH-64E Apache Guardian."

"We have certain air superiority with that E series," said Christina, " I won't ask how you managed to get hold of a latest model American Attack helicopter."

"Let's say that Chuck Manners has some interesting

friends," answered Blackbird, " You can pick up the Apache from Brussels. Not from the airport though, from a separate heliport to the south-west of Brussels. Antanov will know it. We've asked him to fly other missions from there in the past."

"What markings will be flying under?" asked Christina

"USAG - United States Army Garrison - which is useful because its a NATO base."

"I remember," said Christina, 'It's SHAPE, isn't it? Supreme Headquarters Allied Powers Europe."

"That's right, it sounds grand but its only got a couple of thousand personnel on the base there. Think of it as US positioning in Benelux."

"Ha yes. The Americans and their abbreviations Belgium, Netherlands and Luxembourg - all grouped together!" said Christina.

"Well, you'll be an unmistakable profile in the air with that attack helicopter, but as importantly, we've given you the IFF of the other helicopter which will be travelling in from Roslavl."

"So we'll be able to see the other helicopter on its whole route?" asked Christina.

"Yes," said Blackbird, "Although they won't see you - actually with the 64E with all the latest Block III functions they won't be able to see you at all."

"Vassily was most insistent to get the 'copter into Celarus airspace - He wanted the bragging rights. He'll be loading it with some of his hardened soldiers with the intention to kidnap or kill Chuck Manners on the base in Germany. The helicopter won't raise suspicions and the men are going to be in stealth combat gear."

"So, they will be all in black?" asked Christina, "How many?"

"Well, the Sikorsky can carry 11 troops, so I'd expect there to be a full squad," said Blackbird.

"I'd reckon more like eight people, so they are not all tripping over one another. They will also be flying a long way before the mission and those Black Hawks are not as manoeuvrable as an Apache."

"Yes - although don't be deceived by the bulk of the Black Hawk, it is surprisingly fast - about the same speed as an Apache," added Blackbird.

"And a much bigger target," said Christina, "But I'm confused, why all of this help? Is Manners a Russian asset or something?"

"No, but you've managed to stumble onto a huge piece of gangster corruption from Russia. Putin's people at the top are quite keen to stop whatever the Roslavl Bratva are doing. Tima Maximovich may run Gasneft, but he is getting too big for his boots. And he has had Vassily Turgenev as his ruthless enforcer - one who would stop at nothing. If directed by Maximovich he would go after the top positions. I understand the Kremlin is keen to see the whole enterprise end. It is like what Putin is doing with Gavy Yegorin - stripping him of all his companies and his cash. Redistributing it all to his new buddies. "

"So where will we do this?" asked Christina, "If we start

a firefight around the base all hell will break loose."

"I agree," said Blackbird, "we've been scouting the approaches to Panzer Kaserne and think we've found a couple of suitable points before the Black Hawk gets there."

"Their route will be through Poland, but they are likely to go north of Czechia, across Dresden and Nuremberg and south west. It means they will fly over dense woodland before they reach their destination. They can be routed to the north of Schwäbish Hall and then south west for the last part of the journey.

"The forests around that area are ideal for an ambush. Eichelberg's woodland would make an ideal spot."

"I'll run this past Antanov," said Christina, "Also to check whether he's confident enough for an Apache."

"He's flown Apaches before, and we've already discussed it with him. He agrees already with the plan. He says he just needs a good wingman to control the firepower."

"That'd be me then, " smile Christina. I remember they have a chain gun, but also carry Hellfire and Stingers? I assume we'll have the twin missile packs?"

"You will, Archangel, be armed to the teeth."

Ed Adams

Strength

Courage
Conviction
Compassion

Designed for comfort

Christina had not expected to be in Brussels for so long. She had extended her hotel time and waited to hear from Antanov.

He called her on her phone, "You'll owe me after this one, It's tonight." he said, "I'd promised myself I wouldn't get involved in any more of the difficult stuff after I settled into being a regular mole at the EU."

"Have you told Camille?" asked Christina.

"What do you think?" asked Antanov, "Look, they've provided us with some combat gear at the helicopter. We will have to get changed into it. I don't expect us to be ground troops, but you never know."

"God, I hope they don't use Euro sizing," said Christina, "they are all about 2cm smaller than you think."

"No these are NATO F2 - suitable for Americans- designed for comfort. They come with belts and elastic," said Antanov.

"Okay - but more importantly, will our mission also extract Chuck Manners?" asked Christina.

"I've been given clearance to land in the Barracks, but we'd need to find a way to get Chuck to the LZ." Said Antanov.

"What time?" asked Christina.

"It's overnight, we take off from the airstrip here at 22:00. Contact is at 23:30 and we will be able to land at the barracks at 00:00 midnight. We'll be back here before 02:00 dark."

"How about Chuck? He doesn't know yet, does he?" asked Christina.

"No, we've left it to the last moment to inform him. Less chance of information leak."

"Okay, I'll call Jake, he can relay the message via someone else," said Christina, thinking of Amanda, but not wishing to name her.

She picked up her cell phone and dialled Jake. Bigsy answered, "Yes he's just popped outside for a moment – he must have forgotten his phone."

Christina explained the situation. Okay, "I'll go to find him so that he can tell Amanda. What time do you have there? You're one hour ahead aren't you?"

Christina agreed.

"I'll text ACK or NAK to let you know when it's all done," said Bigsy.

Christina smiled, trust Bigsy to overcomplicate YES and NO.

Stinger

They were at the heliport. There was a row of helicopters lined up. The Apache towered over the two domestic choppers. It was already dark although the apron was well-lit as they walked towards the helicopter.

They had allowed an extra three hours to prepare. Antanov wanted to check the chopper, Christina to familiarise herself with the armaments. They would also be told when the Black Hawk left Roslavl so that they would have a confirmed mission.

The IFF system in the Apache was already on and Antanov had selected the code of Turgenev's helicopter. The radar was colourfully alive with blips and Christina could see Antanov studying it.

"Yep, they left on time, they are on their way and logged a flightpath to the north of Czechia, as predicted. They are making good time, they must be flying at top speed," announced Antanov.

"What time do we take off for an intercept?" asked Christina,

"Like I calculated at 22:00," replied Antanov, We want to be behind and above the Black Hawk. It should not see us because we'll be using this E-model's stealth mode."

The minutes ticked around. Christina remembered other missions where she had been expected to wait around, but they were usually when she was already in position, rather than having to fly to a position.

"Okay," said Antanov, "we're going,"

He fired the twin engines of the Apache and as they came up to speed Christina felt the adrenaline kick in.

"Lifting now," said Antanov and Christina watched the reverse ground rush as they cleared some trees and she suddenly saw the orange lights of distant Brussels.

In a moment they were on their way and Christina listened to the rhythmic chop-chop of the rotors carving through the air.

"Contact time will be about 80 minutes," said Antanov, looking across to Christina.

Christina looked again at the Stinger launch controls. They should be able to launch a pack of Stingers towards the target. She did not expect to use the chain gun, and the Hellfire was only for any unexpected ground developments.

"They are through Poland," announced Antanov, "Contact in 20 minutes. That's the advantage of flying a NATO copter, they can breeze across half of Europe in a way I'd never be able to, even in a MiG-21."

"I'm going to start a climb here, said Antanov, They are at 8,000 feet. I want to be at least 1,000 feet higher."

"Helicopters don't like really high altitudes, do they?" asked Christina.

"That's right, the pilot of the Black Hawk is flying at probably the high end of the safe hover zone for such a heavy machine. We can go higher but only hover to around 10,000 feet. Then the air isn't dense enough. But don't worry, I think I can take this up to 25,000 feet as long as we are moving forward."

"Anyway, I suspect he will start a slow descent from about where we are going to intercept him. There he is on my short range radar now. We are on a merged plot. You can look at target acquisition. Fangs Out."

"That's easy on this thing. We have got ATR - automatic target recognition against an MSTAR database. It's already recognised the Black Hawk. It says we are still too far away for a lock, but you seem to be closing fast. I'm arming the AIM-92s."

"Will you fire one or two?" asked Antanov.

"I'll fire the double pack," said Christina, "Mach 2 towards the target . If it tries countermeasures, it will only have seconds to deploy. I still suggest you flip once we've fired."

"You worry about the targeting, I'll worry about the piloting," said Antanov.

"Okay, Missiles selected- Two Stingers, Payload primed, Target Acquired, Padlocked, Ready to fire, count of three, one, two, three, Fox Two, missiles fired, on track, seeking target, target hit. Target immobilised, target destroyed."

"Sierra Hotel, Roger that, moving into Mission Phase Two," said Antanov.

They saw a bright yellow fireball tumbling through the air towards the ground.

"Mission Phase One accomplished," said Christina. The assassins sent to find Chuck Manners had been destroyed. It had been the combined work of NATO, the US and the FSB, something that would not make it into any mission report.

"ETA to LZ is around 12 minutes, said Antanov. "I want to do a spot landing and be out of there."

"Okay, let's hope Chuck is ready for this."

Antanov proceeded to the floodlit H denoting the helicopter landing spot inside the barracks. The late model Apache would be certain to attract stares, and Christina noticed someone taking a cameraphone movie of the landing.

Then, she realised it was the same person running across the 100 metres towards the 'copter and clambered in through the side door.

"Hi Guys, Thank you for the ride," said Chuck, not sounding out of breath despite his exertion.

"Chuck!" said Christina handing him a set of green headphones, "Welcome on board."

"Where are we going?" he asked as he clipped on the headset.

"I've a flight plan logged to Berlin," said Antanov.

"What Tegel?" asked Chuck.

"No - Brandenburg, actually," replied Antanov, "You can disperse with the crowds there, or even take a train. Those people looking for you are gone. Thank Christina for that."

Chuck looked at Christina, "Thank you. That's twice you helped me. I don't know what to say."

"Just store it to pay forward," answered Christina, smiling, "They had sent a whole gunship of people after you this time. I think the FSB are about to send them a *prekratit' i otkazat'sya ot poryadka* - that's a 'cease and desist' order,"

"They are very ceased," added Antanov, "Courtesy of two Stingers."

Christina looked at Chuck in uniform. Here he was an American Colonel, with a silver eagle on his uniform, rescued in a NATO helicopter by an FSB officer.

Antanov revved the engines on the Apache. It was soon back at 2000 feet climbing over the countryside of Baden-Württemberg.

Disproving fake news

Irina played her part. The article was now out there about the staging of the explosions at the Institute. The Manhattanite decided to run the story on its website ahead of the publication of the weekly magazine.

They linked it to stories of fake news, of Russian manipulation and of the hold that the Russian Mafia had over world events. Irina was given a by-line, although so were two better known journalists for the magazine.

Christina recognised that much of the material came from Amanda Miller, although the sources had been anonymised or relocated.

Amanda looked at the copy now spread across several other newspapers, including the Guardian and the Financial Times.

The Guardian created an entire series of graphics to explain what had happened, which looked decidedly well-informed.

The question being posed was who was at the root of the manipulations? Someone on a conspiracy site had also linked the Black Hawk helicopter crash in Germany to the story, although most reports were of a military training mission into dense forest which had gone awry.

A plane spotter expert had produced an analysis of the crashes of Black Hawks, which indicated that an original run of 16 crashes caused the aircraft to be grounded, a further two had exploded or crashed into mountainside, with on one of the most similar crashes by an ROCAF (Republic of China Air Force) helicopter and another at Eglin Air Force Base in Florida. In both cases there were no survivors.

Amanda flicked over the helicopter diagrams but then noticed another small boxout in the Guardian account. It talked about the origin of the original plot. It mentioned that it could have been state-sponsored by Russia and hinted that a well-known Russian in exile in France could have been the source.

Amanda was intrigued by this line. Was someone referring to Tima Yegorin? The story passed the duck test. It walked like a duck, swam like a duck, quacked like a duck. Yes, it was a duck. A story or hint placed there by the Russians.

She decided to follow up via Jake, who facilitated the original story placement. He had been careful to protect his sources and it was better that no-one inside SI6 knew, in any case.

243

Two of Cups

(Reversed)
Imbalance
Broken Communication
Tension

Kremlin anger

Christina was in the office. Someone was calling her phone. She could see it was Fyodor Kuznetsov, her handler.

"Hi Blackbird," she said, cheerily.

"Hello Archangel," he replied.

"What's happening now?" asked Christina.

"The collateral damage from that helicopter escapade," admitted Blackbird.

"The Kremlin is furious with Yegorin for letting Vassily Turgenev mount that mission. They would not have cared if it had all gone right, but instead there's so much trouble.

"First, the discovery of the fake reports, which had been sloppily put together, Russia got the blame for that.

"Then, the hunt for Chuck Manners in the Brussels hotel. The two agents have been identified as part of a Russian team. More blame for Russia, this time running around with guns in the EU Capital of Brussels.

"Then the gunshots in London. A Russian agent has washed up in Tilbury, but it points back to the recent gun shots around Tower Bridge.

"And finally, a 'stolen' helicopter in US Army colours is flown across the Polish border and then into Germany, where it is shot down by a Sidewinder. The crew were all identified as Russian.

"These point to Vassily Turgenev working for Yegorin. The Kremlin are not taking a happy view. It is messing up their stealth influence strategies."

"Stinger, not Sidewinder," said Christina, "It was two Stingers that brought the Black Hawk down."

"It doesn't matter," said Blackbird, "Yegorin is likely to lash out now, to salvage his tattered reputation with the Kremlin."

"Or do something covert," said Christina, "To try to strike a bargain? - So what do you want from me?"

"I think you have done enough. The original aim was to disrupt Yegorin and to interfere with the Celarus plans. I think you have done both, admittedly with more sparks flying than ideal. Right now, I need to stop you from further activities. Now, nothing is pointing towards you, we need to keep it that way."

Christina put her phone down.

Almost at once Jake's phone rang.

"Huh, we are popular today!" said Jake, reaching across.

"Jake? It's Amanda, thank you for getting that story out, it will have helped to clear Chuck and thankfully SI6 are no-where to be seen."

"My pleasure," said Jake, "Although there seems to be even more discoveries in the versions published."

"Yes," said Amanda, "That's what I wanted to ask you about. Do you know who added the embellishments in the Guardian story. The part about a Paris-based instigator?"

Jake replied, "No, I wondered that myself. I know Christina has useful links in Paris, but she would have told me if she was planning to do something like that - she was as mystified as we are."

"Okay, well if anything around that story surfaces, can you let me know? Please." Asked Amanda.

"Sure thing," said Jake, "I guess you are relieved that the complete rescue mission played out so well?"

"Yes, even if Chuck has gone to ground again. I hear he was last spotted in Berlin?"

"Yes, that's what Christina said. She said Chuck would lie low until after the dust had settled. I guess clearing his name is one step along that path, but I don't know whether someone will feel vindictive as a result?"

"Yes, he's wise to stay out of sight for the moment. Thanks for your help."

Amanda hung up the phone.

She turned to Grace. "They don't know. I'm sure they don't know about Yegorin. That Yegorin is in Paris under pressure from the Kremlin."

"Well, we must see if we can put Yegorin under some additional pressure," smiled Grace.

Price of peace

At his home in France, Yegorin had been threatened by associates sent by Mezhkommbank's liquidator - they were threatening his family if he did not pay a $350 million 'price of peace', they told him, the price for making the Russian criminal case against him for the Mezhkomm bankruptcy go away. He knew it was around 1/3 of his liquid assets and that they would have calculated the same.

In the UK courts, Yegorin had been incapable of operating because of the unfamiliar rules and procedures.

Yegorin was accustomed to backroom deals like in his Kremlin past, too accustomed to slipping through the rules and regulations because of his position and power.

Yegorin decided to contact Maximovich to discuss options. In particular, he would like to borrow Vassily Turgenev for a while, to assist him with drawing a strong line under previous events.

Convinced of the righteousness of his position, that he

was the victim of the latest Kremlin asset grab, he believed himself above the regulations of the British courts.

He'd failed to stick to court orders related to an asset freeze and had burned through millions of pounds from an account he'd kept hidden from the UK court. He took a view that he could afford to pay Vassily Turgenev from the same source and that Turgenev's methods might be quicker and more effective than that of the lawyers.

He believed disclosure rules were beneath him; petty compared to the woeful calamity that had befallen his business empire, and only part of a Kremlin campaign to hound and frustrate him at every turn.

Maximovich recognised the handwringing by Yegorin but realised that the Kremlin's spotlight on him could also just as easily turn into a searchlight.

He decided to lend Yegorin his enforcer Vassily Turgenev and make other temporary arrangements. He asked around and was soon introduced to Anatoly Yaroslav, a Ukrainian with access to a fierce firepower.

The Kremlin had become adept at pursuing its enemies through the UK court system, while a PR machine was honed to fill the pages of the UK tabloids with allegations of the Russian oligarch's stolen wealth, even despite his wife's two media interests. Notably, a couple of influential newspapers (The ironically titled Independent and London's Evening Standard) were already in Russian hands, those of the disarming Evgeny Lebedev, son of the billionaire businessman and former KGB agent Alexander Lebedev.

The Kremlin had learned to navigate its way through the UK court system during its victory against Boris Berezovsky, the exiled oligarch who'd become a fierce critic of Putin.

Berezovsky was the fast-talking one-time Kremlin insider who had tried – and failed – to sue his erstwhile business partner Roman Abramovich, a close Kremlin ally, for $6.5 billion in London's High Court.

The judge overseeing the case took a dim view of Berezovsky's claim that he'd jointly owned one of Russia's biggest oil majors, Sibneft, and a stake in Rusal, Russia's biggest aluminium giant, with Abramovich, and that Abramovich had forced him to sell his stakes at a knockdown price.

The current Yegorin situation was like history repeating itself.

Though Berezovsky was recognised throughout Russia as owner of these concerns, the judge said she found him to be 'an inherently unreliable witness' and sided with Abramovich, who'd claimed that Berezovsky had never owned these assets; he'd merely been paid for providing political patronage. It later appeared that a stepson of the judge had been paid around £500,000 to represent Abramovich in the early stages of the case.

Now Yegorin was facing similar treatment although no stolen or hidden assets were found. No fraud claims had been launched in the UK, or anywhere else outside Russia.

Instead, on the basis of a Russian court ruling alone, the legal team had won a freezing order against Yegorin assets and ran rings around him while he sank under a multitude of court orders.

He'd been interrogated over asset disclosures and was found to have given false evidence over whether the sale of his coal business had been conducted by himself or by his son.

It did not seem to matter to the judge that the hard-luck story was that the sale had been forced through at a price that was less than one twentieth of the business's real value. What mattered was whether he had followed procedure and declared all the assets that remained under his control.

Marion

Christina had just seen Hekla back to the airport. Hekla was bubbling with enthusiasm for her brief time in London.

"I'm going to visit again, Aggi…you are still packing so much in - and this is even more exciting than discovering what was in the *Ullarverslun* back on the farm."

"Well that wool store didn't contain wool, anyway!" said Christina, and they both laughed.

"Safe journey!" said Christina.

"Stay safe and avoid mischief!" replied Hekla.

"As if!" answered Christina. They hugged and then Hekla was walking into the Border Control area.

Christina's phone rang, and she answered it, "Hello?"

"Hi Christina? You may not remember me, my name is Marion Charlotte."

"Of course I do, and how are you?" replied Christina.

"I've something I'd like to talk over with you. It relates to the business with Sir Charles Frobisher and Gerhardt Schmidt. Can I see you?" asked Marion.

Christina thought, "Yes, why don't you come to our office. But I don't want any funny business though. I need you to play it straight."

"I will, I will, Circumstances have changed," answered Marion, "You have my word. Look, I would also like to bring Nina Valentine along. You met her at the Ladies' Night."

"Sure, I remember, she was a friend of Jennifer's," answered Christina, remembering the name of the fixer who supplied the women to the Masonic event.

"Okay, let us make it tomorrow. I'll text you a time and location," answered Christina.

Queen of Wands

Courage
Determination
Passion
Joy

Ladies of the Night

Christina had texted Marion with the address of the Cafe Rouge, close to the Triangle office. It had outside tables and served breakfast. She could meet Marion and Nina and could also bring along some reinforcements of her own.

She asked Jake, and he suggested that both he and Bigsy come along. "Bigsy will check for - you know - devices," said Jake.

"I don't want Bigsy patting down two women in the middle of Cafe Rouge," said Christina.

"Oh no, he's bound to have a gadget."

"I hope so," said Christina.

All three of them were sitting drinking coffees when Marion and Nina arrived.

Christina saw Bigsy's mouth drop. He was already in their spell. They all said their hellos.

"Bigsy, behave," whispered Christina, and saw him nod.

"Hello Marion," said Christina; she still remembered when Marion had worked for both SI6 and a Russian clan.

"Thank you for seeing me," she replied, "Nina and I have some news for you. First, let me tell you something. After that dinner with Driscoll, I realised you were some kind of agent, but I guarantee that I didn't pass Driscoll's part in the dinner back to anyone. I know he was killed, but as far as I am aware, it was nothing to do with me."

Christina looked at her, "You swear?" she asked, "Because we had you down as the most likely suspect."

"No, I swear," she said, "And it is the same for Nina. She was a best friend of Gerhardt and narrowly missed being blown up on that yacht."

"Yes, Gerhardt had asked me to stay on the yacht," answered Nina, "I declined and walked back to the dock but about half an hour later the yacht exploded in a fireball at sea. There is no way that it was faulty wiring. Someone must have planted a bomb on board."

"Then we heard about Sir Charles. We both knew him," said Marion,"He was a feature at those big events."

Nina continued, "I arrived in his party on the yacht which Gerhardt had hired. He was his usual buoyant self, but then suddenly decided he needed to go back to London. He walked off the yacht and was going to catch a helicopter back to Nice, and from there fly to London."

Marion nodded, and Nina continued, "We checked, and

it looks as if he got onto a Vassily one-way special at the heliport. Vassily Turgenev is a ruthless mobster. He works for Tima Maximovich and is his enforcer. There's a couple of other well-known businessmen at the bottom of the Ligurian sea, courtesy of Turgenev."

"Did you have anything to do with those cases?" asked Christina.

Nina and Marion both shook their heads.

"You know how it is, we girls that work for Jennifer all talk to one another."

"*A ty russkiy tozhe ponimayesh*'?" asked Christina.

"Yes, I understand Russian, I'm originally from Odintsovo," answered Marion, in English.

"Yes, and I'm from Central Moscow, but I worked in Strogino District, " answered Nina.

"Odintsovo, Strogino - you are both really from Moscow then?" asked Christina.

"Yes, but like many of us, Jennifer Sussex offered us a path to the west and to more money. I knew Marion from when we both struggled to find a living around Strogino and she told me about Jennifer."

"Jennifer's agency - Miel Doux Artists - was only looking for the most attractive women and ones that could already speak good English. We were both selected to come over to London, where we soon discovered a Russian home-from-home although it was significantly better paid."

Nina said, "That's right, the Russians all wanted a second home in London, and were wealthy beyond anything that Marion and I could imagine. Of course, it was stolen money, when the Russian state divided up its natural resources and gave a healthy slice to each of the new owners of the means of production. The men - and for that matter the women - we met were all so rich that they didn't care about anything."

Christina said, "I know Strogino. It's where the dives and pub-crawl bars are situated. It must have been a huge jump up for you to go to London?"

Jake interrupted, "So, we get that you delightful ladies have 'a past', but what is it you want to talk about today? It can't be Moscow reminiscences?"

Marion continued. "Yes, now that we are in London, we are also approached by Jennifer to help out on the bigger and most prestigious events. Those are often hosted by Russians or people who are somehow connected but are often include British establishment people. You know, Members of Parliament, legal operatives, police officers, sometimes athletes, sometimes people from the media, occasional people from music."

Nina added, "Yes, the athletes and music people are usually referred to as 'The Talent' and are there to help bring in the people that are really of interest. The media are there, I think, as an insurance policy."

"Okay," said Bigsy, "So these are big events, in London and have a mix of the good and the great?"

"And the Talent and the Honey," said Nina.

"The Honey?" asked Bigsy.

"That's the ladies," whispered Christina, "Pay attention, Bigsy"

"Oh," said Bigsy, his face reddening.

"We've been asked to come along to a new event," said Marion.

"One where we think we can settle some scores," added Nina, "My friend Natalie was murdered on that yacht."

"We both know people who have been killed under the orders of Turgenev," said Marion.

"Now there's to be a Maximovich fundraiser run for Gavy Yegorin, in London, and Turgenev is being asked to run the security for it."

"I don't think I've heard of Yegorin," said Bigsy.

Christina and Jake both looked at him.

Christina started, "Khramov Gavril (Gavy) Yegorin is a main player. I say is. Was, more likely. He is out of favour with the Kremlin now. I think he is actually under lockdown here in London."

"Lockdown! Ha - you should see it!" said Nina, "He's got a huge house and a ready supply of girls. It's like one continuous party there."

Marion continued, "Yegorin had been forced to hand over his passports to the court and was banned from leaving the UK during a prolonged period of questioning over his asset disclosures as the Kremlin's lawyers tightened the legal net. They wanted to squeeze all the money and assets from him, in something speculated to have been sanctioned by Putin."

Nina interrupted, "And the London lawyers were all bandits too, padding their bills with non-existent work. Russian cases from Moscow's tycoons were easy pickings. Add on the PR firms offering to defend Yegorin's image for £100,000 a month.

Marion looked earnest, "The well-dressed Brits can be cynical about their money grabbing, but it is living off the wealth of gangsters and works its way right through the upper Establishment."

Christina nodded, "Yes, I have seen it a lot."

Marion continued, "Yegorin believes he is in the right about all the stolen assets that - as he sees it - unruly Kremlin underlings are trying to expropriate. Then the car bombs appeared although Nina and I think it was Turgenev or one of his buddies that planted them in the first place. It's ironic that Yegorin is now getting Turgenev to run his security."

Nina said, "We think that the Kremlin see Yegorin as a whistle blower. That is why they are trying to bring him down. Yegorin had long detected the growing influence of Kremlin cash in London. Long before the legal attack started, he said, he'd met a string of English lords who'd guffawed and shaken his hand and told him how great they thought Putin was."

Marion added, "That's a problem, because if Yegorin blows the whistle on some of these people, then Putin's carefully created little empire of influence starts to collapse. And not only here, the same links extend into Washington D.C. as well - close acquaintances of the President - you know what I'm talking about."

Bigsy was busy with his phone.

"Yes," he said, "I've just found this extract…It says 'Yegorin donated to the Conservative Party. All his former friends from the Kremlin kept relatives and mistresses in town, who they visited at weekends, flooding the city with cash' ."

He scrolled down on his phone, " As an example, there's this Transparency International report about his buddy Igor Shuvalov, who owns two apartments in Whitehall Court. It's a penthouse overlooking Trafalgar Square worth £11.4 million. The Washington Times has covered the controversy surrounding Shuvalov's alleged ownership of an enormous $9.4 million apartment in Moscow.

"Igor Shuvalov is married to Olga Viktorovna Shuvalova. The income of Shuvalov's spouse over two years amounted to more than 1 billion roubles: she earned 642 million roubles in 2009 and 365 million in 2008. She is a major business figure engaged in the sale of real estate in the Skolkovo Innovation Center offshore business, and trading in shares of Russian raw materials companies."

Christina added, "1 billion roubles is about 14 million USD, I think."

"Well, it's still a lot, even if it sounds more in Russian," said Jake.

Bigsy was concentrating, "Then there's Arkady

Rotenberg, the Russian businessman and tycoon. With his brother Boris Rotenberg, he is co-owner of the Stroygazmontazh (SGM) group, the largest construction company for gas pipelines and electrical power supply lines in Russia.

Christina interrupted, "It is a comparable situation to Yegorin, except he's done what he was told."

Bigsy continued, "Rotenberg was listed by Forbes in 621st place among the world's wealthiest persons. He is a close confidant of president Vladimir Putin.

"For about ten years, he was formerly married to his second wife Natalia Rotenberg, who is about 30 years his junior and their two children Varvara and Arkady live in the United Kingdom with Nataliya."

"I remember Nataliya," said Nina brightly, "Stunning blonde socialite and quite intelligent. Around Arkady, she looked like his daughter. "

Bigsy continued, "It says they divorced in the U.K. While the financial details of the divorce are private, the agreement includes division of the use of a £35 million Surrey mansion and a £8 million apartment in London. The couple's lawyers obtained a secrecy order preventing media in the U.K. from reporting on the divorce, but the order was overturned on appeal."

Bigsy added, "Rotenberg spread the wealth around though. Igor, his son is a Russian billionaire businessman and Liliya, a doctor living in Germany but she is also the co-owner of the TPS Nedvizhimost which is an investment group that owns shopping malls and entertainment complexes in major Russian cities including Moscow, Sochi, Krasnodar, Novosibirsk and

Ocean Plaza in Kiev, Ukraine.

Bigsy looked at his phone, "The list goes on and on, but as one last example, there's the deputy speaker of the State Duma, one of Russia's most vocal patriots, Sergei Zheleznyak, who has raged against the influence of the West, yet his daughter Anastasia has lived in London for years."

Marion added, "As Yegorin famously said, "They have sorted themselves out very well on this small island with terrible weather. In the UK, the main thing was always money. Putin sent his agents to corrupt the British elite.'"

Nina nodded, "The city had grown used to the flood of Russian cash. Property prices surged and then a series of privileged share orderings to PR and legal firms."

Marion added, "And now we are about to see Yegorin go fund-raising."

Fund raiser

"So, what is the purpose of the fundraising?" asked Jake.

"Leverage," explained Marion, "Yegorin has asked Maximovich to front a fund raiser. If they raise the money, then Yegorin could rise into the ascendency again."

"They will bring along a host of well-known names, most of whom wouldn't notice dropping a few million into the gift box for Maximovich."

"Yegorin can't do this in his own name because it is considered tainted, and anyone appearing friendly with him could also get unwanted Kremlin attention."

"So, what is the point of the money?" asked Bigsy, "It can't surely be simply to bail out Yegorin?"

"No, it will be about setting up a new investment vehicle, co-owned by Yegorin and Maximovich. The purpose of the investment will be to build the new pipeline in Celarus. Basically, to take control of the oil supply into Europe.

Marion said, "Right now, one of the ways that Putin acolytes get paid is by skimming the natural resource revenues that flow across Russia and beyond. It works out to around a 17% tax by all the oligarchs on anything that can be considered a raw resource. It funds plenty of amazing lifestyles. It is why many Russians diversify into property, football clubs and artworks. It makes their wealth relatively illiquid and launders it."

Christina said, "I know this from running security detail: A typical oligarch may have a small stack of apartments in London as well as a couple of show-off places. The 'stack' amounts to 'money at rest' but of course it is also increasing in value in line with the London property market. The Chinese are starting to do the same thing now."

Nina added, "So Yegorin could throw a big spanner in the works by building a pipeline that links the Celarus oil-fields to Europe. And by doing so, also push the US Agenda in Celarus."

Marion added, "Yes, it would massively annoy the Kremlin and could even spark some civil unrest, like the Russian blockade of Ukraine. The Ukraine move was an obvious one by Russia and led to power shortages and a ransom being conducted for extractive companies. In effect the companies were to be turned over to the state and could then be chopped up among the oligarchs. It's a series of well-rehearsed rip-offs and ones that Yegorin has played before when he was in favour. This time it is possible to see the same moves being used in Celarus against Russia.

"But won't Russia intervene?" asked Christina, "Throw

some force around?"

Marion replied, "Yes - Russia could even bomb the partly built pipeline; it wouldn't matter to Yegorin by that time. All it would do would be to intensify the US interest in the region. There would be US and NATO forces crawling all over Celarus before you knew it. Look, the Americans have already established forward positions in Celarus and have Brant building the bases and infrastructure."

"What role do we have in any of this?" asked Christina.

Marion looked at Nina, "Neither of us have any contacts; we don't have access to the state, to police, press or anything. You've already demonstrated that you have high links, like when you visited me, Christina, with your colleague Amanda who said she was from SI6. That's heavyweight influence."

Nina added, "What we do have is invitations and access to the event - we know what it is, where it is and will soon know who is going to be there. We're also completely trusted on the inside."

Marion added, "Yes, and that's something we want to maintain, or we'll end up like Sir Charles and Gerhardt."

Damaged goods

Back at the office, they briefed Clare.

"We'll have to tell Amanda Miller about this," said Clare, "She should be able to mobilise some other help."

"Yes, and to see if she wants to gain anything from the situation," said Christina, "There's a way, you know. "

They conference-called Amanda, to explain what had happened. She invited Jim Cavendish to listen to the call.

Amanda was intrigued to hear Yegorin's name.

Amanda said, "Yegorin is damaged goods. This is substantial risk. He is being punished for trying to exit the tight-knit system that ruled Russia, the mafia clan which no one was ever meant to leave."

"Some say he lost his mind and thought he could leave and work on his own business. The order was given to destroy him."

Jim Cavendish added, "When he left the UK to go to France, Yegorin left behind a number of tell-tale signs. Detectives working for the Kremlin's lawyers raided his Knightsbridge office on a court order issued in the days after his disappearance.

Amanda continued, "His own security must have been terrible. Among the documents, there were several disc drives. On one of the disc drives were recordings from every meeting he held in his downtown Moscow offices."

Jim continued, "One of the recordings shows Yegorin's feelings about Putin and his role in bringing him to power. Yegorin is sitting in his office with Valentin Vitalievich discussing over dinner the tense state of affairs as Moscow hurtled through yet another political crisis.

Amanda said, "In the Kremlin's warren, the former KGB and security men who had risen to power with Putin had been jostling for position, bickering, and backstabbing in hopes that they, or their candidate, would be selected as his successor.

Jim said, "Yes, on the tape we can hear Yegorin and Vitalievich clink glasses and discuss the standoff. The uncertain succession brought back memories of when they'd assisted Putin's rise."

Jake said, "So they'd climbed the greasy pole, but slipped back down?"

Jim continued, "Yes, it seemed to them an age ago. Now they were seen as relics by Putin's KGB allies from St Petersburg. The system of power had changed and struggled to understand what they'd done.

"So, they knew early on, that their days were numbered?" asked Jake.

"Not really; I think they expected to hold on to their gains, not have the ex-KGB come after them to try to grab everything back," answered Jim, "In those days, Putin had appeared reluctant to take the leading role, and seemed malleable and compliant to those who'd helped bring him to power."

Amanda added, "But then, Putin's first term had been drenched in blood and controversy. It led to a sweeping transformation of the way the country was run."

"The writing was on the wall?" asked Bigsy.

"Yes, the bloody writing was on the wall," replied Jim, "Putin faced a series of deadly terrorist attacks, including the siege of the Dubrovka Theatre in Moscow by Chechen terrorists in October 2002 which ended with more than a hundred dead when the Russian security services botched the storming of the theatre and gassed the very theatregoer hostages they'd been trying to free. Putin's battles with rebels from the restive northern Caucasus republic of Chechnya had caused thousands of deaths, including almost 300 who died in a string of apartment bombings."

Amanda said, "Many in Moscow whispered Putin's security services were behind these attacks, not least because the result was a security clampdown that strengthened his power. We considered it a time of mayhem."

Jim added, "Yes, it was a new guard. Putin and the ex-KGB men who ran the economy now monopolised power and introduced a new system in which state positions were used as vehicles for self-enrichment. It was vastly different from the anti-capitalist, anti-bourgeois principles of the Soviet state they had once served."

"No wonder Yegorin is angry," said Bigsy.

"Yes, but we must not forget that he stole wholeheartedly from the Russian people and used Putin to originally secure his power base," said Amanda, "He is a nasty piece of work."

"I'm not sure how we'd fit into this mission?" asked Amanda.

"Well," said Christina, "I think you could make a huge gain if you played it right. Let me explain."

Best cards

Christina began, "Right now, we hold all the best cards. We know about Yegorin. We know he is on the back foot. That his own security was terrible. We also know that he is trying to do a deal with Maximovich.

"Together they can invite an entire group of celebrity Russians to their party in London. There will be A-Listers there too, and 'Honey'.

"We must manipulate the way the event turns out. Maybe round up a few Russians, including Yegorin," continued Christina.

"We'd need some strongarms to do that," said Clare.

Christina continued, "We need to let Maximovich escape. The plans of Yegorin will have been foiled. He won't be able to fund the pipeline, nor will he be able to raise enough money to recover his stolen assets. He will be seen by the Kremlin to have been discredited in both the east and the west's eyes.

"Yes, we need some highly disciplined strongarms if this is to work," added Clare.

Christina added, "Maximovich can emerge as a local hero. He will have rescued Russia without the need for more bloodshed. The status quo will have been maintained. A dangerous opponent will have been quashed.

"Maximovich should get promotion from this. Firmly into Putin's inner circle instead of teetering on the edge of it. And that is where we want him. A highly placed mole."

Christina continued, "We need to trap Turgenev too. He has proved to be a highly effective and brutal security enforcer for Maximovich."

Amanda added, "This outcome would suit both sides. For the Russians, it gets rid of the troublesome and one-time ruthless Yegorin and keeps the current balance of power in Celarus. There will not have been the money raised to build the new pipeline which keeps the oligarchs happy.

"For the Americans it also keeps the balance of power in Celarus, including the US troops and planes stationed there. For Raven, it gives Brant more work to do."

Christina added, "But with powers of persuasion over Maximovich, we can place a mole inside the Kremlin."

"So how would we deploy for such an occasion?" asked Amanda.

Christina said, "I think we have to let Yegorin talk Maximovich into it. They will set a day and then start inviting guests. They will also inform Jennifer Sussex who will mobilise the Miel Doux Agency to provide escorts."

Bigsy said, "Now when they do that, we can have some fun… We'll create a little something for the Minerva Listening Station - just enough to get them interested in the event."

Jake asked, "What about you, Amanda? Will you be able to bring some support to the event?"

"I don't think it will do any harm for us to monitor Yegorin at his place in France," said Amanda, " But to be involved in the main event, I'll need reasonable grounds," answered Amanda, "If there was a plot, or some contraband there, for example."

"Let us worry about that," said Christina, "I should be able to get something for you guys to 'discover'. Ideally, it needs to be something linked to Turgenev. We all have some scores to settle there."

Page of Swords

(Reversed)

Deception
Manipulation
All Talk

Black tie

Bigsy had prepared everything for what was to be the acting debut of the Triangle offices. As well as Jake, Clare and Bigsy, there would be Christina, Marion and Nina present. They had all talked over what they would say when Bigsy magically restored the communications link to the Minerva Listening Station.

Across in Greenwich Peninsula, Pete Burr wasn't certain what he was getting. He was still expected to monitor the Triangle offices from Minerva, but there had been almost zero activity. It was as if the communications had been cut off. Occasionally there would be some footage of people arriving or leaving the offices.

He had also noticed the chit-chat of office banter, but nothing was of any consequence.

Then, one day he saw Bigsy return into the main meeting room.

"I found it," he said, "It was a fuse, well, a power supply actually. The programmable power supply for the second comms cabinet had gone down."

To Pete, this was an explanation. Suddenly he realised what had happened at the offices. Some kind of unit had ceased functioning and cut off the signal back to Minerva.

"Yes, said Bigsy, "I've rebooted the unit. It is supposed to have intelligent management, but the management controller is on the same circuit. If the unit goes down, it can't tell anyone."

Unseen to Pete, Bigsy had just winked to the others. They were ready to put on a show for Minerva.

"So, what do we know about this gala event?" asked Clare.

Jake started, "Well, it's going to be the talk of the town. A-listers abound. They have got a well-known TV presenter to host the show, which is targeted towards Russian magnates with plenty of money.

"It's so blingy, they have ordered extra gold-painted chairs and ornaments. The gathering's official purpose is to raise money for worthy causes, but, it is all about Yegorin's business opportunity, fronted by Maximovich.

"In other words, to get the investors to build the oil pipeline across Celarus and into Europe."

Clare added, "Yes, but there's an auction to win lunch with British politicians, Cabinet ministers and economic operators."

Jake said, "Rumour says it is a replacement for the Presidents Club, which was the appalling club which closed its doors after an expose in the Financial Times."

Bigsy wrote down of a small piece of paper, "I hope they are getting all of this."

Clare shrugged, "I suppose it makes the event all the more appealing, if some of those invited know that other well-known people have already accepted."

Christina added, "It is so non-PC, but in the culture of certain people, this is entirely acceptable. They dress it up as a black-tie evening. And include a couple of well-known TV hosts to do slots."

Bigsy said, "There will be around 300 figures from British business, politics and finance and the entertainment included as well as 120 specially hired hostesses."

Christina said, "The task of finding hostesses for the dinner is entrusted to Jennifer Sussex, founder of MDA - Miel Doux Agency, an agency specialising in hosts and hostesses for what it claims to be some of the 'UK's most prestigious occasions'.

Marion added, " Yes, a couple of days before the event, Ms Sussex will inform the prospective hostesses that their phones would be 'safely locked away' for the evening and that boyfriends and girlfriends were not welcome at the venue."

Nina continued, "The uniform requirements are also more detailed: all hostesses should bring "'black sexy shoes', black underwear, and do their hair and make-up as they would to go to a 'smart, sexy place'. Dresses and belts would be supplied on the day. For those who met the three specific selection criteria ('tall, thin and pretty') the job starts at 4 in the afternoon."

Marion added, "Yes, in the Vinery, where a team of hair and make-up artists will prep everyone for the evening ahead. It needs great self-control, because unlike most hostessing assignments — you can drink on the job."

There was a crackling sound." Oh dear, said Bigsy, "That control box seems to have gone on the blink again."

Bigsy did a double check and then signalled to everyone that Minerva would not be able to hear them any longer.

"You know what, though," he said, "There's a perfectly good pub on the river waiting for us to debrief this."

The Horniman

They all left the office and moved to the pub.

Bigsy looked relieved, "Phew, that was some test of my technology and all of our acting skills!" he said, "Cheers everybody!"

They clinked their glasses together. Jake noticed that they were attracting quite a few stares, with the joint power of Christina, Clare, Marion and Nina in their group.

"Do you ever get used to it?" he asked, "The stares, you know…"

"Beautiful women are like flowers," Marion interjects. "They turn to the sun. But if they don't receive a certain amount of attention, they wither."

Jake added, "That simile has an 18th-century feel; it's about manners, after all, which are always most complicated in times of equality."

"I concur," Nina says. "The most attractive women expect

an attentive gaze that doesn't imply anything other than someone saying, 'You're attractive enough to gaze at.' And the most rewarding thing is if that gaze is returned."

"What does a returned glance imply?" Bigsy asks.

"It implies," smiled Nina, "As they say in the New York State lottery: Hey - You never know."

Christina looked rueful, "Some women assume the male gaze is sinful, hurtful, and evil; that men can never look at women in a different way. But that's not what the gaze is about. Because a sophisticated man would not hesitate to gaze, and then he might be filled with regret and loss, and therefore gain self-knowledge."

Jake added, "Longing makes us sad, but at least it proves we're still alive. Which is why men like spring so much, for the short time it lasts."

"But did we do it?" asked Bigsy, changing the subject, "Did we make the story interesting enough for the listeners?"

"I can't imagine they wouldn't want to pass it on.," said Jake, "All that stuff about black shoes and sexy underwear - it's too salacious."

"Let's just hope they were recording and believed that bit about the fuse box or whatever it was that Bigsy was talking about," said Clare.

Pete Burr reacts

Pete Burr was listening. He was used to the daily ritual of finding a few files from the Triangle Office, seeing a few people come and go and the ritual of early morning office banter. Then, usually after they had all collected their first coffees from the kitchen, it would all go quiet.

This day was different. The one called Bigsy had found a technical hitch in a cupboard and was triumphantly saying he had fixed it.

That could explain why the recordings had been so weak from the offices.

Some kind of technical overload.

Today's meeting was coming through as clear as a bell. And there were a couple of extra people in the office too.

They seemed to be talking about a big event which was to be held in London.

A fund-raiser of some kind, but with some dubious added attractions.

Pete listened to the recording. There were many moments within it of interest.

- The missing Russian Yegorin's business opportunity, fronted by Maximovich.
- A new pipeline for Celarus.
- An auction for lunch with British politicians.
- That the event would be non-politically correct.
- TV hosts as comperes.
- Black tie event with 300 guests.
- 120 specially hired hostesses, wearing black shoes and told to wear black underwear.
- Jennifer Sussex, of MDA - Miel Doux Agency, to provide the hostesses.
- The Vinery, to prepare everyone with a team of hair and make-up artists.

But shortly after this the recording had stopped. Bigsy was implying that the control unit had failed again.

Pete knew enough to know that the Vinery was in the Lanchester Hotel, a very fashionable hotel in Mayfair. He had visited it once with his then girlfriend, for a company event. The ballroom was like something out of opulent Soviet Russia and the company had thrown quite a party. Yes, Pete could see this being the scene for some Grade-A frolics.

He called to Olivia Lang and she walked over with Emily Karankawa. Pete thought to himself that this could be awkward. He ran through a description of what he had heard, and Olivia looked very interested.

"This could be a great win for us, to bring down Yegorin, who is someone that the UK and Russian authorities have been hunting.

"It could even make up for that business with the American Colonel," added Emily, "You remember, where those two dead Russians were found in his hotel room and he escaped on a Canadian passport."

Pete remembered that although Emily and Olivia were friends, there had been an increased rivalry since Olivia had been slated for promotion but then had it taken away again after the Chuck Manners incident. Emily, on the other hand, had been consistently reliable and was now a grade higher that Olivia. Pete looked at the two women standing next to him. He thought of the description that one of the women in the meeting and used, 'Tall, thin and pretty'.

They both were.

"I've an idea," he said, "You could both infiltrate the event and collect incriminating evidence. Recordings to use as collateral."

They both looked at him, somewhat shocked.

"What, infiltrate as escorts? You have to be kidding?" said Olivia.

"No, think about it for a moment," said Emily, "They need 120 women for that evening. We know where it is, what is expected to go down and even who is hiring the extra support staff. If we wanted to put someone on the inside this could be the way!"

"No, I'm not doing it," said Olivia.

"Okay, I'll find someone else," said Emily, "I know we can make a difference to this operation. I will ask Anne-Marie Bristow."

Pete smiled; he knew Anne-Marie. She fitted the description too. Tall, thin and pretty.

Three of Coins

Teamwork
Collaboration
Building Together

Energy Sector

Back in the office in the Galleria, Bigsy had been busy researching the energy sector in Russia. He'd called everyone together for a PowerPoint presentation of his findings.

"This is terribly formal!" joked Jake.

"Well, there's a lot and I don't want to miss anything," said Bigsy, " I've cut and pasted the web pages into the deck - so it is a bit messy."

He clicked to the first image.

"The present Russian vertical structure of power has clear roots. Today, the political and economic structure in the country is usually referred to as a state corporation or a system of bureaucratic capitalism."

"It's a closed political system which is resistant to foreign attacks, the merging of political and economic elite and strategic areas of the economy controlled by a bureaucratic corporation and isolated from the influence of foreign capital."

"Yes, we were briefed on this when I was back at the Academy," said Christina, "The late Russian oligarch, Boris Berezovsky, said that seven bankers controlled about half the economy of Russia."

"That's right," said Bigsy, "When during Putin's first tenure a new model of government-business relations started forming, the dominance of the so-called oligarchs was replaced by representatives of the political elite who ran the five largest Russian gas, oil, transport and nuclear energy enterprises responsible for one third of the country's GDP. "

He showed a diagram of the enterprises which included a pie chart showing how much of the economy they made up.

Christina added, "I ran security details for some of them when they were meeting foreign businesspeople. Out of that came the term silovak. The term means a system when former members of power structures have high posts in the civil service and also perform important functions in major state companies and therefore can always employ administrative resources when dealing with business competitors. In Britain that clown of yours would say you'd say you have your cake and eat it."

Bigsy moved to the next image, "Yes, that was the trick, enterprises like Gazprom, Transneft, Sberbank, VTB Bank, Rusnano or even Rosneft have members from nearly all groups. Similarly, in the Government or Presidential Administration all clans compete."

Bigsy nodded and move to the next image, "This shows that Putin's Russia signals a new interaction between politics and business, where groups of political elite take over control of major businesses and strengthen the centralisation of the political system, because the idea of a strong Russia is the compulsory unifying element of the entire political elite."

Jake interrupted," So Putin has control and these semi-state businesses are happily skimming away a slice from the top of all the run-rate business."

Bigsy added, "And that's a considerable amount when you think of the types of businesses involved. Oil, Gas, Electricity, Finance."

Christina agreed, "Yes, Putin's policies were aimed at regaining the power from Yeltsin's old-man oligarchs - where necessary crushing the oligarch and substituting one of his own.

"The most English example I can think of was Berezovsky himself, who was exiled to Surrey, where he described that he would mount an opposition to Putin. Instead, in 2013, he was found hanged in his home. Open verdict was declared."

Christina continued "But dig back and you'll find other things. I happen to know he was targeted by FSB hitmen in 2007 and fled the UK on advice from Scotland Yard. Then he came back to the London Hilton where a hitman known to Berezovsky was detained and later deported back to Russia.

"Still with Berezovsky, there's the well-known case of the Polonium 210 killing of Alexander Litvinenko, which happened in 2006. Litvinenko was one of Berezovsky's closest associates and UK government sources suspected a Russian state sponsorship.

"I only know that 'Dmitry K' had been speaking openly about the plan to kill Litvinenko that was intended to 'set an example' as a punishment for a 'traitor'. And then shortly Litvinenko's death Russian Federal Protective Service officer - FSO - Andrei Lugovoy was called back to Russia.

"Then, in 2008, Berezovsky's close friend and long-time business partner billionaire 52-year old Arkady "Badri" Patarkatsishvili, collapsed and died in his bedroom after a family dinner at Downside Manor, his mansion in Leatherhead, Surrey, England."

Christina looked around the room, "Surrey is a dangerous county for Russian exiles. But don't you all look at me like that, this stuff is all known to SI6 and the police. They just have to choose whether to act or not. Sometimes there's a whole domino effect if one person is toppled."

Clare said, "I find it incredible that first Berezovsky's closest associates Litvinenko and Badri are killed and then he is found hanged."

"That is just one story, there are many others, like double agent Sergei Skripal and his daughter Yulia, famously poisoned in Salisbury with Novichok, " answered Christina.

Bigsy flipped the PowerPoint and continued, "The development of political oligarchic capitalism during Putin's rule took a turn towards state capitalism. That is what is happening right now as the Kremlin attempts to crush Yegorin."

Jake nodded, "And Putin made sure that in such a system the private businessmen keep control of their companies, but only after having accepted the fundamental condition – loyalty to the political system and loyalty to Putin."

"So, Putin created the New Society Agreement," said Christina, "With it, the state ensures the immunity of property rights and balance between different interest groups, and businesses pledge loyalty to the state."

Bigsy added, "Yes, it says in this report that Russian models of safe business and politics can be various: private businesses can benefit from 'hidden' protectionism (for example, the largest Russian oil company, Lukoil) or a company can be run by top-level bureaucrats and politicians (or their groups) even though formally it wouldn't be legal. This is how the second largest oil company, Rosneft, operates."

Bigsy found an item on the screen, "When Sechin became Executive Chairman of Rosneft, the company was only ranked sixth in the country in terms of oil extraction.

"But Sechin and Rosneft are said to be the ones who ruined the private company Yukos. Rosneft took over Yukos' main extraction centres and became the second largest oil company in Russia.

Christina nodded, "Yes. The Yukos case served as a message to all independent oligarchs and businesses about the new rule for the games set by the Kremlin.

"Simply, it was, 'Disobey at your peril.'

Christina added, "I was providing security to some of those early enforcement talks. The creation of Putin's ruling system was highly influenced by the state's growing interest in the country's economy and the appointing of politicians to the management of state companies or corporations."

Jake added, "It's not that different from what Raven was trying to do with Bernard Driscoll, nor the ways that the Minerva station is trying to gather Kompromat on British politicians. There must be a similar mechanism operating in Washington D.C. and targeted at the American establishment."

Christina continued, "That's where Putin has the leverage to control the competition between different groups of the political elite. And the control he uses to guarantee stability is corruption.

"In order to create a loyalty system and decrease the risk or regional separatism, he made a double move: on the one hand, he created the relations between annuity receivers and providers, on the other hand, he drastically expanded the bureaucratic apparatus – from 2000 till 2012 he increased the number of bureaucrats by 65%.

Christina added, "That price of corrupt relations is a sum equal to 17% of Russia's GDP. Nearly as much as the UK's VAT."

"What? and all of it is payola?" asked Jake, "The skimmed money is going straight into the pockets of the Russian elite?"

"Exactly," said Christina, "And then, in turn, to buy football clubs, shopping centres and large-scale apartment blocks in the west. Notably in London, but plenty of other spots as well. London is just, well, decidedly friendly towards the influx of money."

"That's right," said Bigsy, " I thought London was turning into Little Beijing, but it's still Little Moscow at the moment. All these Russians have their families living somewhere in London."

Christina added, "But when they say they need to crush someone in the name of patriotism, they say it sincerely. It's just that if it's London they're targeting, they will get their families out first."

Bigsy put up a London map, "There's plenty of well-heeled Russians living in London now, he said, Let's just zoom in on the Queen's back-garden."

He put up an aerial shot.

"Kensington Palace Gardens. Just behind Buckingham Palace, it includes Kensington Palace where Wills and Katie hang out. But look at their street. Compound of the Russian Embassy. Leonard Blavatnik, Roman Abramovich. The neighbours include the Mittals - the richest man in Britain and the Ecclestones, complete with their car turntable to avoid reversing.

Then he flipped to another chart, "A few years ago, an analysis by estate agency Knight Frank estimated that almost a tenth of all buyers at the top end of the London market came from the former Soviet Union. Rival estate agents Savills calculated that Russians like to buy the biggest houses of any group of purchasers. Average house prices in Kensington have risen eightfold over the past two decades, at least partly thanks to the influx from Russia.

"In 2011, a Ukrainian bought the world's most expensive flat – the penthouse at One Hyde Park – for £136.4m. Five months later, a Russian bought Park Place, a stately home near Henley-on-Thames, for £140m. Russians who acquired homes valued merely in the tens of millions barely deserved notice.

"Among those lesser buyers was a banker who moved to London in 2008. He and his family came on tier 1 investor visas, which provide successful applicants with residency in exchange for an investment (of, at the time, £1m) in government bonds.

"Over eight years Russian citizens made up 764 of the 3,396 people who paid for these so-called golden visas – making them the second largest group of applicants, after Chinese citizens.

"Of course, I don't have up-to-date figures and with the recent turmoil in the world I suspect things are changing, but it is still a good general indicator."

"So, live in London on proceeds from State crime in Moscow?" asked Clare.

Christina added, "I used to overhear people talking, when I was on security detail. They used to say - with absolute sincerity – how great it is they can get so rich in Moscow. They go and work for the state to earn money. Ministers hand out licences to make money. And of course all this comes from the boss …

"The first conversation Putin has with a new state employee is, 'Here is your business. Share it only with me. If someone attacks you, I will defend you … and if you don't use your position as a business you are an idiot.' "

"These are now like people who have drunk blood. They can't stop. Now it is state officials who are the businessmen."

Moving parts

"There's a lot of moving parts to this," said Christina, "For one thing, we will need something to warrant Amanda being able to send in some heavies. Look, I don't want to risk asking my handler to get something. It will likely leak back that there is something happening."

"To insulate Amanda from this, I guess we'll need to use Chuck," said Jake, "Who has gone back into hiding."

"Not necessarily," said Bigsy, "Remember our old agreement regarding the website, where we can essentially call him like Batman?"

"Oh yes, I had almost forgotten about that," said Clare, "We should use it now. What was it we have to mention - A Square?"

Bigsy nodded, "Yes that's right. I will work it onto the home page. I'm quite sure that Chuck will see it."

"Then, who and how will we get to the event?" asked

Christina, "I guess I can ask Antanov again, but I really don't want to get him involved."

"Maybe he could get us the invitation. We could send someone else in his place and you, Christina, could be the plus one. At least you will know what to expect."

"Good idea," agreed Christina, "You know, no offence, but I think this would be a good play for Chuck. He'd know how to handle himself if things got tricky."

"What about Marion and Nina?" asked Clare, "Won't they get invited anyway?"

"Yes, I expect they will, but I think we should not implicate them further. After all, they tipped us off about this."

"So how do we get close to the action? Invited into the main auction?"

"I don't know. If it is like the Ladies' Day, they will run it in the main event, but I have a feeling that for this there will be a side room somewhere and an extra layer of security, probably run buy Vassily Turgenev."

"Turgenev plays hard-ball, so I think we should be prepared for Amanda's team to help in that area," said Christina, "We'll just need the reasons for Amanda arriving with force."

"I think you'll need some special comms too," said Bigsy, "I've been tinkering with some new walkie-talkies recently. They use Tetra, which is the same stuff as the police and emergency services, except there's all these extra bands. I think we could use a few slim-line hand sets for this mission."

"I thought Tetra made milk- cartons," said Clare.

Bigsy replied "No that's Tetrapak. Tetra is radio designed for use by government agencies, emergency services, for public safety networks, trains, transport, and the military because it keeps on working and goes through walls and tunnels and so on. To make it work properly, we will need to install a base station in a store cupboard or somewhere around the meeting zone. Then everyone, even the military, will be able to use it, provided we divulge our secret channel and key."

"That sound very useful," said Christina, "Now we just need the just cause for Amanda to go barging in!"

Two-helicopter household

Amanda had asked Grace Fielding at GCHQ to dig around on Yegorin. She called back on a video link.

"Hi," Grace smiled, "More about your mysterious Russians. Yegorin first gained French citizenship in 2009, and knew French law protected its citizens from extradition to Russia.

"Then he fled to the relative safety of his villa high in the hills above the bay of Nice, a fortress surrounded by an impenetrable high iron fence, a team of bodyguards and a battery of security cameras at every turn.

"Of course, he still had the entire French Riviera on his doorstep, so it was hardly a hardship to be in exile. Notably, he had a couple of helicopters, and would cross over to Nice Airport to fly to European capitals whenever he felt the need. We obtained the flight logs and he makes extensive use of the facility."

"A two-helicopter household?" asked Amanda.

"Yes, one for the family, silly. The villa is really high in the hills. Pretty but isolated," Grace smiled, "It was the arrival of Moscow rules in London, where the Kremlin could twist the legal process to suit its agenda, where the larger issue of expropriation of Yegorin's multi-billion-dollar business empire could be buried in the detail of rules."

"Lawyers tying people in knots?"

"Yes and getting rich in the process."

"Of course, Yegorin was no angel- in fact, he was one of the very bad people in the lead-up to Putin's power."

"But he's been erased from the photographs now?"

"Exactly, you'd be hard pressed to know he even existed. Curiously enough, Berezovsky gets most of the 'credit' for Putin's rise."

"And then there is the little matter of the missing money. It was not at all clear what had happened to the $700 million he'd been accused of siphoning from Mezhkommbank.

"A New Zealand trust he'd set up to hold tens of millions of dollars in properties, including his Chelsea home, was later found to be a sham."

Amanda said, "For all his flaws Yegorin insisted he had been caught in a Russian state vendetta pursued through the UK courts. The Kremlin seemed intent on quashing any notion that he'd ever been well-connected in the Kremlin, or that he could have any knowledge that could be damaging to it?"

Grace replied, "The people I have spoken to just say he was a blatant crook. But Yegorin had worked at the heart of the Kremlin and had been privy to some of its deepest secrets, including how it was exactly that Putin came to power.

"He literally knows where the bodies are buried."

"That's why the Kremlin is after him, then."

"To be honest, I'm amazed they haven't sent him a polonium parcel by now," said Grace.

"I'm equally amazed that he thinks he can make a comeback from this position."

Incoming

Jake's phone beeped; an incoming text.

"What's the matter, can't get enough of me?" asked Chuck in a text to Jake.

"Hi Chuck, we think you are in the clear now over that fake news about the Institute bombing. How would you like to get even? We've found the culprits and are planning to bring them down."

"Okay," said Chuck, "Let me get to you, New office isn't it?"

"Yes," replied Jake, "Let me send the address."

...

Page of Coins

Ambition
Desire
Diligence
Craving New Venture

Carrying

Pete Burr was quite excited at the prospect of going on an assignment. It sounded as if it was to be to one of the most politically incorrect events in London for the coming year.

He'd had to draw a compromise, though.

When Emily Karankawa and Anne-Marie Bristow had applied to Miel Doux Agency, they had been accepted straight away, especially with their back-stories about working in public relations for a call centre. He had been a much tougher sell. MDA wanted females for the event. Initially he was turned down, but then it transpired that MDA wanted 12 men as well as the women. He had been shortlisted for a call-back and had to answer one awkward question about his orientation.

But he was now in and could go with the two women to the event. There was a strength in numbers which he was sure would prove useful.

The three of them had all proved somewhat sheepish

about revealing their plans to Minerva. But if it worked the way they hoped, they were sure that they would each get a promotion.

They had also worked out how they would gather information. They had acquired some voice recorders which looked like USB sticks and could be attached to their key rings. They were perfect for the task and would not be confiscated by security in the way that a mobile phone might be.

Pete received the same information as the ladies about what to wear for the event. He was also expected to show up at 4pm, for an event that started some three hours later.

Chuck arrives at the office

"It's Chuck!" called Jake, excited to hear that Chuck was downstairs in the lobby of their offices.

"He's on his way up."

Chuck arrived, gave a brief slap on the back to Jake and asked," So what it this about? I guess you are still dealing with that Raven crowd?"

They walked into the office area and he greeted each of them with a smile, saving a smiling salute for Christina.

"So what is the mission?" he asked, looking at Jake.

"Well, it's party time," began Jake, "Gavy Yegorin will be in town at the party being hosted by Tima Maximovich, who is the Head of Russian Infrastructure. Here's the twist. Maximovich's usually enforcer is Vassily Turgenev, who is being loaned to Yegorin to securely manage the evening. Turgenev is the person who sent gunmen after you."

"Okay, I can see that," said Chuck, " But what is the purpose of the party? Not just for old times' sake?"

"No, it is to look for backers for an oil pipeline project in Celarus, to add to the investment to be made by Yegorin."

"That sounds distinctly dicey," said Chuck, "Yegorin is betting against the Russian state."

"He is, but he is also being hunted by them. This would be a fantastic way for him to throw a huge spanner in the works. If he can build the pipeline, then the Russians will lose a substantial slice of energy business."

"Energy business which the Kremlin oligarchs skim to make their own private money?" guessed Chuck.

"Exactly," said Jake.

"So, it is likely to be backed by others on the Kremlin hit list. As Putin is tidying the Kremlin, there must still be people who are looking over their shoulders, even now."

"Yes, although we think Yegorin will want look further afield. Non-Russian backers too. We think he has asked Maximovich to use his Masonic connections to pull in a wider audience. He went to Michael Tovey, MP to set up the invitations. Tovey suggested the same facilitators as at Raven's Ladies Day. ISMC seem to be handling the production of the event again, although it can't be with Gerhardt nor Frobisher."

"Why would Maximovich do this? - Get involved - I thought he was still in with the in-crowd at the Kremlin?"

"Yes, we thought so too," said Christina, "It is possible that Maximovich is trying to smoke out some of Yegorin's allies, which would make it easier for the Kremlin to know who to go after."

"So, I assume you involved Amanda Miller in this?" asked Chuck.

Jake added, "Oh yes, and she says she will bring SAS troops along. But, she says she will need a sound reason to intervene, like they are plotting a coup, or have some signs of terrorism in the building."

"What something like guns or explosives?" asked Chuck.

Jake nodded.

"Did I mention where I've been visiting?" said Chuck, "I needed to top up my supply of olives and hummus."

"Middle east?" hazarded Bigsy, "Or Borough Market?"

"Ha ha. It was Jordan and I discovered a little something extra whilst I was there. The Russians have been supplying Jordan with Barkas."

"What is it, a type of clothing?" asked Clare.

"No, it's a weapon," said Christina, "A hand-held grenade launcher. Very compact and made in Russia. Based on the RPG-32, I seem to remember."

"Top marks," said Chuck, "The Russian company Bazalt made them, but now supplies them as assembly kits to Jordan. They are called Nashshab in Jordan. They like them so much they built their own factory to manufacture them."

"And they are easy to get hold of?" asked Christina smirking.

"Let's just say the Jordanian security at the factory is a little less reliable than that in Russia."

"Chuck, does that mean you've brought a grenade launcher to London?" asked Jake, somewhat incredulous.

"No - I didn't bring it, I had it shipped, complete with Lithium battery warning stickers on it."

"You don't intend to use it at the party?" asked Clare still looking alarmed.

"No, I think it will make a remarkably interesting accessory though, something for Amanda Miller's people to find. The beauty of it is that the whole RPG-32 is small and would easily fit into a cupboard, with a couple of defused grenades. We can get it in a small wheeled suitcase."

"Excellent," said Clare, "Not that I'm condoning bringing high explosive into prestigious central London hotels, but this does ensure that Amanda can bring her SAS posse into town."

Jake said, "Now Chuck, we'll need you in a tuxedo for this event. Properly James Bond. Christina arranged for you to go along, under Antanov's name - Antanov Chekeryn. Antanov is a senior mason and used his contact with Michael Tovey to get us two invitations to the event. That's for you and Christina."

"So, I'll be going with Christina? Well, that will set the

tongues wagging!"

Christina smiled, "And I assume we'll both be carrying?"

"Possibly," smiled Chuck, "Will you have that fancy little handbag of yours?"

"Possibly," smiled Christina in return

Part Three – Riddle of One

The Hangman's Beautiful Daughter

The natural cards revolve ever changing
Seeded elsewhere planted in the garden fair
Grow trees, grow trees

Tongues of the sheer wind
Setting your foot where the sand is untrodden
The ocean that only begins
…
Earth water fire and air
Met together in a garden fair
Put in a basket bound with skin
If you answer this riddle
If you answer this riddle
You'll never begin

Robin Williamson

Tower

Upheaval
Disaster
Foundational Shift

Through the Yard of Blonde Girls

Pete Burr arrived at the Lanchester. He was a little early but had black shoes and rather self-consciously he'd been out and bought some new black underwear. It has cost him a small fortune, because he'd first bought Hugo Boss. A three pack had cost him £36, but when he'd tried them on, he realised that the logo was vastly too prominent in white around the waist-line. Then he'd bought another set of three Armani boxers. They had the logo on the side, in a contrasting colour, but it was, at least, grey. He'd worked out that it had cost him £72 to get one serviceable boxer brief.

Now he was inside the Vinery, where everyone was to get ready. It was already busy in the room and several of the women were unselfconsciously changing into their evening outfits. The women had all been provided with the same outfits. A black dress, with a wide belt and see-through side panels. He noticed that some women were given red shoes instead of the black ones they had been asked to bring.

Then he noticed that a few of the women were asked to wear a different outfit. A black, sleeveless top, with a white collar and impossibly tiny shorts, together with a black leather belt. Then he saw one of the other men and he realised that the shorts outfit worn by the women was the same one that they expected the men to wear.

"Don't freak out!" said Emily laughing. She had just walked into the same scene of chaos, "You know you have the legs for it!"

Pete was taken away by one of the makeup artists. "My name is Lucy," she said, "Not bad, but I'll need to see your legs." A few minutes later Pete found himself in the outfit and Lucy peering at his legs.

"It's gonna have to go," said Lucy, and switched on a hair trimmer, "Usually I'd suggest wax, but we haven't got time here, so we'll use this and then some spray tan over there."

Another woman approached and left a box of disposable boxers for spray tanning. Pete was thinking about how little of this he had suspected a mere half hour ago.

"I see you are almost done," called over another guy, with blonde spiky hair. "It's a great way to get a makeover!"

Pete decided he'd not ever seen this many almost naked women at one time. Now he had to cross in front of them to the tanning area. That old Jeff Buckley song was flittering through his mind.

> *'Through the yard, through the yard of blonde girls.*
> *Through the river and the sea.*
> *Gold sharks glittering.'*

Mercifully, he noticed that there was one booth marked 'Men' and several marked 'Women'. He was soon sprayed a uniform tanned colour and emerged, after cautiously putting his shorts and shirt back on.

'You've got innocence in your eyes.
Even in this world of lies, you're still hopeful.
Very sexy. Okay, okay.
Fear we may come.
Fear we may come.'

"You are lucky," said Lucy, "You get to wear flats. This outfit has white deck shoes. Go over there and collect some."

'Fear we may come.
Fear we may come.
So run, run, run, run, run, run, run.'

Lori Kramer and Audrey Clark must have attended something similar he was thinking.

He could see that Lucy was rushed off her feet as more of the hosts had started to arrive. He looked at his watch. It was only just four o'clock. Things were going to get busier. Then, as he walked back to a table with some bottled water, he caught a glimpse of himself in a long mirror.

"Oh. My. God," he thought, "This seemed like such a good idea."

To stay focused, he imagined Jeff Buckley's guitar sizzling and swirling and the way Buckley pronounced 'glittering' the second time.

Anne-Marie and Emily came across and joined him. They now looked almost like a stage act in the outfits that had been provided. He noticed that Anne-Marie looked a little tearful.

"This is exploitation on a grand scale," she said, "I'm shocked - this would never happen in Washington."

"I'm not so sure," said Emily, "There's a planet of lively bars between F and H Street and around the Logan Circle."

Anne-Marie looked back, "Despite living in D.C. I have only ever been to the H Street Festival in that area. It's a bit too edgy at night - I'll take your word for the misadventures!" she said. The others noticed she looked a little brighter.

"Oh and there's that Mansion on O - you must have been there?" asked Emily.

Anne-Marie replied, "I have - we went there as a family once. A whole row of houses knocked into one and then filled fit to bursting with artworks. I remember seeing some Lennon and a Janice Joplin piece and a couple of famous guitars, plus paintings and books, it was incredible - and exhausting in a good way!"

Lucy came over, "Time for the talk - No offline arrangements, no gratuities, no handling, you can drink as much as you like; this has to look disreputable but maintain a high standard. You get any trouble, find one of the women in red shoes, they will help you get out of it. It will get more ragged as the night runs. Think about the average man powered by two litres of wine - you have to be sweet as you tell them to sit down. Now put on these wrist bands."

She looked at Pete, "And the same rules for the men. Now practice smiling and looking happy, everyone!"

Bolo

It was arrival time at the event. Chuck and Christina climbed from their taxi and made their way to the main line for entry. Christina had decided to wear the same blue gown that she wore to Raven's Ladies Night, but this time with a bright red sash.

Chuck had already told her how stunning she looked. "And Chuck, you look very dashing in the tuxedo, said Christina. "I like the American touch of the bootlace tie."

"It's called a Bolo actually," said Chuck, "I got this one when I was in Albuquerque."

"I love the turquoise stone and the red and black motif on the surround," said Christina.

"Yes, it's quite powerful Navajo symbolism, I got it from my friend Tom, - his real name is Atsa Tahoma - that's 'Eagle by the Water's Edge' - Bigsy and Clare have met him, we were all in the desert together at the time."

They both looked at the line. Christina looked in her

Mulberry bag. "Here, put this on," she said. It was the insignia that Antanov had left in her apartment when he moved out. Christina knew it signified high Masonic rank.

Chuck clipped it to his jacket and almost immediately a man approached him.

"Would you like to come this way?"

Chuck nodded and the two of them walked around to a side entrance. Christina was used to this now, although this time she noticed there seemed to be some heavier duty security on the doors. She could sense that one of the guards had a pistol too and caught in Chuck's eyes that he had the same thought.

To Christina's surprise, they were whisked past the security and directly into the event. Once again, the side entrance had jumped the queue and they were already in the thick of the reception.

"We'll need to find our table," whispered Christina. She noticed Chuck was checking the number of exits from the room and the likely location of any side rooms. She was doing the same and when she found their table she briefly walked across to take a look.

"We'll rotate ourselves 90 degrees, then we have a view across the whole room, she said and moved the name tags from the table to adjacent positions.

"There," she said, "That's much better."

Then she took her phone and surreptitiously took a snap of the entire table plan for the room.

A band struck up a fanfare, and then a Toastmaster walked out. He brought everyone to order and asked that they applaud the hostesses, who would be coming out right now.

More music as 'Good as Hell' by Lizzo blasted from the speakers and the hostesses sprang out, accompanied by cheers and whoops from the attendees. To Chuck's eye, they were all pretty although he could see that many looked as if they were students trying to earn a buck.

Christina noticed one in particular. She was Anne-Marie from the Minerva station. The plan back at the Triangle offices when they staged their mini play script had obviously worked. Christina wondered just how many from Minerva were present.

Emil Pozharsky

The Toastmaster had urged them all to be seated. Christina noticed that this event skipped the formality of the Ladies' Night.

She was on a table with Chuck and six others. Two of the couples were chatting to one another in Russian. The two men were talking about Maximovich's offer and commenting that the last time he'd suggested something the return for investors was an almost instant doubling in the share price.

She decided to speak to one of the wives. These women looked like wives rather than escorts provided by Miel Doux Agency. "This is quite an event!" said Christina brightly to one of the women.

"Yes, Emil insisted we come over specially for it," answered the woman, "We came in from Nice last night. We are staying in this very hotel, so it won't be a long journey after the event," she said, "I'm Marisha and these are our friends Lev and Karine Oblonsky"

Marisha looked at Christina's brooch. "That's a very

pretty brooch," she said, "Where did you get it?"

"Oh, my partner got it," said Christina alluding to Chuck, "He's quite high up in - you know - the Masons." She gestured towards Chuck and the insignia pinned to his jacket."

"Oh, I see, I don't think Emil has realised, let me nudge him."

She spoke some Russian to her husband, who suddenly looked around startled, "My goodness, My name is Emil Pozharsky - I had no idea, let me welcome you, I am in the Nizhny Novgorod Masonic Temple although nowadays I spend a good deal of my time in France."

Chuck smiled, "Nizhny Novgorod, ah yes, home of Maxim Gorky. But surely you should join the French Masons if you spend much time there?"

"I know, I should, but thankfully my contacts via Nizhny are sufficient, and still get me invited to this lovely event."

Chuck and Christina realised, but were too polite to say, that Emil Pozharsky and Lev Oblonsky must be others of the exiled Russians, in a comparable situation to Yegorin. Maybe there were seeds of an uprising against the Kremlin's use of strong arm tactics?

See Emily play

Emily had been paying attention since the event started. There were many people present and to her surprise many of the men had brought their wives. She wondered how much this would cramp the style of the others, but to be honest, she was rather pleased.

She had been allocated a table which contained two married couples and two other men who were with escorts. Behind her was a pair of large exit doors and in front of them stood a security man.

Her job was playfully keeping the table served and to be jolly at all times. There was an outer circuit of red-shoed hostesses whose role seemed to be to ensure the black-shoed hostesses were occupied all of the time, but that the guests were not crossing the line.

Between courses there was entertainment and a rather crude comedian had just come on.

Emily regarded it as respite and could look over to where Pete was looking similarly relieved. So far, she didn't think they had managed to find much of interest for their recordings. She looked further around the room but could not work out where Anne-Marie had gone. She must be working behind the scenes or something.

Emily decided that the lull while the comedian was on would be a good opportunity to look around. She carefully snuck over to the big double doors, pressed the bar and was soon in the outer corridor, itself a wide space capable of holding most of the participants that were now seated in the event.

She looked across the way and saw another door, which she entered. A small side-lit room, but with a coffee station ready for use. She was about to pour a coffee when she heard a noise behind her. It was the security guard from outside. He had followed her into the room.

Now she had to decide what to do. He approached her and she could only think to smile. Then he grasped her around the waist, and she realised what was on his mind.

There was a click as the other door to the small room opened.

"Vassily!" said the guard, "Yes, Igor, what are you doing away from your station with this pretty little thing? Didn't you read the emails? You know that the second ballroom is being used for the auction and that it starts in about five minutes?"

"And you, what is your name?"

"Emily," she answered.

"Well Emily, I think you had better accompany me into the other ballroom. We cannot have you telling everyone what is going on before we've had the meeting. But do not worry. We'll find a few more like you to join us after the meeting."

Emily followed Vassily Turgenev into the second large room. It was another ballroom but this one had been set up with chairs and tables in rows. Each table separated from others with a total of around 50 tables in the room.

Emily noticed several of what she assumed to be Turgenev's 'heavies' spread around the perimeter of the room. She resigned herself to being stuck in this room until after the auction or whatever took place.

Wheel

Fate
Karma
Destiny
Fortune Cycles

Criticism

"So why did you come over for this event?" asked Christina, looking first to Lev and then to Emil.

Lev Oblonsky replied, "For me, my entire life, the truth was equivalent to freedom. I earned money not for riches, but for freedom. How much can you really spend? But a certain independence gave me one thing: I don't need to lie."

This all sounded too good to be true to Christina. She wondered what was coming next.

But as the conversation continued, it became apparent the two men believed that the president had become surrounded by yes-men, all of whom proffered lengthy toasts to Putin, telling him he had been sent by God to save the country, while they served at his pleasure.

Yet it seemed to Oblonsky that these yes-men understood the deep hypocrisy of the system, the sham democracy represented by the Kremlin's ruling party, United Russia, and how deeply corrupt it had become.

"Look at the people around VV – that's Putin - who say Vladimir Vladimirovich, you're a genius!" Oblonsky continued, "I look at them—but realise that they don't believe in anything."

Emil Pozharsky added, "These new men understand it's all crap. United Russia is crap, elections are rigged, even the president is a gangster. They know all this, but then they go on stage and say how great everything is. They make toasts which are also total crap, total lies."

Chuck interrupted, "Do you think you should say these kinds of things in here? Someone might be listening."

Emil said, "No, this is the one place we can say these things. We've come along here tonight to support Yegorin. He's being chased by the Kremlin. The latest in a long line of people positioned to fall under the wheels."

Lev said, "Yes, these bratva gangsters sit and tell stories about how they have always been together, ever since they were sitting on the school-bench.

Emil added, "But at the same time the guys sitting in the office next door are saying, 'As soon as he comes out, let's finish him off.' It could be financial ruin, a death threat to his family, a murder or a staged suicide."

Lev said, "The ones who have power are stealing from all sides, and then they come out and speak about how Putin is fighting against corruption. I look at them and think, this is the end. VV was always asking, "What is that word beginning with s? Sovest – conscience."

Emil added, "They don't have time for conscience. They don't understand it. They forgot the word and what it means. They've gotten totally messed up."

Chuck looked intrigued, "But aren't there people here who are part of that system?" He asked, "Ruthless, and conscience free?"

Lev nodded, "Yes, I'm not sure why Yegorin is using Vassily Turgenev's people here for security tonight. They are people that will push you off a building and then go for a cool beer. To be honest, if I'd known that then I might not have come along."

Karine looked at Marishe, then said to Lev, "Lapochka, don't get too wound up about all of this. Like you said on the way here, we can always just leave if we don't like it."

Christina smiled at the use of Lapochka - sweetie pie - when Karine spoke to Lev.

Lev continued, "All the achievements of the Putin era so far—the economic growth, the increase in incomes, the riches of the billionaires that had turned Moscow into a gleaming metropolis where sleek foreign cars filled the streets and cosy cafés opened on street corners—boiled down to the sharp increase in the oil price during the Putin years, they agree."

Chuck asked, "But hasn't it got more difficult now? The Americans, The Saudis, NAFTA, manipulating the prices and disadvantaging Russia?"

Emil interjected, "In the 2000s, the oil price was $50 to $70, and we were happy. Then when it topped $150 the only thing they decided was to skim even more from the top. Enough skimming to buy stacks of apartments in London or villas on the French Riviera. The state is doing nothing with the money. They could have transformed the country's infrastructure. But everything, all the money, all the materials, will be stolen if we build roads.

Oligarchs put it into property because it makes it difficult to steal."

Lev continued, "In the 2000s we gave the boss such a smoothly oiled machine. Everything worked. And what did we get? We didn't understand that he wasn't going to drive things forward. I thought he was liberal, young"

Emil said, "But it turned out he was from a different species."

 Lev agreed, "Yes. They are different people. They are different, special people. This was something we didn't understand. The person who understood this very well was the prosecutor general."

Christina interrupted, "But surely for people to turn out this way they would have needed some special indoctrination?"

"Oh yes," said Emil, "The Akademies, which took the young children away and indoctrinated them. They learned how to play fast and loose with the truth and with many kinds of weapon and fighting skill. Probably most of Vassily's people have come through the Academy structure."

Lev said, "That's right. They had a tiered system. There were 'the grunts' who were the strong arms for enforcement. Then the more able people were made into various agent types and embedded. The elite were promoted and given code names and a licence to operate anywhere, often on fake papers."

Lev said, "Yes, the prosecutor general told me, 'You understand, the guys from the security services, they are different. Even if you were to suck all their blood out and then put on a different head, they would still be different. They live in their own system. You will never be one of them. It is an absolutely different system.' I'm afraid that it is where Vassily Turgenev comes from."

Chuck asked, "So Turgenev is a necessary evil?"

Lev said, "No, he is only plain evil. He has left a trail of bloodshed wherever he visits. I won't be surprised tomorrow to read about some kind of shoot-out in London if he is here running security."

Emil said, "The KGB - nowadays called the FSB and the GRU - had forged an alliance with Russian organised crime long ago, on the eve of the Soviet collapse, when billions of dollars' worth of precious metals, oil and other commodities was transferred from the state to firms linked to the KGB."

"So, it was all planned then?" asked Chuck.

Emil continued, "Right from the start, foreign-intelligence operatives of the KGB sought to accumulate black cash to maintain and preserve influence networks long thought demolished by the Soviet collapse. They would run secret meetings protected by the very best security and cut deals about how many percent they would take off the top."

Lev said, "Yes, It's true that for a time under Yeltsin the forces of the KGB stayed hidden in the background. But when Putin rose to power, the alliance between the KGB and organised crime emerged and bared its teeth."

"Are we sitting in the jaws this evening?" asked Chuck.

331

Anne-Marie

The event continued. Chuck and Christina watched as everyone enjoyed fine wine, good food and dubious comedy acts. Then a band was announced. They would be playing a set for around 40 minutes.

Chuck and Christina looked around. This was surely the time when some of the 'investors' would be scooped up and shown to another session.

"Hello," said someone in Christina's ear, "I think we've met before."

Christina turned. It was Anne-Marie in her hostess outfit. Christina had to make a snap decision whether to blank her or not. One look at her face and she decided she would talk.

"Yes, but I think this place is a lot more dangerous than Wagamama's restaurant," she said, referring to where they had previously met.

"Look, I'm worried, can we talk, please?" Christina noticed how American Anne-Marie sounded.

"Let me introduce you to my colleague, he is also American."

Chuck turned and said, "Hello little darlin' what seems to be the matter?" He could see Anne-Marie almost burst into tears.

"Look I've got to keep busy," said Anne-Marie, or the women with the red shoes will be over. Can you look like you are asking me something?"

"Yes, in that case I demand that you show me the way to the ladies rest-room," said Christina, " I want you to accompany me the whole way there and then wait whilst I re-apply my lip liner."

Chuck smiled. This wasn't what he'd joined the US Marines for.

The three of them made their way outside, Christina looked suitably unapproachable and Chuck quietly glowered as he followed them. It had all the theatre of a domestic dispute being handled by one of the hostesses.

They made their way to the rest room and Christina pulled Chuck inside.

"Chuck, get in the cubicle, so you can hear us, but if we are disturbed, you'll be hidden," said Christina. Chuck guffawed as he locked himself into the cubicle.

"Okay, now tell me what is going on," said Christina, "Don't tell me you are involved with all of this?"

"Yes, I am. Look, you know I work for the CIA out at

Minerva listening station. We heard that there was to be some sort of deal constructed here tonight, fronted by one bad Russian and supported by another. It links up with Brant and the work that is going on in Celarus. I came along with two of my colleagues to find out what was happening."

"Now, one of my colleagues, a friend named Emily has been apprehended by the security here. I know because I followed her when she went out to snoop around. She didn't know I was following but was soon caught by a guard, who put his hands all over her. Then I saw her being taken through into another room - it is the second ballroom - this place is huge.

"They said they would keep her there until after the meeting had taken place. They said it would be in a few minutes, so I ran back outside. That's when I recognised Katarina here. She was around at Minerva with Anna a couple of weeks ago." She sounded breathless as she continued.

   "I knew, from what you had said that you were good in a tough situation and frankly I didn't have anyone else to turn to."

Chuck's voice came from the other side of the stall door. "Anne-Marie you have done so many things wrong. Things that would never stack up in a CIA agent's field book. Fortunately, this time you have struck lucky, so I think we will be able to help you."

"You said two of your colleagues. Where is the other one?" asked Christina.

"I don't know," answered Anne-Marie, "He's one of the men hosts here. He has on a tiny black top and some white micro shorts. There's only about twelve of them here. I guess I'd describe him as the one who looks most like a fish out of water,"

"No good," said Christina, "You'll have to find him yourself, I assume he is still in the main room. We're going to the other ballroom and will keep a lookout for Emily. Is she dressed like you?"

"Yes, and with long dark brown hair."

Christina called to Chuck, "You got that, let's get moving."

Chuck opened the stall and came out. He made directly for the door of the restroom.

"Wait!" hissed Christine, "Let me look first. Okay it's clear."

 Chuck was once again aware of Christina's guardian powers as all three of them emerged into a dark corridor and walked back towards the two ballrooms.

Ed Adams

Dry run

Emily sat at the back and watched the second ballroom fill up. The security officer Igor was being kept busy by a door. Emily had already decided she would need to get away from him. She hoped that Anna-Marie or Pete would have noticed that she had gone.

She was sitting close to a small group of men, who were talking about the event. She decided that they were the organisers and finalising who would say what. Then a woman appeared, "Hello Trudi," said one of the men, "Hello Miller, you've been over here all the while?" she asked.

"Yes, Gentlemen- I'm Miller McDonald and this is Trudi Hartmann, from my Company ISMC."

"Ah, we have heard much about you," said one of the men, "My name is Khramov Gavril Yegorin, but you can call me Gavy."

   "And I'm Timur Maximovich, call me Tima." said another man.

"And hello again, "said the last man, "You'll remember when we met at The House of Commons, Michael Tovey,"

"Ah yes the Member of Parliament, " said Trudi, "I'm pleased to meet you all."

"Let us check the running order then," said Miller McDonald.

Emily sat quietly, at least she should be getting all of this recorded on her covert microphone.

"I'll briefly open and then pass over to Trudi. She will paint a picture of the fantastic opportunity which this presents to this privileged audience."

"Then Michael can add something about what this means to the UK, getting the security of a pipeline to ensure regulated energy costs into Europe with the bolstered stability to the UK."

"I'd like to remind people that Brant is a spin off from the British Company Raven, too"

"Yes, although, strictly speaking Brant is Belgian," said Miller McDonald.

"Yes, but a British angle will go down well in the sales pitch," said Tovey.

"Right, then who? One of you Russian gentleman, I think. And this section should be partly in Russian too. You can recap over what has already been said and then add any additional Russian points as well. I suggest Tima presents the case, and we keep Gavy in reserve."

Tima looked at Gavy. "Are you okay with that?" he asked, "Yes, I know why, the Kremlin's ceaseless chasing of me won't do our case any good. It's better to come from you, Gavy."

"Right, that's settled, then when Gavy finishes I'll take over again and explain to everyone what they need to do. We'll have prospectuses and other paperwork stacked up at the back of the room."

Emily knew right away that the meeting had been rehearsed by Miller McDonald, Trudi Hartmann and Michael Tovey and that the others were being used to bring in 'colour and texture'. It was a setup.

Ed Adams

King of Swords

Head over heart
Truth
Discipline

Tetra codes

Outside the meeting, Bigsy had been using the communication gear to listen to what had been happening. He had booked into the Lanchester the previous day and even arranged on-site parking for his small van.

The van was a 'Bigsy special', kitted out with a Tetra repeater station and several concealed microphones spread around the hotel. He had used his best High-Visibility jacket to walk the various devices in after Turgenev's people had run their sweep of the floor.

Additionally, he had had to improvise a cleaning bucket to contain the RPG-32 which Chuck had provided. Bigsy had never seen one of these grenade launchers before, but Chuck had assured him it was safe and that the detonators for the grenades had been removed in any case.

Bigsy had put the device in a cleaning cupboard, behind a row of cleaning products. He thought it was well-enough hidden for 24 hours unless the whole hotel went on a sudden cleaning rampage.

Bigsy sat in the back of the van with Clare and Jake. They had direct communication to Amanda and in turn Amanda was using the same Tetra communications to talk to the SAS soldiers parked around the corner from the hotel.

Amanda had retrieved a plan of the Lanchester, and the soldiers also had a copy. The exact position of the concealed grenade launcher was explained to the SAS team and the two ballrooms were both known together with the ways in and out.

All it would take now was a coded signal from Christina and they would deploy.

Sell it loud

It was time for the start of the principal event. The dinner had been served and now the investor recruits had been shepherded towards the second ballroom. Inside the ballroom, Emily realised that only a small percentage of the attendees were being invited and considered that the rest of the event must have been a camouflage to get these investors in.

Just outside, Chuck and Christina were drawing similar conclusions. They had to make a speedy decision about whether to be inside or outside of the event. They both decided it would be better for them to be inside but seated near to the back. Anne-Marie had pointed to Emily inside the room, although they both realised, she seemed to be the only hostess present.

"You'd better stay outside," urged Christina, "It will draw too much attention if you go inside."

They slipped in thought the doors, noticing that the security people were present at each exit from the room. Christina estimated that the security detail were all carrying concealed handguns, by the way they fidgeted with what were probably underarm holsters.

"Give the security detail the job of preventing pistols and what do they do?" whispered Chuck. Christina nodded. It could get very ugly in the room if anyone pulled a gun.

Christina still had her Mulberry, within which she still had her compact weapon of choice, the Sig Sauer MPX.

Bothe she and Chuck were counting the number of security people visible, but also aware of two double doors at the end of the room, which could conceal more gunmen.

"That's where they will have any heavy fire-power," whispered Christina, "This is a classic GRU strong-arm setup. They will probably have a sub behind those doors, and maybe a couple of rifles too."

"They say that London is pretty-much gun-free, yet somehow they seem to move in quite a lot of fire-power."

"Yes, it is dismantled and then sent in with high value goods - electronics and camera accessories. Who would notice an extra pole or two in a disassembled TV camera tripod, for example?"

They noticed some movement. The first of the speakers had come to the stage. Christina vaguely recognised him. Then he spoke with a strong American accent, "Hello, my name is Miller McDonald, from ISMC. Welcome everybody. We are here to facilitate this evening's event and this special privileged meeting for potential investors in this unique business opportunity."

"I recognise Miller McDonald," said Christina, "I didn't

speak to him, but he was present at the Ladies' Night at Raven. I guess he was manipulating the occasion for Raven. They didn't have a special event like this though."

"Or not one that you were invited to?" asked Chuck, "Remember there's still around 200 people in the other ballroom."

"…and now let me hand you over to Trudi Hartmann, who can give you the facts and figures."

He left the stage, and an immaculately dressed woman crossed the stage. Christina admired her choice of outfit. Power dressed in a sharp blue tailored suit, with tan shoes. Hair worn down. The tiniest hint of jewellery.

"Darker hues to be taken seriously," thought Christina.

Trudi began to talk and explain the virtues of investment in the new pipeline. That this was no ordinary fundraiser, and everyone should expect to see their initial investment double within two years and then a healthy 18% yield every year that the pipeline was active.

"If it looks too good to be true, then it probably is too good to be true," whispered Chuck.

Next it was Michael Tovey's turn. He played the earnest Member of Parliament and offered praise that an erstwhile British company - Raven - was involved in the development of the new pipeline.

"He is being somewhat economical with the truth," muttered Chuck, "Raven sold off Qube and made Brant - which is a Belgian Company - they are trying hard to conceal this now."

"Although, ironically, probably half the security here are on Brant's payroll," whispered Christina.

It was Maximovich's turn. He took to the stage and spoke with a polished English, but still a Muscovite edge,"This investment will be a great opportunity for all of us, " he said, "we can support the realistic rebalancing of power. It will be like a blow to our oppressors. We can fight with financial measures instead of staging a coup. We don't need to use guns and bombs to shift the balance of power in Celarus.

Maximovich continued, "Even though we spend much less on security than other countries, this does not mean that we are ready to compromise our combat readiness. Our equipment must be better than the world's best if we want to come out as the winners. This is not a game of chess where we can sometimes accept a tie."

Chuck said to Christina, "This smacks of a declaration of conflict along the Celarus borders."

"Working with military friends continues to play a key role in securing peace in Celarus. Our American allies, including those deployed at the new Brant-constructed airbase and perimeter border stations — are guarantors of peace and stability in that country. We have also fielded other weapons systems as well and tested them during exercises and in combat conditions."

"I can't see how Maximovich has managed to get the agreement of America to play along with this. It sounds more like an elaborate bluff, " said Christina. She looked around the audience and could see they were lapping it up.

"Yes. He is saying that Celarus is armed to the teeth along the borders with Russia, with mainly American forces," answered Chuck.

Maximovich continued, "We can all see that the arms control regime is disintegrating, which is a serious concern. Since last November, Washington has been creating new ways with its engagement under the Treaty on Open Skies. The prospects of extending the New START are also under consideration."

"He's trying to play both sides," said Chuck, "He wants this new Russian-backed pipeline, but he expects the Americans to defend it."

Maximovich shifted forward on the rostrum, " All of this is taking place as the U.S. expands the capability of its global missile defence system. A well-defended pipeline will be assured if we take our diplomatic mission seriously alongside the development of business. "

"War-mongering," breathed Christina.

There was clapping and 'Eye of the Tiger' rose from the sound system.

"Wrong tune," said Chuck, "It should be Eve of Destruction,"

Cristina looked at Chuck. "Now?" she said.

"Yes. Now," Christina fiddled in her handbag and pressed the signalling button on her phone.

"They will be in here in 20 seconds," she said to Chuck, "We need to be as close to those doors as possible,"

She gestured to doors behind her, close to where Emily was sitting. They indicated to Emily to follow them as they stood close to the closed doors.

Then a bang. A flash-bang stun grenade had been thrown into the middle of the floor. The security guards looked around. A door at the other end of the room burst open, and as Christina had predicted someone came in carrying a machine gun.

Then four of the smaller side doors burst open together. Soldiers in black combat gear entered the room. There was a short chatter from the sub machine gun and then two separate shots fired followed by silence.

A loud voice came from a different direction to the speakers that had been used during the presentation.

"This is a Police Announcement. Everyone remain calm. This is a raid under circumstances outlined in the Police and Criminal Evidence Act 1984 (PACE). We have the power to enter premises and search them to either arrest someone, seize items in connection with a crime, or both."

Chuck was aware of several people moving towards the doors. He knew there would be even greater force outside. He could hear the rattle of firefight and the clink of metal as bullet cartridges hit the floor.

Everyone else remained seated, looking shocked, but as if this was some kind of extended floor show. Chuck noticed one person edging along a wall towards a door. Emily stood and pointed to the individual. Emily called out to Christina and Chuck, "It's Vassily Turgenev!"

The man pulled a pistol and took aim towards Emily. There was a further rattle of bullets. Christina had fired cross the room towards Turgenev. He was now pinned back against the door, having been hit by several of Christina's bullets.

Christina dropped the weapon as three SAS men came over to her. "She's with us," barked Chuck. "We are the people you have been listening to on the inside. Chuck Manners"

The squad leader made a hand gesture to the other two men, who relaxed. "Colonel Manners?" He asked, "Yes, said Chuck - he saluted, "And she is my plus one."

Christina knew why Chuck had said plus one. It was a lot simpler than trying to explain why he was with an FSB agent.

"You'll need to check in that cupboard," said Chuck quietly, "You might find there's some explosive in there, brought by Turgenev and Yegorin."

The squad leader walked across to the cupboard signalling to a couple of his men to follow him. They gingerly opened the cupboard, aware that it might be booby-trapped.

Nothing. Just packs of cleaning material.

"Behind them," whispered Chuck, motioning with his head. One of the soldiers toppled a few of the cartons with his gun. Suddenly, they could see the Grenade launcher and on the floor a couple of grenades.

"It's enough to blow a hole through the wall of the hotel,

or with the launcher it could rip a hole in Parliament or The Palace," said the squad leader.

Chuck looked around the room. The guests were being marshalled into one holding area and the security men into another. A military paramedic was wound dressing Turgenev, who looked as if he was in a bad way.

"We are getting clearance for emergency services to come inside," crackled across the radio.

Streets of London

Amanda Miller had been monitoring the whole engagement from outside, in a specially established communications vehicle.

Amanda had been asked to take Sir Stafford Peters along. The head of the Department for External Security on a live mission. This would never have happened in Bernard Driscoll's day.

However unheard of, the stakes had risen because of the complexities around this situation.

A CIA Listening station, Brant Subcontractors, Russian ex-KGB, Celarus oil fields and pipelines. American bases. A presumed terrorist device.

The price of gaining access to heavily armed British forces and a FALCON Communication unit was that Sir Stafford had to sit in the same vehicle. The Army had done a smart thing and set up the unit to look like a film location shoot, which meant they had brought along a second huge caravan truck which included a lounge and a catering area. It was all parked in a side street around the corner from the Lanchester, on double yellow lines.

Amanda had heard the gunshots but could also hear Chuck talking and referring to Christina.

"They all seem to be safe, " she said into the Tetra, for the benefit of Clare and Bigsy.

"Roger that," replied Bigsy, pleased he could, at last, do outgoing comms from the Tetra radio.

"What have we got?" asked Sir Stafford Peters.

"Well, they have caught the organisers, embarrassingly including MP Michael Tovey. Thanks to Maximovich it looks as if they were inciting an uprising- we could even consider it inciting a military coup."

"The bomb successfully implicates Turgenev in something deeply unpleasant and Yegorin is now a spent force. We can bring him in, linked to Maximovich. Everything that took place is on the recordings, thanks to the recordings we gained from the hidden microphones."

Sir Stafford looked worried, "I'm just not sure how much of this we want to advertise as occurring on London's streets."

"Now we need to do a deal with Maximovich. Tell him we'll make sure that Yegorin and Turgenev carry the can for everything. Tell Maximovich that he is free to continue so long as he provides intelligence to us. Explain that if he doesn't then we'll leak what he did to the Kremlin and he will then soon find himself in a similar situation to Yegorin."

"This is good work, Amanda,"

"Thank you, Sir Stafford."

Sun

Joy
Success
Celebration
Pleasure

Containment

Christina could see that the military had the inside of the ballroom under control and containment. Vassily Turgenev now had several paramedics tending to him. She assessed the gunshot wounds from afar and decided he would live. Her prime objective had been to stop Turgenev from letting off a shot towards Emily after she had identified him to the military.

"Turgenev and Yegorin have been captured, and most of Turgenev's men have been rounded up - at least the ones in the ballroom and through in that back room. It will be interesting to see how many of them come from Brant and have been supplied to this event," she said to Chuck.

Chuck nodded, " I think this will see the disgraced closure of the Minerva Listening station, in any case."

Chuck turned to Emily, who had regrouped with Anne-Marie and Pete. He couldn't help smile when he saw Pete's outfit.

"You three are very lucky to have come out of this

without a scratch," he said, "You were playing with fire. But I suppose you'll need to think of a story now that will get you off the hook for being implicated through Minerva."

Anne-Marie looked at Chuck, "Look I don't know why you helped us, but thank you. I know your friend helped save Emily. We are regular US citizens caught up in something far bigger than we expected."

"Come, come now," said Chuck, "We know you work for the CIA and that your friend Pete works directly for Brant. We can cut you some slack, but you must co-operate."

"What kind of slack?" asked Emily.

"Well, we'll want to say that you helped us identify the bad people. That you gave a tip-off that Yegorin was here. That you knew about the terrorist plot."

"Most of that is true. We knew about Yegorin, although not that his enforcer would be using a bunch of Brant contractors to run security at this event. We didn't know about the explosive either."

"Well, you'd better start practicing your story," said Christina.

"Why do you want us to do that?" asked Pete, somewhat indifferent to the situation.

"Well, it's easy really. You can go down as part of the conspiracy, just another three names on the Minerva roll-call of disgrace, or you can come out of this as saviours of the situation."

"Why would you do this to help us?" asked Emily,

Christina answered, "Ask Anne-Marie, she knows me already from a small meeting at Wagamama's close to your offices. She knows that I am quite a tough lady and my friend here is even tougher. - But we do not want our names mixed up in this. If the story of what happened can be told with just the three of you, then it will be a much preferable outcome,"

"What that we worked it all out by ourselves?" Asked Pete, now looking interested, "This could be promotions all round, if we play the story right. Olivia will be pig sick that she didn't get involved."

Emily and Anne-Marie looked at one another and smiled, Emily spoke, "Oh goodness, Olivia might even be seen as a part of the problem!"

"Or we could save her and then she would always be indebted to us." added Pete.

Loose end

Once the area had been secure, Chuck and Christina and the three from Minerva could cross back into the other ballroom. There was a similar scene in the master ballroom. The SAS had moved in although the security staff had surrendered under sheer weight of numbers.

No shots had been fired and Chuck could see that there was unease rippling around the room. It contained many senior people. Both those invited by the Russians and an additional selection of captains of industry, MPs and A-listers.

Chuck noticed that the military presence in this room had been offset by Metropolitan Police, who had also run security tape around much of the area.

Chuck looked at Christina, "They'll want to process these people and let them go as quickly as possible... There's too many well-known faces in here."

Emily and Anne-Marie looked over to the left-hand side of the room. There were fifty or more of the hostesses sitting together on the floor. They both noticed how matter-of-factly they seemed to be taking it and realised that for the hostesses this must be part of a way of life. Pete spotted the blond guy that he'd seen on the way into the event.

"All in day's work, I just hope they pay us for the full time here," he called over to Pete. He noticed that Pete was with Emily and Anne-Marie and that they were able to move around freely with Christina and Chuck.

"You take care," said Pete, "Sorry I couldn't tell you, but I'm a special agent,"

The blonde guy looked incredulous, but then noticed Chuck's pistol, which he had placed back in a shoulder holster.

The entourage of Christina, Chuck and the three Minerva people slipped out through a side door guarded by a police officer. Chuck explained they needed to speak to the controller of the operation, Amanda Miller.

...

Evidence

Once outside, Chuck looked for the military security detail. He saw one officer and engaged him in conversation. Then he walked back to the three from Minerva.

"Look, I've arranged for you three to be taken to a secure area. You will be guarded there until the heat from this dies down. You are not under arrest and are free to walk at any time, but understand me, you will be better in the Army's care for the next 24 hours. The holding area is inside the Lanchester. Three hotel rooms, upper floors I'm told."

The three looked at one another, "Well I'm in," said Pete, "Is room service included?"

Then Emily, "Well it does sound like a sensible idea, me too."

And Anne-Marie nodded her agreement.

Chuck heard them talking, "Yes, room service is included, but no booze, I'm afraid. Enjoy your stay."

Christina said, "Good, that's one less thing to worry about, Let's find Amanda now, and Bigsy, for a debrief."

Christina pulled her smartphone from her bag and texted "All OK. Meet at Amanda's location." The message would travel to Bigsy's comms van, also containing Jake and Clare.

They reached the street and walked to where they knew that Amanda had parked her convoy of vehicles.

"It looks so different now," said Christina, "with all these military buzzing around. Before it looked like a typical London street with a few film trailers parked along it."

Chuck agreed, and they both made their way to the now overtly guarded entrance to the hospitality vehicle.

Chuck gave his details to the sentry, and they listened as there was some communication interplay. The sentry then waved him and Christina through towards the entrance of the caravan.

They climbed a couple of steps and then entered a well-decorated environment. At the far end, around a small table were sitting Amanda and a suited man who they took to be Sir Stafford Peters.

Amanda and Chuck were still both in their finery and so the effect was more of a James Bond entrance rather than two combat veterans entering the room.

Amanda stood as they entered.

"Chuck, Christina, Well done! - You do not look as if a hair is out of place! That was an amazing operation."

"Yes," agreed Christina.

They all looked over to Sir Stafford. It intrigued Christina to know whether he felt it had been good value for money.

"Indeed, a very well-executed operation," he said, "And now we have Maximovich where we need him. As for the Yegorin and Turgenev, they will get what they deserve. And we can close Minerva Station, which was a cheeky attempt by the Americans to get on our soil in any case."

"Yes, all of that is good," said Christina, "But I'm still suspicious. In the Nordic stories of *Þiðrekssaga* there's a dragon. Sigurd can slay it, and smear his skin with its blood for protection, but he must always watch out for the sword Mimung, which can still cut and defeat. And for the shape-shifting that Sigurd may choose in order to get his way with Brynhild."

"That's like The Ring Cycle?" said Amanda.

"Yes, but you see my point. There's still someone running this, beyond Maximovich, Michael Tovey or ISMC."

"It's not over 'til it's over," said Bigsy.

"I agree," said Amanda, "We will need to interrogate the principal players to find out what they know."

Hanged Man

Sacrifice
Suspension
Release
Martyrdom

(Reversed)

Stalling
Fear of Sacrifice

Mainstream Media Attention

They all soon discovered that they could not run a major assault on a famous landmark hotel in London, without it attracting the MSM – the mainstream media and getting cut-through.

Amanda had sought advice from a PR Agency to cover what information they released, and a selection of slightly posed pictures of SAS soldiers going about their business. Amanda's intention was to deflect the event's cut-through potential by getting it classified as terrorism on London's streets.

By doing so, she would capture Turgenev and be able to dispense rough justice. Yegorin would also fall squarely under UK jurisdiction with these charges and be less likely to gain a Russian extradition, which would anyway send him to his doom. Yegorin would understandably play along with this, being caught somewhere between the devil and the deep blue sea.

The PR Agency said the story had wrap-up potential.

The Agency suggested a positioning speech, by someone in authority and the next day a press conference was conducted with The Mayor of London. It was a passionate speech about the event and emphasised that Londoners had brought it all under control. The event was characterised as an incitement towards a coup and the plotting of a bomb placement.

There was tribute paid to the police and special forces who intercepted the conspirators and then to the emergency services for their swift, professional response.

The large swathe of attendees in the master ballroom were mysteriously absent from the story. It was briefed that there was a coincidental second event occurring in the master ballroom.

Ominously, wording was added that there will be more armed and unarmed officers on London's streets in the days ahead to reassure everybody as they go about their normal business. Londoners owed the police and security services a huge debt of gratitude.

Then, "Terrorists have tried to sow fear, hatred and division in our city before. They have never succeeded and will not succeed now. London will not be intimidated or cowed by terrorism.

"Rather, we will redouble our efforts to stand resolute, defiant and united in the face of such evil. Terrorism is an act of complete cowardice and we will pursue and bring to justice anyone who might have offered support."

"There will be earnest questions for the government to answer in the weeks ahead about how this plotting could have happened and whether it could have been prevented."

"I will continue working closely with the police, authorities and government to reassure our communities and ensure that all possible measures are put in place to protect Londoners. I have no doubt that in the coming days Londoners will once again show the world exactly why our capital is the greatest city in the world. We will not let anyone divide us or disrupt our way of life. We will defend our values—and we will never let the terrorists win."

Interrogation outcomes

Amanda had called the Triangle members to her offices in Vauxhall Cross.

"This is exciting!" said Clare, "We are going to Spy Central."

"It's less exciting if you've already been held there for several days," replied Jake, remembering his time detained there when Clare and Bigsy were travelling around Arizona with Chuck.

Christina and Chuck had assessed their chances of getting in and out of SI6 without being detained on 'other matters', but Amanda had given her word.

They all met Amanda in an entrance lobby, where Amanda asked each them to be photographed and issued with badges. "You'll need to be accompanied," she said, "Everywhere, I'm afraid."

They moved through the building's security system and were eventually in an upper floor meeting room.

"The system will record this automatically. There's nothing I can do to stop it," said Amanda.

"Would you like me to stop it?" asked Bigsy, "Only I have this little app on my phone that duplicates IP addresses, it'll confuse the heck out of your devices in here and they will all hang."

"Thanks, but no thanks," said Amanda, "We should really have confiscated that on the way in."

"You did take my other two phones, " said Bigsy, "that scanning booth on the way in is surprisingly efficient."

"Okay, this is my colleague, James Cavendish and we've another colleague Grace Fielding on the Polycom."

"Hello," said Grace's voice.

"Hi," chorused several of the attendees.

"Right, let's get to it."

Amanda began:

"Slide 1: What we know. We have seen the attempts to break into the commercial arrangements of Brant. The sell-off from Raven was extraordinarily successful and investors in Brant made about double their original stake holding."

"Slide 2: Brant's shareholding has reduced, because of the early profit-takers, but there seems to be several large blocks still held. It includes the sizeable block holding by Gasneft, a Russian company."

Slide 3 : One of the largest business opportunities for Brant is in Celarus, a country that borders western Russia. Oil discoveries there were made by American exploration and the United States agreed to place US planes and military in Celarus.

"That's American planes right along Russia's borders," said Jim

"Slide 4: Unknown forces have been creating some interference in Celarus. There have been acts similar to those affecting Qube in Syria. Skirmishes which ensure the continued presence of the American forces."

"Qube was the offshoot of Raven which was made into Brant when Raven divested Brant," said Jim, "They were operating in the same way."

"Slide 5: Brant offers a range of services. Oil exploration, extraction, packaging, movement, trading - these are the same services as Raven. Then it offers security services (that's a quasi-military force) and construction of large infrastructure. Like the pipeline building, but also military camps and roads."

"The old idea to blow up place and then repair it is a well understood American business model from the early 2000s," said Jim, " a kind of Kellogg Brown & Root and Halliburton type of manoeuvre."

"Oh yes, the Iraqi oil wells, featuring Mr Dick Cheney," said Chuck.

"Slide 6: Brant has other interests too; it appears to be supplying the outsourced contractors to the CIA Minerva listening station in east London."

"And yes, these outsources seem to be coming with a distinct Russian flavour?" said Jim.

"Slide 7: And Minerva has been used continuously to target British MPs and Captains of Industry - faster than lobbying, using sleaze and slush to compromise them."

"Slide 8: So, who is pulling all the strings? Why would Brant be positioned to win the contracts in Celarus? Who really owns Brant? The Belgians? Raven? Or the Russians?"

"Well, Raven even seemed to be using the Freemasons," ventured Christina.

"No, too obvious, a smokescreen," interrupted Grace from the speakerphone, "It's a clever idea, and can bring in contacts, but then someone else is taking over the manipulation. Meanwhile we can all run off to try to investigate the tirelessly secretive Freemasons."

"I think I agree with that, " said Christina," My friend Antanov was none the wiser about any plans by Brant of anything to do with Celarus or Russia."

"Slide 9: Our questioning of persons of interest," continued Amanda., "These are the 'net nets' from the interviews. What everyone said, boiled down to a line or two - I'm going to hand over to Grace for this part."

"Okay," said Grace,

"Slide 10: old players. I wanted to start with the people who were involved when this all started.

"1) Bernard Driscoll- the rude and hapless Minister who

was compromised by the efforts of ISMC, acting on behalf of Raven. We think he was killed by the Roslavl Bratva run by Tima Maximovich. If so, that would have been orchestrated by Vassily Turgenev.

"2) Sir Charles Frobisher - threatened by Turgenev. Then disappears after saying he is going on a helicopter flight to Nice airport from Monaco. Likely death at sea caused by Vassily Turgenev.

"3) Gerhardt Schmidt - blown up, with seven others on a yacht off Monaco. Almost certainly an American smart mine attached to the vessel. Suspect Vassily Turgenev.

"That just about rounds up the deaths under suspicious circumstances. We could add the fire bombing of The Triangle Works in Hoxton to that list and the couple of attempts to shoot Chuck Manners."

Christina interrupted, "The attempts on Chuck were from FSB agents. Low level - their code names were Puffin and Auk. They worked with another agent, who also shot at me near Tower Bridge. I think the body was washed up near Tilbury."

"Oh," came Grace's voice, "I had no idea it involved you, Christina. You are not on cameras nor give any trace. It looked as if the extensive firepower used in both cases was a 9mm submachine gun?"

Christina said, "No comment."

Grace continued, "Let's move on to the captures from the Lanchester. Slide 11:"

"4) Vassily Turgenev - a nasty piece of work. Has no direct

connection with Russian intelligence, but has been an enforcer for mainly Maximovich for around ten years. There is a bloody trail left from his endeavours. In interrogation he didn't give us much, except when he was under Midazolam because of the severe injuries from 9 mm bullets in the Lanchester.

"Under the tranquillisers, he rambled, but did that he had been pleased to even the scores with Driscoll, Frobisher, Schmidt and a couple of other names. He described the yacht explosion as one of the best fireworks displays he had seen. He described the Driscoll car crash as hilarious - something from Mr Bean."

"5) Yegorin - a true Russian gangster - one of the people that put Putin into power. He calls Putin 'VV', by the way."

"VV - Vladimir Vladimirovich," said Christina.

Grace continued, "Yes, and now Yegorin plays hard-done-by saying that metaphorically the Kremlin have held him by his ankles and shook him. They want all his hard assets, and his money. He's put the money into various hiding places and that has just made the Russians madder. That is why they are pursuing him through the English Courts. They seem to think that they have some kind of hold over elements within the legal profession. That and excellent PR outlets for what they see as 'the truth'."

"He said metaphorically, but I could see Turgenev trying exactly that ankles trick, " said Christina.

Grace answered, "Yegorin wanted to cut a deal with us, because he is frightened of extradition to Russia. He says his time will be limited if he goes back. We are leaving him to hang for a while longer," said Grace, "And hold that thought about influencing the English Courts and the link back to Minerva.

"6) Michael Tovey, MP - Now that was interesting. At first he made out that he had been dumped in a similar manner to Driscoll. Our people believed him until they unearthed a significant Foundation Fund in the Caymans. He had made the same stupid mistake as Driscoll and was funnelling money into it by a well-known bank. We think Tovey is further up the decision tree than he is letting on.

"7) Miller McDonald, MVP in ISMC- This is the outfit that has facilitated the various celebrity events. They seem to be more or less a fixer to Raven. Gerhart Schmidt also worked for them. Miller, a Texan, seems to be quite high up in the company, but aside from fronting the event in the Lanchester seems to be clean.

"He certainly looked like a tanned, drive-by handshake to me, " said Chuck, thinking back to the presentation.

"8) Trudi Hartmann, a VP from ISCM and a close ally of McDonald. Some say they are sleeping together. She gave the introduction presentation for the oil pipeline investment, but otherwise seems untouchable."

"She was polished, has the moves and the power dressing to add credibility to the session. They also gave her some time to position the arguments," said Christina.

"Slide 12: The others - Yes - while we were processing everyone at the event a few other names surfaced. A Marion Charlotte, who said she knew and had been out with Driscoll and had met Chuck, Christina even Amanda.

"Then there was Nina Valentine a friend of Marion, who seemed to know Gerhardt Schmidt, Maximovich and Yegorin. She said she'd never forgive Yegorin for blowing up the yacht in Monaco. She said she was supposed to be on it and her friends were, plus Gerhardt. Oh yes, and Nina also knew all of you, from visiting the Triangle in Galleria.

"And a curious turn up was a couple of people from Smooth Pebble, which is a kind of Californian PR agency. Han Yoon was the SVP and said he had coached Raven's board on ways to handle the divestment to form Brant. He also knew Sir Charles but wasn't aware he was missing.

"Then there was Brittany Krasnigor, a very self-confident American, who had met the Raven board at the same coaching session as Han Yoon. She was surprised that Smooth Pebble were invited to the London event, but decided to come along 'to see the Brits at play' as she put it.

"Ha," said Jake, "Is she a psychologist or something?"

"Great guess," said Grace, "Behavioural Psychologist, PhD, from Harvard.

"She said she hadn't said anything to Han Yoon, but had been darkly disturbed by the Raven pre-divestment meeting. She reckoned that Frobisher and the other had deliberately put a 'B-Team' on to lead it. She said it was like passing the rudder of the ship to a blind captain. She reckoned that there were other games afoot and that Raven to Brant was just the opening move of a more complex game."

"The Narrenschiff - Ship of fools, " said Christina, "A friend of mine told me to watch out for it."

"But wait - there's still one person we havn't talked about," said Grace.

"Saving the best for last?" asked Jim.

"Yes, you could say that," answered Grace, "But I'll pass the deck back to Amanda."

Amanda continued, "Slide 13: Kasharin Timur (Tima) Maximovich, who is the Head of Russian Infrastructure. He was asked to set up the Lanchester session for Yegorin and did so because of Yegorin's leverage towards him. "

"Leverage? Friendship or threats?" asked Christina.

"Probably all of the above, Yegorin knows, literally, where the bodies are buried," answered Grace, "It was because of Maximovich's inflammatory speech that we could send the SAS into the meeting. We needed something as well as the discovered explosives which implicate Turgenev, but the speech could implicate one or both of Yegorin and Maximovich."

"Creating the prisoners' dilemma?" asked Jake, "Who betrays whom?"

"No, they will both treat it as 'every man for himself', said Amanda, "They are caught too tight and both could expect execution by Russia if they play their cards badly."

Jim said, "That's where Maximovich has an escape. He can say that he was setting a trap for Yegorin and Turgenev. That it was best to find the anti-Kremlin

Russians and this was a quick way to flush them out in a single sweep. We can even help write the script for him."

Amanda added, "Then the Kremlin would be very pleased with Maximovich and move him to the inner circle for such a daring act. Especially as it looks as if the Kremlin had no hand in it."

"That's how we can position a threat over Maximovich and ask him to become our mole."

Judgement

Reflection
Reckoning
Awakening

The Maximovich trade

Maximovich had been placed in a secure detention centre, out in the Surrey countryside. A sweeping drive led to the main building, which was a repurposed stately home.

Amanda and Jim Cavendish arrived and walked through the large wooden door, with a smaller door cut into it. Amanda glanced to the door frame. Sure enough, a ring of small circular indentations. Apotropaic marks cut into the door to ward off evil spirits.

"Look - these ward off the witches," she said to Jim. He glanced over, "As long as they ward off the Russian bogey men too," he said as they walked in.

"We are here to see Maximovich, " explained Amanda flashing a badge, " We are Amanda Miller and Jim Cavendish."

"Ah yes, Ms Miller, Please, come this way. You'll be entering the secure part of the site, so be prepared for some security rigmarole. I expect you'll be used to it, coming from Vauxhall."

They walked through a metal detector and then into a small cubicle where they were body scanned.

"All good, you can leave your phones in the secure boxes and then follow me," said the guard.

They were both issued with freshly printed computerised badges.

"Here's the lanyards for the badges, they are proximity sensitive so they will let you through doors that you are allowed to go through. Just watch out for a green light - not a red light which means stop."

They walked through a couple of corridors including one which smelled of fast-food and then another of detergent. A sharp left turn and they were in a small lobby area with three metal doors.

"It's like one of those quiz shows," quipped Jim.

"He's in here," as the metal door swung open revealing another locked door.

"You will need to use your pass for the second door," said the guard.

They entered and could see Maximovich seated at a small table. His arms were out in front of him and appeared to be chained to the table via a small metal loop.

"More questions?" he said, "Haven't you got enough answers already?"

"Hello Tima," said Amanda, "This time we come with a

deal for you."

"I don't do deals," he started.

"Well, you'll have to listen in any case. We want to set you free. But there is a price. So far no-one knows that we are holding you. Outside you can be seen as the man that brought Yegorin to justice. It will play well in the Kremlin and could save you from being chased the way of Yegorin."

"We know he has got something on you," bluffed Jim, "We even know what it is, but we won't be talking about it to anyone."

"Not if you play along with us," continued Amanda, "We want you to tell the Kremlin that you orchestrated the raid. That it was to catch Russian dissidents. They will believe you."

"I've been waiting for this," said Maximovich, "You English are so predictable. There's a price for me turning against Yegorin."

"Yes, but if you don't, you'll be turning against your families." said Jim.

"Blah-blah-blah, I've done this stuff too you know, let's cut to the chase. I'll need money and a safeguard," said Maximovich, "Both Yegorin and Turgenev go to Russia. You deport them on terrorism charges. Maybe trade a few people the other way?"

"That would represent death to Yegorin," said Jim.

"He can take his chances. I have stuck out my neck for him with this last thing. Look where it has got me. I need him off the scene. And Turgenev, for that matter. Otherwise he'll send a surprise package around to my home."

"Surprise package?"

"Yes, a gunman or a bomb. Maybe some poison. He's not that particular. Then I can go to the Kremlin. Say I engineered the take-down. They will believe me, but only if I'm not missing for too long. A week in hiding after that Lanchester incident is believable. Then I need to surface in somewhere like San Tropez. I can explain everything about hiding. But you'll need to get Yegorin and Turgenev moved fast. And offer me a sweetener, for the inconvenience. Maybe a million a day in detention. There. That's my offer."

"That's too much," said Jim.

"Okay, I'll be kind, Dollars. Final Offer."

Amanda and Jim remained poker-faced. They had been given a budget for this by Sir Stafford Peters. "Twenty million is the maximum. That's Pounds."

So far they were on day six. A couple more to fix everything. Eight days was eight million US, at the exchange rate that was about £6.4 million.

"Okay," said Jim, "We agree. How do you want to do this?"

"I want someone Russian that I trust to pick up Yegorich and Turgenev. Helicopter from the field behind this building. To an airstrip - military is fine - then on to Moscow. A Russian plane. I want to hear from the pickup they have all arrived. Then, show me a fund transfer, get me a private jet to LFTZ-La Mole out by Saint Tropez and we are done."

"Okay, although we'll want you to stay in contact after that."

"I understand, you expect me to be a double. But I need to be careful first. You only want infrequent high-value from me. Not lots of noise. Are we done?"

Amanda and Jim rose. They decided it was best to leave when Maximovich thought he was on a high.

Kamov Ka-60

It was early morning. Amanda and Jim waited on the field behind the stately home for the helicopter to arrive. They had done everything that Maximovich had asked. They had even transferred the £6.4 million to a bank account in Liechtenstein. Now there were two more things left to do.

To move Turgenev and Yegorin back to Russia via helicopter and then onwards by private jet to Sheremetyevo airport.

Then, some eight hours later, to move Maximovich to an airstrip from where he could catch a private flight to Saint Tropez, where he would resurface with a great tale of sunshine and powerboats and an additional $8 million in his pockets.

The Kamov Ka-60 circled once and then landed.

"Noisy," said Chuck, and Christina nodded. She was having flashbacks to when they used similar helicopters in Archangelsk to make short runs into the Dvina Bay and the White Sea, where they would stop on the flatlands of the Dvina River delta to practice various kinds of military field craft. It was where she had first met Antanov, when he piloted the craft to take their unit back to the Academy.

They looked out and saw Amanda and Jim shepherding Turgenev and Yegorin to the helicopter. Turgenev still looked in a bad way. He had sustained four bullet wounds to the leg from Christina. Only her shooting accuracy had kept him alive. Yegorin looked as if he was quietly going mad. He had let his beard grow long and his hair looked wild.

"He looks finished, " said Chuck quietly and Christina nodded. From a distance they could see Amanda and Jim saying a last few things to the pair as they climbed aboard the helicopter.

A large metal door was slid closed, with Christina thinking she did not remember that the door there even closed on the ones they had used in Russia, and then the helicopter started to rise in the air.

Christina's phone rang. It was Blackbird.

"Archangel. The helicopter ride is a trap," he said, in Russian, "Maximovich has got a word outside, to his new enforcer, Anatoly Yaroslav. Yaroslav is to take the plane down. We heard it today because we have been monitoring Yaroslav's line."

"Why are you telling me this?" asked Christina, also speaking in Russian, "Do you want me to stop it."

"No," he said, "I want to make sure you are not deciding

to take a ride for old times' sake. Riding shotgun. You know the kind of thing."

"No, my feet are both on the ground," replied Christina.

"Yaroslav has access to firepower," said Blackbird, "It will be final."

Blackbird hung up.

Christina looked at the helicopter which had circled once before taking its heading towards the airfield where the jet was waiting. She looked around the field. There were several outcrops of trees. In the distance she could hear metallic scraping. Then a loud bang and she noticed the orange flash from behind the treeline.

She and Chuck watched as two white finned missiles headed towards the helicopter. There was a bright light as the first one struck and then a second orange light as the second one reached the target. Three or four seconds later the sound arrived, ominous and loud. A mix of explosion and metal sheets being torn apart. Then a short pause and a further noise as the helicopter hit the ground, or, as Christina gauged it, hit some trees in the middle distance."

"That was a Pechora, I think," said Chuck, "Where does anyone get one of those in Surrey? This is like the wild west."

Christina nodded as she looked toward Amanda and Jim. They were both running to the same part of the field where Christina and Chuck were standing, so they could get a better view.

"It must be Maximovich, " said Amanda, "He didn't want to take any chances. That was ruthless."

Jim nodded, "We will have to cover this up from the public," he said, "But it does still reinforce Maximovich's position with the Kremlin."

"Who do you think did this?" asked Amanda. Christina kept quiet.

"We need to find out who Maximovich has hired to replace Turgenev; he seems to be from the same barrel," said Jim.

"Do you think Maximovich knows what has happened?" asked Amanda.

"I mean he's in that building and that explosion was so close he could hear it."

"No, he's got some kind of link to outside," said Jim, "Maybe it is through his wife."

"Do we have any way of capturing the launch vehicle?" asked Amanda.

"If that was a Pechora 2M, they have the advantage that you can pull curtains along the side of them and apart from the odd-looking forward cab, they look like a regular haulage truck," said Chuck, "It'll have melted into the traffic."

"What would a soviet SAM be doing in Surrey?" asked Jim.

"I know, I was wondering the same thing," answered Chuck.

Saint Tropez

They decided not to talk to Maximovich before his departure. Eight hours later another helicopter arrived, this one a sleek modern-looking business craft with a Gatwick address on the door.

The original timings were to allow time for the other Russians to get back to Moscow.

Maximovich walked out.

"I think my reputation will be good for the Kremlin," he said, "And that there are no loose ends. Now I must find my sunshades for sitting outside Le Sénéquier."

He climbed aboard the helicopter, which revved for takeoff. Amanda, Jim, Chuck and Christina looked on as it took off, circled and then flew away, in the same general direction as the other craft had done during the early morning.

They waited until it was a tiny speck on the horizon and then moved back towards the house.

"Job done!" said Chuck, "Except for the tidy-up."

Christina looked towards him, "I'm not so sure," she said, "I can't help think there's still something else here. That we have not followed the whole trail, even now."

"I worry that the route leads into Moscow," said Amanda.

"Or maybe that is what they want us to think?" questioned Christina.

"Well, they've burnt all the links, that's for sure," said Chuck, "I think we must be careful now, because Maximovich seems to have traded up for his enforcer. Anatoly Yaroslev seems even more menacing than Turgenev."

"What about your friends?" asked Amanda, "The ones that work in that Triangle thing?"

"They'll want to know what happened, that's for sure," said Chuck.

"And probably over a few beers," added Christina.

"There should probably be some closing theme music about now," said Chuck.

"I can hear it," said Christina.

Providence at a top table in London

It was a busy reception. Drinks, canapés, a few celebrities, including some A-listers. Songs from a well-known pop band. An inspirational speech from a well-known football team manager.

Off to the side was a compact room. In different times they would have filled it with cigar smoke. Nowadays just the dark-suited men.

"We still need Brant, " said one.

The others nodded.

"Who can we use to manipulate it?" asked the second voice.

"Someone we can control. A puppet."

"I have the very person, a clean skin, " said a third voice.

"Well, let's invite him into the club." Said the first voice, as if concluding the discussion.

Your Cards

World

393

Fulfilment
Harmony
Completion

Ed Adams

Judgement

Reflection
Reckoning
Awakening